Death and Breakfast

— A Mystery —

Gordon Inglis

Death and Breakfast
— *A Mystery* —
Gordon Inglis

killick press
an imprint of Creative Publishers

St. John's, Newfoundland
2001

Le Conseil des Arts | The Canada Council
du Canada | for the Arts

We acknowledge the support of The Canada Council for the Arts for our
publishing program.

We acknowledge the financial support of the Government of Canada
through the Book Publishing Industry Development Program (BPIDP) for
our publishing activities.

Cover: Joanne Snook-Hann

∞ Printed on acid-free paper

Published by

CREATIVE BOOK PUBLISHING

a division of 10366 Newfoundland Limited
a Robinson-Blackmore Printing & Publishing associated company
P.O. Box 8660, St. John's, Newfoundland A1B 3T7

FIRST EDITION

Typeset in 10.5 point Centaur

Printed in Canada by:
ROBINSON-BLACKMORE PRINTING & PUBLISHING

National Library of Canada Cataloguing in Publication Data

Inglis, Gordon

    Death and breakfast : a mystery

ISBN 1-894294-38-6

    I. Title.

PS8567.N4546D42   2001   C813'.6   C2001-902222-0
PR9199.4.I54D42   2001

Contents

DEATH AND BREAKFAST

I

THURSDAY NIGHT

*J*ENNIFER MOVED ALONG THE SIDE OF THE LARGE OAK dining room table, assembling the last set of pages. She squared the edges of the little sheaf of paper by tapping it on the tabletop, passed it to Alan, and sank into the chair across from him with a sigh. Alan fastened it into the last cardboard cover and dropped the completed booklet on the pile.

"That's it," he said. "We'll put them in the rooms in the morning."

Jennifer ran her hand over the top copy. "It would have been nice if we could have used a colour printer . . . "

"Oh, for God's sake, Jen! It's perfect. It's *better* than colour. More dignified." Alan divided the last few drops of tea from the pot between their two mugs, put Jennifer's into her hand and clicked his own against it. "Here's to a successful murder."

Her answering smile was wan. "I'm frightened!"

"Me too. Scared to death — but we can't let it get us down. We'll be okay once it starts."

"Easy to say."

"Come on, Jen, this is no time to mope. We ought to be knocking back champagne instead of cold tea." He put down his mug and reached across the table to take her hand. "It's like a play, right? The set is perfect, we've got a good script, we've got a great cast . . . We're not

1

exactly over-rehearsed, I'll admit, but we're in as good shape as most shows on opening night. All we have to do now is let it roll."

Jennifer grimaced. "But there are so many things that could go wrong . . . "

"Sure, and some of them will, they always do. But we can handle it. We can handle anything except if the theatre burns down."

"Oh, thanks a lot! That's one I hadn't thought of. You certainly know how to cheer a girl up!"

"If you're going to imagine disasters, you might as well make 'em big. Listen, by tomorrow afternoon we're going to be so busy we won't have time to worry." Alan's grin turned into a wide yawn. "Speaking of which . . . "

"I won't sleep a wink." Jennifer swirled the dregs of tea, staring down into her mug. "I keep thinking about the people in the village — how are they going to react? I mean, when the guests are all here, and . . . "

"We probably shouldn't call it 'the village' for a start. They don't like it."

"Oh, dear! I've done it again, haven't I? It's all those Agatha Christies, and the mysteries on PBS. Why should it matter so much?"

"I guess it's just that words mean different things to different people. And I think 'the village' sounds patronising to the people in the Cove."

Jennifer had been trying to smile, but her eyes suddenly filled with tears. "I'd so hoped they'd like us!"

Alan played for time. "Who?"

She retrieved a crumpled tissue from the pocket of her jeans and blew her nose with an impatient gesture. "Oh, for Heaven's sake! Who do you think? The people in the . . . the Cove, of course."

"Ah, Jen, they like us all right . . . "

"They *don't!*" Jennifer wailed. "They *hate* us! They hate my English accent, and they hate me because I say things like 'the village', and they hate you because you come from Toronto, and they hate both of us because we bought this place. It doesn't matter how long we stay here, we'll always be outsiders, and . . . "

Alan moved around the end of the table and slid into a chair beside her, putting his arm around her and gently pulling her head onto his shoulder. "Jenny, love, you're exaggerating. You're dead tired, and you're worried about tomorrow, and it's all piling up on you. This is a small town, and everybody knows everybody else, and we're newcomers. But it's like anyplace: some people are friendly and some aren't. Mostly, they're curious about us, I guess. And we've made some really good friends, haven't we? Ernie's mother thinks you're wonderful, for one, and then there's all his aunts and uncles — that's nearly half the population, right there. And there's Faith . . . "

Faith Carter would probably never know the anxiety she had caused them in their early days in the area. They first heard her name as 'Fate,' but from the beginning Jennifer was fairly sure that it was 'Faith', while Alan argued that it could really be "Fate", perhaps a bizarre rural nickname. The two would sound identical when pronounced by people from the local area.

Alan and Jennifer avoided the issue by using "Mrs. Carter" at first, but that could only last so long. Especially when they learned of her virtues and wanted to hire her they had to use her given name, but local residents were fully familiar with what they thought of as "mainland" accents; they knew exactly how outsiders would pronounce 'Faith' and 'Fate', and would judge accordingly: the newcomers could not afford to get it wrong.

Alan tried to force a solution by playing up his outsider status and asking her outright what her first name was. "They calls me Fait'," she said, which did not help at all. "I 'lows it could of been worse. I might've been Ope."

"Ope?" Alan said.

"Ope or Charty. I figures I got the best of d' tree."

Alan, thoroughly confused, reported the conversation to Jennifer, who heaved a sigh of relief. "That settles it," she said. "It's 'Faith'." Alan insisted on a little more explanation before he accepted the verdict.

All this flashed through both their minds in the momentary pause before Alan finished, " . . . she likes you a lot."

"I don't think her husband does, any more," Jennifer said, straightening in her chair and wiping her eyes.

Alan's face hardened. "Steve? What about him?"

" I didn't want to tell you before because you've had enough to worry about, but . . . well, Faith says he's been drinking again, and he's been threatening all kinds of things."

"What things?"

"You know how he gets when he's been drinking. Faith's at her wits' end. She says he's been telling people that he's going to come up here tomorrow when the guests are here, and — oh, I don't know — do something awful . . . "

Alan pushed his chair back roughly and stood up, turning away from her. "Let him try! I'll deal with Steven bloody Carter. But I'm glad you told me. I don't think he'll actually come, but I'll be ready if he does."

"Oh, Allie, don't you think we should just give him some more money? Just to keep him quiet until . . . "

Alan turned back to face her. "Jen, listen. We divided the responsibility, right? You've got your stuff to handle, and I've got mine. Steve's one of mine, and I'll handle him, but I can't do it if I have to argue with you as well."

"I know, but . . . "

"Just remember what he's put us through!" Alan waved a hand at the pile of booklets on the table. "Thanks to him, a couple of weeks ago we were about ready to phone all those people and say, 'Sorry, folks, it's all off. Your refund is in the mail.' Only there wouldn't have been enough in the bank to cover the cheques.

"The only reason we're on schedule tonight is because I spent a week racing around pleading with bureaucrats while you were working about twenty hours a day. My God, Steve shouldn't be threatening us, we should be threatening him!"

Alan sat back down beside Jennifer and hugged her again. "Faith isn't complaining about money, is she? She knows that what we've paid him is more than fair for the work he did. And Steve knows it too, when he's sober. He's got a real problem with the booze, and I wish we could help somehow, but giving him more money would only make things worse." A sudden thought struck him. "He isn't threatening Faith, is he?"

"No. She'd never stay with him if he did that. He makes her life hell, one way or another, when he's drunk, and he gets into scraps when he goes to St. John's, but she says he's never lifted a hand to her or the kids."

"So things could be a lot worse, right? Steve's just . . . being Steve, and anybody who's dealt with you knows you're not patronising, even if you are English.

"Come on, now, this is the moment we've been waiting for! This is where all our work pays off!" Alan waved expansively. "I mean, just look at this place. Look what we've done!" Jennifer moved her head against his shoulder in a reluctant nod and reached out to touch the edge of the table in front of them, a magnificent sweep of old oak that would seat twenty people easily, its polished surface glowing in the light of two glittering fixtures that had once been a dangling mass of cobwebs and dust. It was hard to believe that the first time she had seen it, the table had been in two pieces and covered in paint. Now, she had to look carefully to find where it had been re-joined. She let her eyes wander around the big room. Everywhere she could see similar transformations, from the decorated plaster of the high ceiling to the dull sheen of the wide floorboards.

It seemed incredible that there was a time when they didn't even know the house existed. Their first inkling came from a close friend who was also a real estate agent. Ruth had caught them both at home in the historic area of St. John's at lunch-time one vicious January day nearly a year and a half before.

"Listen," she had said, "there's a place I think you ought to see. I haven't seen it myself, but . . . well, I just think you ought to look at it."

When she told them how many rooms it had and where it was located, in a tiny outport well off the beaten track, they shook their heads. But they knew that Ruth had an uncanny instinct for historic properties, and they were prepared to listen to more.

"Okay," she said. "I had a call from this guy in Boston. Did you ever hear of the Cranmers?"

Alan and Jennifer shook their heads again.

"Shame on you. Looks like I have to teach you some Newfoundland history. Again. Well, okay. The Cranmers were a big merchant-and-shipping family in England in the old days. They were involved in the migratory fishery before there was any settlement to speak of, and some time in the early eighteen hundreds a branch of the family set up an operation here. They bought fish and outfitted fishermen all over the Northeast Coast, had all kinds of ships, traded all over the place. Back in about the eighteen nineties they built this humungous house in — wait for it — Cranmer's Cove.

At the time, there were a whole bunch of them, and they all lived there. They owned everything and everybody in the area. Lived like English aristocrats: stables, riding horses, the whole bit.

"In the twenties, when the fishery was going downhill, some of them branched off to the States, to Boston, and got into business there. Started in fish, of course, then moved into other things. Now it's some kind of conglomerate — shipping, real estate development, supermarkets, you name it. But some of the Cranmers still own a big chunk of the family firm.

"The Newfoundland operation just wound down, and family members either died or went off to Boston. For the last forty years or so, there's just been this one old brother and sister in the big house in Cranmer's Cove, neither of them married, living on their piece of the family fortune and getting crazier and crazier. Everybody else was gone. Sad, when you think about it.

"Anyway, apparently a week or so ago the old lady died — they were both in their nineties — and the old man just gave up and died, too. This guy who called me from Boston is a great-nephew or something, and he's delegated to wind up the estate. He never knew the old folks, and he's never been near Newfoundland. Anybody in the family who actually knew them is either dead or too old to take much interest.

"So there it is. He wants to get the place sold, clew up the estate, and get back to building supermarkets or playing golf or whatever he does. He's been in touch with the lawyer here who's handling the will, and she put him onto me. I told him there isn't much of a market for big old houses out around the bay, but I also told him that I had some clients who might be interested. He's coming down sometime soon to look at the place himself and sort out the will. He wants a quick sale."

"Yeah, but listen, Ruth," Alan said, "how far is this place — what is it? Cranmer's Cove? — how far is it from town? Must be two and a half, three hours anyway. And how many rooms did you say the place's got? That's not a house, it's a bloody hotel!"

"So what's your point? What's the matter with you two? Haven't you been babbling on about an outport bed-and-breakfast since last fall? Where's your sense of adventure? We're talking real live history here. I've been asking around a bit, and apparently the old pair didn't do anything much to the place except fix the roof when it leaked, so it hasn't been messed up. And it's full of old family stuff. It'd be worth going through it just to see it! And if you aren't interested in the house you might at least pick up some old furniture. Chappy from Boston didn't sound like the type to want to ship anything back with him." She patted her purse. "And I've got the key."

"What have you got in mind?" Alan asked suspiciously.

"Go out on the weekend and look at it, boy! We'll go together. I'd love to see it!"

"Not me," said Jennifer. "I've got a report due next week. I'm spending Saturday and Sunday in front of the computer."

"I've got a lot of stuff to do, too," said Alan. "And I don't want to go driving all the way out there in this weather. Probably get snowed in for a week."

"Mainland wimps. I don't know why I bother with you at all. If you were real Newfoundlanders, now . . . "

"Listen," Alan said, "real Newfoundlanders are too smart to let themselves get suckered into something like this. You're just trying to take advantage of our innocence."

"And, anyway, I'm not a mainlander," Jennifer said. "I'm English. D'you want some lunch?"

"I haven't been eating lunch since Christmas. And English is worse. I'll have a cup of tea, though. Brits make good tea. You'll be sorry when some smart operator buys the place for peanuts and gets an ACOA grant to turn it into a health spa.

"I *have* got it right, haven't I? You *are* the same couple who've been talking about a bed-and-breakfast out around the bay all winter?"

"Well, yeah," Alan said, "but . . . "

Jennifer finished the thought: " . . . we weren't thinking of anything on that scale."

"But you *are* looking, right?" Ruth said. "I didn't just dream that up?"

"Listen," said Alan. "This whole thing started right here, at this table, back in . . . I don't know -September?"

"Yes," Jennifer said. "We were right here, having a late candlelight dinner, and we started talking about the fact that we've been in this house for twenty years now, and we were both about to turn fifty . . . "

"Oh, God," said Ruth, whose own fiftieth birthday was not far off. "Spare me the agonizing details."

"You weren't here when we fixed this place up, were you?" Alan said. "You never saw what it was like when we moved in."

"That's right," Ruth said. "We went to Brampton in 1972, and stayed there for ten years. It was okay at first, and kind of exciting, but after a while I just couldn't wait to get back home."

"Yes," said Jennifer. "There's really something about this place, isn't there? The pull is strong enough for people like us, but it must even stronger for people who were born here. We used to say that we both fell in love with St. John's before we fell in love with each other."

"It was the theatre scene that attracted me," Alan said. "I came in '75, and got into set design and construction. I wanted to write plays."

" I came for the painting, and especially the printmaking," said Jennifer. "All kinds of exciting things were going on here. I'd gone to art school in London, and spent some time in New York and Montréal, but St. John's seemed to be the place it was all happening.

"You know my office on the third floor?" Jennifer gestured toward the ceiling and Ruth nodded. "That was supposed to be a studio. It wasn't supposed to be full of filing cabinets and computer stuff, it was supposed to have easels and smell of turpentine. I haven't done any serious art in years."

"Yeah," said Alan. "You can't make a living in the arts — or very few people can, anyway. Jen had to take her job with the Department of Education, and I had to get into the renovation business — furniture at first, and then whole houses. You know my office on the first floor? That wasn't supposed to be the head office of a contracting company, it was supposed to be a place for me to write. There's a couple of play manuscripts in there someplace, but I couldn't tell you where."

"So you bought the house and did it up and had to take real jobs to pay for it," Ruth said. "Very touching, I'm sure. But what's all that got to do with an outport bed-and-breakfast?"

"We're getting to that," Alan said. "Give us a break. So we were having our candlelight dinner, and we were talking about all that, and how we were spending all our time working, and not doing the stuff we really wanted to do, and we got this great idea."

"Stop," said Ruth. "Don't tell me, let me guess. You were going to get a big old house out around Brigus or Harbour Grace and turn it into a bed-and breakfast!"

"Right," said Jennifer, undeterred by Ruth's ironic tone. "Alan and his crew would renovate it, and I'd decorate it, and we'd get a local couple to run it in the summers. We'd have Newfoundland art on the walls, serve Newfoundland food, and generally give tourists an experience they could talk about when they got home."

"Right," said Alan. And then in the winter, we'd both take a week or two off at a time, and we'd go and stay out there. Jen could get back to her art, and maybe I could get back to writing. And on weekends, we'd have friends from town out, and we could have leisurely dinners, and talk in front of the fire, and they could stay over, because we'd have all the rooms fitted up to rent in the summer. You were on the top of the visitor's list."

"Sounds great," said Ruth. "I can hardly wait. So why aren't you jumping up and down when I come up with a place?"

"We told you," Jennifer said. "We were thinking of something a lot smaller and a lot closer to town."

"Listen, if there's one thing I've learned in real estate, it's that you can't think yourself into a house. You have to look at places, and they give you something real to think about."

Ruth left shortly after, but Alan and Jennifer talked about the old house in Cranmer's Cove several times in the next few days, and when her report was finished Jennifer called with a few questions.

"I was just going to call you," Ruth said. "Mr. Cranmer is coming down from Boston to see the lawyer about the will and have a look at the house. I'll be driving him out there on Thursday. I told him you people weren't interested, and he said" — she put on an exaggerated American twang — "he said, 'Wall, *git* 'em innarested, Honey. I wanna get this over with.' He said that if anybody showed any interest at all, I should get them to come out with us. That's not usual, for the vendor and the purchaser to look at a place together, but . . . "

"What's all this about 'vendor and purchaser'?" Jennifer said. "I told you, we're just sort of interested in the history of the place."

"Oh, don't pay any mind to that. Just real estate jargon. Anyway, I can hardly tell him you're just sightseeing, can I? Now, do you want to go, or what?"

In the end, Jennifer and Alan agreed to drive out by themselves and meet Ruth and the man from Boston at the house. It was another wicked January day, with a bitter northeast wind moaning over the drifted snow under high, thin cloud, and the sun creeping low across the southern sky, looking as small and cold as the moon. By the time they left the highway on the road to Cranmer's Cove, they were wondering why they had come.

They had no trouble finding the house. They could see it from a mile or more away as the road dropped down toward the sea. It stood out starkly against the snow, perched on a hill against a vista of slate-grey sea and sky.

"God, it *is* big, isn't it?" Alan said.

They drove up in front of the house and stopped. On their right, to the south, the land fell away sharply to a small bay, the steep snow-covered slope leading down to a restless grey sea two hundred feet below. Freezing spray had streaked the black rocks to a surprising height. The little bay was formed by a narrow, rocky headland on the right, and a piece of the main peninsula on the left that rose as it extended eastward to a low, brush-covered crest. Ahead, the road curved downward to the left then looped right again, following the only moderate slope leading to the larger bay formed by the headland that stretched away ahead of them and another to the north. Although it was invisible from where they sat, they knew that at the end of the road the tiny

12

community of Cranmer's Cove nestled at the base of the cliffs, its hundred-odd houses, small fish-plant, school and church a colourful jumble along the shore. To their left, Cranmer House stood on a low hill. Behind it, a ragged line of bushes and rocks marked where more cliffs dropped down to the sea on the northern side of the peninsula.

The driveway up from the road was drifted in, but its entrance was marked by two stone pillars, and its line by a row of huge poplars, their bare limbs black against the grey sky. Beyond the eastern row of trees a row of poles was nearly hidden, carrying wires from the road to the house. There was no sign of Ruth and the man from Boston, so they pulled off the road onto a patch of drive that had been blown clear of snow and sat looking up. The house was an architectural oddity; Alan's practised eye could pick out features of a whole catalogue of styles, but the nineteenth-century builder had somehow shaped them into a whole that was harmonious in spite of its strangeness.

"Those trees are magnificent," Alan said after a moment.

"If they're alive."

"Oh, they're alive. The bark looks healthy. Need to be cut back a lot, though. The entry's impressive, isn't it, off-centre like that? The driveway goes right under the portico, see. And I like the way the verandah goes out on both sides."

"Ghastly paint job," said Jennifer.

"The colour's all wrong, for sure, but it's been kept up. I'll know better when we get closer, but it looks to me as though there's been a lot of scraping and painting and replacing boards over the last hundred-odd years. Even in this climate, you know, wood will last a long time if it's properly cared for and if you don't let rot begin to spread. The old geezers must have spent plenty for repairs along the way. And they've had workmen who knew what they were doing."

"It's sad to think of them hanging on all those years, and now they're gone and the house is just . . . just *there*. They must have had enough money to live someplace more comfortable. Did they think the family was going to come back and live here again, I wonder?

"There's garden on both sides, and probably out back, as well. See the bushes under the snow? They need a lot of cutting back, too."

Their conversation was interrupted by the arrival of Ruth's car. Mr. Cranmer was something of a surprise. Without realizing it, they had both built up a picture of the American businessman as television hero — tall, handsome, greying at the temples — all the clichés. He turned out to be short, bald and overweight, and he spoke with the accent and delivery of a bad stand-up comedian. Getting out of the car, he seemed to take the wind as a personal affront. "Jesus Christ!" he said, gasping. "Do people really live in this country? All year round?"

"This isn't so bad," Alan said, somewhat defensively. Although he complained bitterly about the weather himself, he did not like visitors to treat it with anything but admiration.

"Yeah, right. The polar bears must love it. Let's get out of this wind."

Ruth had a key for the back door, and they waded through the drifts around the side of the house. At the back was a large open space, drifted in with snow, which Ruth explained had once been a stable-yard. The stable buildings had been reduced in size over the years, and modified to provide garage space for several cars, a large storage shed for garden equipment and a workshop. Ruth pointed out that with a few loads of gravel the stable-yard could be a useful parking area.

They kicked snow off the few stairs leading to the back door, and Ruth put her key in the lock. When the door closed behind them they felt a momentary relief, turning down coat collars and brushing snow off boots and trouser-legs in the entry porch, but as they opened the inner door and moved into the kitchen an eerie stillness settled around them with a chill that felt almost colder than outdoors. The silence was broken only by the low moaning of the wind. The pale winter light through the dusty windows gave a feeling of being under water. No one spoke as they began to look around.

The house was exactly as the old people had left it. Clearly, they had been living only in the huge old kitchen and a few small adjoining rooms that had once been servants' quarters.

"Probably couldn't manage the stairs," Jennifer murmured.

"Probably couldn't *find* the goddam stairs," Cranmer said over his shoulder, pushing open a door into the huge panelled dining room.

They wandered through high-ceilinged chambers like explorers in the ruins of some lost civilization. The old people's living space had been clean and tidy, but most of the rest of the rooms were a bewildering dusty jumble, crammed with the accumulation of a century. The place had been built to house several families of Cranmers; on the upper floors it was possible to identify sitting-rooms and nurseries as well as conventional bedrooms. Jennifer was struck with sadness when she realized that some of the rooms had never been lived in.

At some stage in their descent into eccentric seclusion, the old people had made various attempts at re-organization: the dining room had apparently been used as a workshop, and some rooms had been packed full of furnishings while others had been cleared to the bare walls, but if there had been any rational purpose behind these arrangements it was not now apparent. They had also made liberal but decidedly unskilled use of paint, favouring enamels in a particularly revolting chocolate brown and a sickly yellowish green that suggested decaying vegetables. The painting had been done indiscriminately on woodwork and furniture and was unfinished in many places, so that the overall effect was as though some alien growth had been creeping through the house, plastering itself to exposed surfaces.

Behind the dust and clutter, though, Alan could see that the plaster walls and ceilings were sound and dry, and the floors were solid and as even as could be expected in a hundred-year-old building. Aside from a bit of misguided and now out-dated "modernization" in the living quarters, there had been none of the structural butchery that he was used to in old city houses: no mutilated woodwork or tacky gypsum-board partitions. And under the sagging coats of dreadful paint he could discern a wealth of monumental old furniture from a dozen European traditions and eras.

When they were alone for a moment in an upstairs sitting-room, Alan was as excited as Jennifer had ever seen him. "There's a fortune in old furniture here," he whispered, "and it hasn't been messed around too much. Whoever sawed that dining room table in half ought to burn in hell, but even that is fixable."

"But that vomitous paint!" Jennifer exclaimed. "It's everywhere!"

"All to the good. It disguises what's underneath. Listen, the old geezers hired good workmen to keep up the outside, but I think they did most of this stuff themselves. And I don't imagine they did a lot of cleaning and sanding. When paint like that is slapped on directly over old varnish, it isn't too bad to remove."

Cranmer said little except for occasional exclamations of bemused astonishment and complaints about the cold. He paused for a moment in the doorway of the library, surveying a tangled pile of chairs, tables, and wardrobes that blocked access to high shelves of musty books in dark-coloured bindings, then snorted and moved on. He showed a flicker of interest in the billiard room, but snorted again in disgust when he saw that the legs of the massive old table had been given the brown paint treatment. Ruth shepherded the group through as though it were a three-bedroom split-level in Mount Pearl, but Alan and Jennifer could see that she was bubbling with suppressed excitement. "Look at her," Jennifer whispered to Alan. "Look at the way she's touching everything, running her hands along the bannisters . . . This place has really got to her!"

At the door, as they gathered to leave, Cranmer shook their hands formally and said, "Okay, that's it. I'll talk to Ruth here on the way back. If you're interested, get in touch with her. Now, let's make a run for the car."

Alan and Jennifer were silent for the first part of the drive back to the city. "He'll never find a buyer for that place," Alan said finally. "God, imagine if it was a couple of hours outside of Toronto or Montréal! Or even in Nova Scotia someplace. In the right place it could be the finest private hotel in Canada. But you couldn't do it here." He waved a hand at the snow-covered barrens.

Jennifer, in the passenger seat, had taken the highway map from the glove compartment and spread it on her knees. "The Department of Tourism has spent a lot of money in this area lately," she said.

"Not in Cranmer's Cove."

"No, but it's still an authentic fishing community, even if the cod are all gone. That 'Outport Heritage' development is just here." She put her finger on the map. "They're spending millions on that. It's going to be quite a place when they're through. And there are the whale watching and iceberg-spotting tours out of here."

She touched the map again. "Eco-tourism is a growth industry, they say. And that ski area development is just over here. Downhill runs and cross-country trails. And that golf course the federal government built in the national park . . . I've heard that a lot of people go there." All the sites she mentioned were within a half an hour's drive of Cranmer's Cove and Cranmer House. "Watch the road," she said, as Alan craned over to look.

They talked about it all the rest of the way home, occasionally reminding one another that it was all just fantasy. They did, however, talk to Ruth again a few days later. "That place is fantastic!" she said. "I've never seen anything like it!"

"Okay," said Alan. "We know that. We were there too, remember? What about Cranmer?"

"He's a businessman," Ruth said. "He knows plenty about real estate development. I didn't have to educate him the way you often have to do with people with a house to sell. He stayed an extra day, checked economic statistics, population figures, talked to people at Tourism . . . "

Alan and Jennifer felt oddly deflated at the idea that the man from Boston had been doing the same calculations that they had. "What did he decide?" Alan said.

"Well, he knows there isn't going to be a big line-up of buyers. He says that if he can sell it as is, contents and all, for a half-decent price, he'll do it. Otherwise, he'll transfer it to his company, have it boarded up, and let it sit. 'Who knows,' he said, 'maybe someday there'll be some development in that place. I don't figure it'll be in my lifetime, though.' He isn't terribly impressed with the place his family came from."

"Contents and all, eh?" said Alan.

"Yes, except for one stipulation. Anybody who buys it will have to agree to go through it with his agent, and any personal papers or business documents will be packed up and sent to him at the buyer's expense. I don't think he's really much interested in the family history, though. I think it's just a businessman's instinct to keep any stuff like that to himself. Too bad, in a way. I know some archivists and historians who would just love to get their hands on some nineteenth-century merchants' records."

"What's his idea of a half-decent price?"

Ruth named a figure, and Jennifer and Alan looked at one another glumly. Mr. Cranmer had certainly done his homework. The sum was ridiculously low for such a building, but it would make converting it to its only possible modern use, as a small luxury hotel, a risky enterprise indeed considering the location.

"You could always make him a counter-offer," Ruth said. "But listen, you two, I hope I haven't got you started on something that's going to be . . . I mean, when I told you about it I didn't have any idea what it would be like. That place is incredible! But to do the stuff that would need to be done to it . . . "

"We know," said Jennifer.

In the end, Mr. Cranmer came down in his price by about as much as they thought he would, and the project took over their lives completely. They sold or mortgaged their houses in St. John's; Alan sold his contracting business. Jennifer gave up her job with the government and they moved out to Cranmer's Cove and began work. Jennifer had received a small inheritance a few years earlier on the death of her mother; they'd been saving it for a trip to Europe, but it went into the hotel development instead. They negotiated loans from banks and loan guarantees from government departments, and every penny went into the renovations.

They had thought that renovating their house in the city had been hard work, but it was nothing compared to this — a year and a half of fifteen-hour days filled with the sound of hammers and the scratch of sandpaper, meals out of tins with everything tasting of paint-remover. Alan's ex-employees from the city arrived with sleeping bags and tool boxes, shaking their heads at the sheer size of the task. People from The Cove scraped, sanded, washed and shifted furniture, glad of the chance of work but convinced that the newcomers were completely insane. The peculiar arrangement of old-fashioned dressing-rooms and nurseries among the bedrooms upstairs allowed the creation of spacious guest rooms with bathrooms *en suite,* and the servants' quarters near the kitchen became a small private apartment for Alan and Jennifer.

The big trees in the drive were pruned, their leaves came out in glorious green, then turned brown and fell again. The garden shrubberies were clipped and trimmed, and inside the house the smell of paint-stripper gave way to varnish and new paint.

It all cost money: a lot of money. As Alan put it, they mortgaged everything but their souls, and they hadn't had any offers on those. They simply had to make the place pay, and the murder they were planning seemed like a good way to start.

They had been sitting quietly at the big dining room table for several minutes, too tired to move and lost in their own reveries, when Alan suddenly leaped to his feet. "Listen, there's one more thing we should do before we go to bed. Stay right there." He darted out into the hall and up the broad, elegant staircase. In a few moments he was back, panting a little, to offer Jennifer his arm with a courtly bow and lead her out the front door and down the curving drive. "Don't look back," he said.

Jennifer knew that upstairs he had been switching on lights in some of the rooms. She knew what he was doing and why he was doing it, but she played along, and began to feel better in spite of herself. About a hundred yards from the house Alan stopped, disengaged his elbow, and put his hands on her shoulders. "Now," he said, and gently turned her around.

The house loomed over them at the top of a gentle slope, silhouetted against a diffuse, grey blur of moon-light filtered through a low bank of moving fog. Built in the eighteen eighties, the rambling three-storey struc-ture was a curious blend of architectural styles: a jumble of curved bays, turrets, dormers and decorated eaves, surmounted by an ornate cupola and widow's walk, a feature common enough in New England and the Mari-time Provinces, but unusual in Newfoundland. The few lights Alan had turned on glowed mysteriously, dim-ming and fading irregularly as wraiths of vapour blew past.

Jennifer was about to speak when from behind them a high, demented shriek sliced through the padded silence of the fog, dropping in pitch and trailing away in a despairing moan. They both shivered involuntarily and moved closer together. Seconds later, like an echo, a faint answering howl came from farther along the shore.

"Fantastic!" Jennifer whispered. "If you didn't know those were fog alarms, they'd scare you half to death! They sound like dinosaurs!"

"How do you know what dinosaurs sounded like?"

"I feel old enough to know at first hand. But they sound like what I think dinosaurs must have sounded like. Is that better?"

"What kind of dinosaurs?"

"Oh, shut up. The house is gorgeous with the moon-light behind it like that! I wish the guests could see it like this!"

"They will, provided the weather people have got it right for a change. The fog is supposed to burn off tomorrow morning, so they should have sunshine for the drive out from St. John's, and then more fog in the evening, so tomorrow night should be pretty much like this. Saturday's supposed to be clear again. I don't know about Sunday, but by then it won't matter — they'll have a murder to worry about."

Jennifer gazed raptly toward the house. "It really is fantastic, isn't it? It seems ages since we've done this. Remember how we used to come out here about three times a day, looking at it in all different lights? I'd practically forgotten how great it is."

"Well, we've had a few other things on our minds for the last while. But never mind, we've brought it off. From now on, we'll be able to come out any time we like. Right at the moment, though, I'm about ready to collapse in an unsightly heap on the driveway. Unless you want to carry me in, let's go to bed."

Arms around each other's waists, they started toward the house. "Feeling better?" Alan said.

"Yes. Thanks. I still don't think I'll be able to sleep, but I'm all right."

Behind them, the fog alarms screamed insanely at one another through the grey dark.

II

FRIDAY

*T*HEY SLEPT UNTIL SEVEN O'CLOCK, WHEN THEY BOTH found themselves suddenly, widely, and irrevocably awake. The fog had still been there when they woke but the wind had dropped, and the scene outside the windows had started as a murky grey, paling to luminous silver as the sun burned through. Now Jennifer stood at the kitchen window, entranced. The back garden was bathed in translucent vapour glowing with brass-coloured light, the trees a series of vague yellowish-grey skeleton shapes growing more distinct as she watched. How could anyone want to live anywhere else?

She glanced at the kitchen clock and shook her head impatiently. Nine-thirty, and the last time she had looked it was nine twenty-eight. Faith would be arriving around noon to start the food preparation, and they couldn't reasonably expect the guests to arrive until four. What on earth were they going to do in the meantime?

Part of the answer came almost immediately; the outside door opened and a voice in the drafty entry-way called, "Anybody home?" A fatuous question, but Jennifer brightened.

"Simon! Good morning! And don't you look nice!"

The tall young man in the doorway blushed and grinned. "Mom gave me this stuff when I was home last," he said. It was entirely typical that his mother should have chosen a pair of cream-coloured corduroys and a white v-necked pullover, an outfit more suited to the 1950s than to the turn of the twenty-first century. It was also typical that Simon should wear them even when his mother was miles away, and typical that he should look wonderful in them.

Jennifer felt a familiar blend of emotions: amusement, exasperation, and a powerful rush of affection, most of it maternal. It still didn't seem possible, but she had forced herself to admit that if things had worked out differently back when she was young, she could have a son or a daughter of Simon's age. Or older. Quite a bit older, in fact.

"You're all fancied up early," she said. "You must be really anxious. You don't have to leave until one-thirty or two at the earliest." It was hard to resist teasing him a little, and the young man responded predictably, blushing and stammering.

"Oh, I know, I know," he said. "I know. I just thought I'd come by and see if there was anything that needed doing . . . "

Jennifer laughed. "I'm sure there are dozens of things, but we can't think what they are. We got up at seven. We've been used to having a big breakfast, but this morning we couldn't eat anything. We've been wandering around, dusting things that are already dusted, and shifting chairs an inch or two one way, and then shifting them back. We had about six cups of coffee. I think Alan's out raking the back parking lot, for heaven's sake. Have you had breakfast?" There was something about Simon that made women want to feed him.

"Well, sort of. I didn't feel much like eating, either."

"How about some tea and a piece of toast?"

Jennifer busied herself with the kettle and toaster. Sometimes it seemed almost impossible that Simon could have become so much a part of their lives in so short a time, but it was only a little more than a year since she had answered an unexpected ring on the newly-repaired doorbell one evening when she and Alan were tired, sweaty, and thoroughly sick of stripping paint. She had no idea who might be calling, and first she had thought that the tall young man in a clergyman's black suit and white collar must be some sort of joke cooked up by their theatrical friends back in St. John's. She looked past him into the darkness for the others she fully expected to be giggling in the shadows, but when the young man introduced himself as the priest at St. George's in Cranmer's Cove, she knew that no actor could play the part with such apologetic diffidence. And even then, on the chilly, dark doorstep, she had felt an urge to feed him.

She had made a big pot of spaghetti sauce earlier in the day, and she and Alan were just about ready to quit for the night. So Simon had come in, they'd put on the pasta and opened a couple of bottles of the last of Alan's home-made wine, left over from when he had time to do such things, and they ended up talking for hours. They learned that Simon was from St. John's, was twenty-six years old and fresh from the Anglican seminary, and was finding it very difficult indeed to be in charge of an outport parish where virtually everyone was at least nominally a member of what they still tended to call The Church of England.

What Simon might have learned she did not remember, but he came back, and soon he was spending most of his evenings at Cranmer House, helping with the renovations. He wasn't exactly handy, but he made up for it in enthusiasm.

Jennifer tended to mother him from the beginning, and once they got to know one another Alan treated him like a much younger brother, teasing him unmercifully, especially on religious subjects. Both of their families had been Anglican, but neither she nor Alan had been near a church for most of their lives. At first they felt that they ought to start going to St. George's, but Simon made it very clear that they should not do so out of friendship but only for genuine religious reasons, so they had turned up once at Christmas and once at Easter, which seemed about right. They had the feeling that Simon found their agnostic company a bit of a refuge from the sometimes oppressive low-church piety that most of his parishioners thought they should adopt when dealing with a clergyman, especially a young one.

"I don't know what we're going to do until the guests start to arrive, " Jennifer said, pouring the tea, "unless we both have a nervous breakdown. This is all your fault, you know."

It was typical of Simon to look guilty and puzzled for a moment before recognizing the teasing tone. "Well, I mean, I guess I did suggest it," he said, "but you people worked it all out . . . "

"Yes, but it *was* your idea. Don't try to get out of it." At one of their late suppers, surrounded by plaster dust and the smell of paint-stripper, she and Alan had been fantasizing, as they often did, about what things would be like when it was all finished, and Simon had suddenly blurted, "You could have a murder!"

He was an avid fan of the British mysteries that played weekly on American public television, and he was excited by his own inspiration. "People have them at dinners, you know. Some friends of my parents' had one in St. John's. You can get the whole kit — there's an audio tape and everybody gets a sort of script, and everybody has to play a character. Somebody's been murdered, you see, and one of the people at the dinner is the killer. Everybody has to try and figure out who did it. Everybody has to give out information and ask questions according to their character, and it turns out that pretty much everybody hated the victim, and could have murdered him — or her, I guess. It was a man in the one I went to." When he remembered, Simon made every effort to be non-sexist.

"They had me playing a clergyman," he added, ruefully. "I think that's why they invited me. I'd rather have been the murderer, I think. But it was a lot of fun, really."

"We'll do it," Alan had said. "But only if you'll come along and play a Pentecostal pastor."

"No, I'm serious," Simon insisted. "It could be like one of those English mysteries — guests at a weekend party in a country house, everybody going around suspecting everybody else. Like the dinner thing, only people would have more time to work it out, and they wouldn't need scripts. You could do it on a long weekend. It could be a real old-fashioned mystery!

"Thousands of people read mysteries, you know, and watch them on TV. I bet if you advertised it all over the place you could get people to pay a fortune to be in the middle of one!" One of the many things that Simon could not quite come to terms with was the idea of the rates they would have to charge for rooms in the new hotel. He was always looking for ways of justifying the price.

The more they thought and talked about it, the more real the idea became. It fit the house perfectly, and their theatrical links in St. John's made a whole range of advice and assistance available. And they needed something to give the new hotel publicity, something that people would remember about it. Obviously, they couldn't do it all the time, but the long weekends would be plenty for a start: the 24th of May, July First, Labour Day, maybe Thanksgiving . . . Maybe when it was all running smoothly, they could go for ordinary weekends. And they were bound to get some free publicity.

At the time, the next 24th of May weekend had seemed far enough in the future to be part of the fantasy, and whenever they sat down together for a meal the idea of The Murder took on greater shape and solidity. Advertisements were placed, and requests for reservations trickled in. They wouldn't have all the rooms ready, but there would be enough for a reasonable selection of guests. Theatre friends would help them put the mystery together, and the whole thing would be a test for the operation of the hotel, with Faith in the kitchen, her two surprisingly obedient teen-aged daughters as chambermaids, Alan and Jennifer playing the gracious hosts. When everything was running smoothly they could involve more people and fill more rooms.

Most of their friends in St. John's wanted to be involved in one way or another, and among them a scenario began to take shape. Two of the guests and at least one of the hotel staff would be actors. The two false guests, who would pretend not to know one another, would arrive with the real guests on the Friday afternoon. Along with their colleague on the staff, they would spend that evening and part of the next day setting up a situation of conflict, drawing in as many of the real guests as possible so that suspicion could fall in several directions when, some time on the Saturday, one of the actors would be murdered. Any of the three could be the victim, and the motives could range from sexual jealousy to blackmail to theft of a valuable necklace, all depending on how things developed with the genuine guests. Alan and Jennifer would assist the development of the plot as needed. Simon was excluded from the script-writing, partly because he was inclined to wax enthusiastic over unworkable ideas, but mostly because if he didn't know the plans he could mix with the guests on an equal footing of ignorance. And although neither

Alan nor Jennifer wanted to say so, there was always the danger that if he knew too much, Simon might blurt out some key piece of secret information at the wrong time.

Paying guests would be part of an old-fashioned mystery. They'd have a long weekend in a charming old country house, three memorable dinners, and a chance to play amateur sleuth. On the Monday morning, they could hash out the mystery — in the library, of course — have a nice farewell lunch, and be away by mid-afternoon.

And now the day had finally arrived. Jennifer swallowed and put down the piece of toast she had been about to bite into. Simon was not eating either, and kept glancing at the clock. She reached out and took his hand for a moment. "Poor Simon," she said, "you're as worried about all this as we are, aren't you? And you've got your own reasons to be excited and nervous, besides. Don't worry. I'm sure everything will be fine. I'm really looking forward to meeting her." The last two statements were not strictly true, but the sentiments were genuine.

It had taken several weeks and a lot of late dinners with wine before Simon had got around to mentioning Marion. He had met her in Ottawa at a conference on the feminization of poverty, and again in Halifax at a meeting on the Oppression of Women in the Christian Church. They had communicated a lot by e-mail, and met a few more times when it was possible. Marion was a graduate student in the Women's Studies programme at the Ontario Institute for Studies in Education, and — although it might have been redundant to say so — a militant feminist. Alan had amused himself, if no one else, making up outlandish names for the next conference where Marion and Simon could meet, and speculating luridly on what they might do there.

She was from St. John's, too, as it turned out — or

from Mount Pearl, which is much the same thing — but they had not met until the conference in Ottawa, facts that left Jennifer unmoved but which Simon seemed to find intensely fascinating. They were very different in many ways, Simon confided. For one thing, Marion did not believe in organized religion, although she professed a strong respect for what she termed 'spirituality' of almost any other kind. In any case, it was their shared interest in social issues that drew them together. She was . . . well . . . a bit impatient with societal unfairness. She had firm opinions on most things, and could be quite . . . *sharp* with people who disagreed with her.

Once he had started, Simon could not stop talking about her. Jennifer was apprehensive from the beginning. She couldn't bear the thought of Simon being hurt, and the young woman sounded daunting, to say the least.

Well, she would soon find out. About a month before, with everyone working flat out toward The Opening and problems cropping up every half hour, Simon had confided one of his own. Marion was going home to Mount Pearl for a week or two at the end of term before plunging into fieldwork back in Toronto. She intended to fly to Stephenville, visit the Women's Centre there, then take the bus to St. John's. The bus could stop at a service station on the Trans-Canada near the road to Cranmer's Cove, Simon could meet her there and they could spend a few days together before she went on home.

The catch was that Marion could not, of course, stay at the rectory And Simon had not got around to mentioning the fact to her.

It was not that she wouldn't understand the reasons; it was more that she would understand them all too well. She would understand them to be outmoded and repressive patriarchal convention, an insult to women in general and herself in particular, something that no sensible person would put up with for a moment. He had a strong feeling that if he were to tell her that she could not stay at his place, she would not stop at Cranmer's Cove at all, and quite possibly would never e-mail him again, let alone speak to him.

With more than a little misgiving, Jennifer came to his rescue. Simon had already been written into the weekend mystery and was very much looking forward to it even though he would be playing a clergyman again, since he was to be himself. He had already mentioned it to Marion on e-mail. He could explain that Cranmer House was a bit short on guests since not all the rooms would be ready for occupancy, and that she would be doing his friends a great favour if she would stay — at no cost — in one of the rooms that was not quite ready, and take part in the weekend's events.

Simon would never be a party to any sort of deception — except for the necessary fiction of the mystery weekend, of course — so it was fortunate that this plan was made up mostly of the truth. He accepted it immediately, and was immensely grateful. When he reported that Marion had accepted the offer, his relief was so apparent that it almost made up for Jennifer's misgivings.

And now, the big day had arrived. They both raised their heads to look at the kitchen clock, and laughed as they caught each other doing it. "Oh, dear," said Jennifer. "I don't know how we're going to get through the day. What time do you have to meet the bus?"

"It's supposed to be there around three," Simon said, "but it could be earlier. Or later. I thought I'd leave here by about one-thirty." It took about an hour to get to the Trans-Canada.

"Maybe you should go at one-fifteen. Give yourself

lots of time. Let's go and find Alan, and we'll all try to eat something."

*   *   *

Inevitably, after the hours of fidgeting and waiting, the arrival of the bus at around four p.m. caught them off guard. Simon was long gone and, by this time, presumably on his way back with Marion. Alan was in the bathroom when he heard two sharp toots of a horn from the front gate, followed a moment later by Jennifer's cry of, "Oh, God, it's them! Where are my shoes? Oh, Alan, hurry!"

They had visualized the moment a thousand times: the two of them, carefully but casually dressed, standing in the elegant doorway as the minibus entered the grounds, Alan descending the stairs with dignified composure to greet the guests as they left the vehicle, Jennifer remaining by the door to welcome them as they came up.

In the real-life version, the minibus was moving slowly up the curving gravelled drive as they burst out the front doors. Alan shot down the stairs clawing at his fly to check that it was zipped, stumbled on the last step and nearly fell under the wheels as the bus rolled to a halt. Jennifer burst through the door behind him still trying to kick one of her feet into its shoe.

Alan had time only to register a fleeting impression that the roof-rack seemed to be piled with a remarkable amount of luggage before the door opened and the driver called out, "Here we are, ladies and gentlemen, Cranmer House."

He stepped down from the bus and greeted Jennifer and Alan formally: "Good afternoon, Ms. Foster, Mr. Davis," but before turning back to help the passengers disembark he flashed them a conspiratorial wink and grin. Terry Byrne was one of the younger generation of St. John's actors, a rising star on the St. John's stage and already a seasoned professional. He was of medium height and build and not startlingly handsome, but he had a deep, resonant voice, and that indefinable quality called 'presence'. He had studied acting in England, and an anecdote from those days told of one of his fellow-students complaining that whenever Terry came on, he took over centre stage. The instructor had explained that the whole thing was beyond his control: wherever Terry was *became* centre stage.

For his role as bus-driver and general factotum, Terry had fitted himself out with a grey uniform cap and jacket, and in a dozen subtle ways had become the character he was to play for the rest of the weekend.

According to the script Alan was to greet each guest by name. He had been studying the dossiers he and Jennifer had prepared, but as an elderly woman made her way slowly out of the vehicle and another began to follow, he found himself tongue-tied. Terry took over without a missed beat.

"Miss Gilford," he said as he assisted the first guest to step down onto the gravel drive, "this is Alan Davis, your host for the weekend. Mr. Davis . . . " he produced the second old woman as though he was presenting her for an award " . . . Mr. Davis, the Misses Gilford: Miss Alexandra and Miss Katherine." Alan shook their hands and mumbled a greeting, and Terry turned to Jennifer who was standing rigidly at the top of the stairs, a look of sheer panic frozen on her face. With his back momentarily to the guests, he flashed her another broad grin and a wink. "Ladies, Jennifer Foster, your hostess . . . "

Jennifer broke free from her paralysis and came down the stairs to welcome the two women and lead them up to the house. Terry turned to back to the minibus, giving Alan the same reassuring backstage grin as they faced one another again across the open doorway.

Alan's confidence began to return. The Lapierres, the young couple from Montréal, rather surprised him by emerging with a tiny golden-haired girl about a year old who gazed at him appraisingly from her mother's arms with large, solemn eyes, a thumb fixed firmly in her mouth. Their letters had said nothing at all about a baby. Their few words of greeting also left him puzzled: the accent did not sound anything like the Québecois he had been expecting,

He shook hands with an older couple, and suddenly realized that the bulky and rather supercilious man he was greeting was the last person on the bus. Alan steeered the man toward the stairs and wheeled back to Terry. "Where is she?" he demanded in a loud stage whisper.

"Listen, Alan, she's not here . . . "

"I can see that!" Alan hissed. "As soon as everybody got off the bloody bus and Sheila didn't, I figured it out right away. Where the hell is she?"

"Alan, listen," Terry said soothingly, "it's going to be all right. There was a bit of trouble, but she'll be here. They both will."

"But, goddammit, they were supposed to . . . "

Alan was no longer whispering, and Terry gave a warning jerk of his head toward the house, where the last guests were being ushered into the hall by Jennifer, who was looking over her shoulder anxiously, also wondering why Sheila was not among them. "Listen, Alan, just shut up, will you? I have to get all this stuff inside, and you have to get in there and help Jennifer get the people settled. Let's get that done, and then we can talk, okay?" As he spoke, Terry began to loosen the straps holding the luggage on the roof.

They both turned at the sound of tires on gravel and

saw a conveyance much too large to be called a camper
moving ponderously up the driveway like a misplaced
cruise ship. "Christ!" said Alan, smiling weakly in the
direction of the massive vehicle and trying unsuccess-
fully not to move his lips. "I suppose that'll be the
MacEwens. They said they were going to be driving, but
I thought they meant a car. Will that monster get around
the back, do you think?" There was a small parking area
for cars in front of the house, off the main driveway and
screened by shrubbery. Alan and Jennifer's van was
there, and Faith's car, and Alan had intended that the
MacEwens would park there, too, but there was no way
the small area could accommodate the vehicle that was
coming up the drive. It would have to go in the overflow
parking area at the back, where the minibus was to park.
Fortunately, there would be room for both.

"I was behind that damn thing for about a half an
hour on the road," Terry said, "but it never occurred to
me that it might be coming here. I finally got past it on
the flat stretch, out on the barrens. They call those
things 'recreational vehicles', but I can't think why.
They're certainly no fun for other drivers."

Alan was still gazing fixedly at the huge machine.
"Derm is supposed to be driving, too," he said, "Why
isn't he here? Is it connected with Sheila?"

Terry turned back to the suitcases. "For God's sake,
Alan, pull yourself together and start acting like a host!
Go and show that monstrosity to the parking lot and
welcome the . . . the MacEwens, if that's who they are,
and then get inside and help Jennifer. Tell them I'll
come out and pick up their luggage from that thing once
I've got this stuff inside. If I'm going to be a lackey, I
might as well do it right." He reached out and shook
Alan's shoulder gently. "Listen, Alan, boy, calm down.
Every show has glitches. If you're going to fall apart

every time something goes wrong, you're in the wrong business. Now, get going!"

Alan did as he was told, and soon found himself walking backwards along the driveway by the side of the house, making pointless beckoning gestures at the driver of the big vehicle. He was watching the wheels and the driver was watching him, so it came as surprise to both of them when a chrome-plated excrescence on the camper's roof snagged a wire leading to the house and wrenched it from its attachment with a splintering sound. Before either could react, whipped across the driveway and draped itself in a tree, an insulator and a piece of clapboard swinging gently on the free end.

The driver apologized rather stiffly, clearly feeling resentful toward Alan for not warning him about the wire. Alan said that it was all right, but inwardly felt that anyone who would drive such a monstrous vehicle ought to be alert for anything overhead. He assured the occupants of the van that no harm had been done, although he had no idea what the wire was for.

* * *

Terry sat slumped at the kitchen table smoking a cigarette, a large mug of tea in front of him, his face shining with perspiration. His uniform jacket hung on one corner of a thumb-back chair and his cap on the other. Faith Carter bustled about filling plates of tiny sandwiches and biscuits. Terry took a noisy sip of the hot tea. "Lovely. Saved my life. I can't believe the amount of luggage those people have got! You'd think they were going to be here for a month. Those Lapierres, now, the couple with the baby . . . "

"Isn't she a little love?" said Faith. "I seen her through the hall door when they was coming in. Like a little doll, she is. I didn't know there was going to be a baby."

"Neither did Alan and Jennifer. She's got enough baggage by herself to give me a heart attack. Crib, play-pen, box full of toys, four hundred thousand diapers, suitcase, and all up three flights of stairs. Lucky the rooms are big, is all I can say. And the parents — would you believe an oboe and a bassoon?"

"They seemed like real nice people to me."

"Musical instruments, Missus. I never thought I'd get it all on the bus. Had to tie half of it on the roof. I'm not doing this again, I can tell you." Faith put a few of the sandwiches on a small plate and placed it in front of him. Terry grinned at her appreciatively, popped one of the little triangles into his mouth and followed it with another sip of tea.

"Lovely," he said again. "Then I had to go out back and get more stuff out of that honking great camper. Did you see the size of that thing? Ontario plates. I think Alan said they're from Ottawa, but I suppose that's not their fault. You know what they've got inside?"

"What?"

"Furniture."

"Yes, well, I expect they would, wouldn't they?"

"No, I don't mean regular camper furniture. I mean stuff like this." He tapped the pine table in front of him. "A bunch of old chairs stacked up, an old kitchen table taken apart and tied up against the wall, a chest of drawers, a couple of old washstands . . . they must have bought it someplace to take home. I didn't think there was any old furniture left in Newfoundland. You can't move around inside there, sure. They must have been staying at motels."

"People used to come around here on times when I was a youngster," said Faith, "buyin' up old furniture." She brushed a hand over the pine table-top with a reminiscent smile. "We had a table and chairs like this in the kitchen at home. I remembers when Mam got a chrome set from the catalogue. My dear, she was some proud of that! She left the plastic covers on the seats till it wore off, so they wouldn't get dirty. She was so glad to get rid of them old chairs she broke 'em up and burned 'em in the stove. Dad took the old table down to the stage to cut fish on."

"My God, girl, there's people in St. John's would give their right arms for some old pine furniture. That's the Newfoundland heritage you're talking about."

Faith sniffed. "If that's the Newfoundland heritage, you can keep 'un. Give me a nice formica top any day." She stroked the table-top again. "This looks nice, though, with the paint all stripped off and a bit of varnish on, don't it? Ours at home, if you'd knock a chip off it, you'd see about six different colours. Sometimes we'd look at 'em when we didn't have nothing else to do. I remembers one time when me sister Eleanor says, 'Mam, I don't remember when the table was blue!' and Mam says, 'That was before you was born, girl.' I remembers that because El's older than me, so it must have been before I was born, too.

"But you're right, you know. A fella from St. John's seen that old table of ours down to Dad's stage, all covered in blood and gurry, knife cuts all over the top, and he give 'im ten dollars for 'un. Got a bit of line from dad, tied the old table on top of his car and drove off, happy as you like. Dad thought it was a great joke. Took us all to Clarenville and bought us pizza."

Alan burst in through the swinging door from the dining room. "Faith, is Terry . . . oh, there you are. They're all settled away for the moment. They'll be getting together in the Library in fifteen or twenty minutes to have some tea and coffee, and get things started. We've got a few minutes. And you'd better not let Jennifer catch you smoking in the house. We'd better go outside."

Terry got to his feet, put on his jacket and picked up his tea and his cigarettes. In the garden, Alan grabbed him by the arm. "Now what the hell is this? What happened? What's going on?"

"Now, try to take it easy, Alan." Terry disengaged his arm and sat down wearily on a bench. "I'm sure they'll be here, and as long as they get here before dinner . . . "

"But they're not even supposed to know each other! If they arrive together . . . "

"They won't. They know what they're doing. Derm's going to arrive by car, the way we planned. Sheila's going to call from someplace out the road, and I'll go and get her."

"She'll do what?"

"She'll call, boy. You know, on the phone?"

"Oh, my God!"

"What?"

"She can't call. The phone's not working. That big RV snapped the wire off going down the side driveway. I didn't know what the wire was, but I tried the phones when I went in, and they're all dead. I had to go down to Hancocks' to call the phone company and they say they can't get anybody here for a couple of days."

"You didn't happen to give Derm and Sheila an alternate number, did you?" Terry caught Alan's expression and hurried on. "Anyway, they're good at improvising. Sheila'll have some story for why she wasn't at the airport and how she got a lift out here. She'll probably just arrive and say she hitch-hiked from the highway, and she'll probably send me for her bag. She's going to enjoy treating me like a lackey."

"She better not try it on Faith."

"Sheila can be a pain in the arse, but she's not stupid.

She'll get along with Faith like a house on fire. Stop worrying, boy. It'll be okay."

Alan paced back and forth. "By God, it better be *better* than okay, or there might just be a double murder. I could strangle the two of them! Of all the bloody, irresponsible . . . "

"Listen, Alan, they really want to do this right for you. We all do. We know how much it means to you. It isn't their fault that the telephone isn't working."

Alan slumped down on the bench, suddenly deflated. "Yeah, I know, Terry. I'm sorry. I really appreciate all you've done. You look great in that hat and jacket, by the way, and you really saved the day out there when you arrived. I just froze up. Couldn't say a word. It's just that . . . "

"Look, forget it. I've seen stage fright before. Had it myself, believe it or not. And I know the kind of strain you're under. And they *are* being bloody irresponsible, but they've got problems of their own. We haven't got much time, here. You want to hear the story?"

"Yeah, I guess so. Will it make me feel any better?"

"No. But it's probably better than going around wondering."

"Right. Let's have it."

"Okay. Now, as I said, we really wanted to do a good job of this. We wanted it to be a success for you and Jennifer, and we liked the idea for its own sake. It was kind of a challenge. Only we didn't quite know how to go at it. You know, Sheila and Derm and I have worked together before — we've done collectives, and we've done scripted plays, and we've done improv, but this isn't quite like any of them. It's a bit of everything."

"But we had it all worked out . . . "

"Well, yeah, but we're going to have to be doing a lot of stuff at the same time. And it's a different kind of thing when there's only a few people in the audience, and you're right in along with them. Everything's going to depend on which guests we can get involved, and what we can do with them. We've got to make up our minds pretty fast which scenario we're going with, then we've got to stick close to the plot so the mystery works out, and get the right clues planted and all that stuff, and we have to improvise a lot with the guests. So we figured we'd better work up our own characters a bit more.

"So in the last couple of weeks we started doing some rehearsal. You know, building up the parts, figuring out how the characters would relate to each other — Sheila coming on to Derm, and Derm getting interested, and Sheila coming on to me, as the younger man —" he leered lecherously like a 1920s matinee idol — "and Derm getting pissed off, and all that.

"So everything was going fine, but then all of a sudden it turns out that Derm and Sheila had started getting into a bit of heavy rehearsal when I wasn't around. If you see what I mean."

Alan considered this for a moment, unsure where it might lead. "Well," he said, "it's not the first time something like that has happened when people are rehearsing for a show."

"No, of course not. But the point is, it hasn't happened to *them* for quite a while. I mean, back in the good old days I keep hearing so much about, back in the seventies, I gather you were all at it all the time."

"Well, we were all pretty young . . . "

"Right. That's the whole point. This ain't the seventies any more, is it? Derm has been with Marg since . . . I don't know — must be ten or twelve years. Maybe more. Long before I got into the theatre, anyway. And, if you'll remember, a couple of years ago they celebrated the fact by getting married. Seems to me you and Jennifer gave them a nice refinished bookshelf for a wedding present. And they've got the two kids and the house Gower Street and a half share in the cabin at Brigus, right?"

"Right," said Alan.

"And Sheila and Phil have been together for damn near as long, and they're partners in the production company and the house on Walsh's Square and the van and the two dogs and God knows how many cats. I mean, we're talking major commitments here."

"Yeah," said Alan. For a moment he was seeing his own generation of the St. John's arts community through Terry's eyes. When Alan had first come to Newfoundland in the early seventies, and when Sheila and Derm and the rest of them had been creating their exuberant, socially-conscious collective productions, living in an intense little world of work and ideas and shifting personal relationships — when all that was going on, Terry was . . . where? Not even born yet, for God's sake! And times had certainly changed. Alan looked up at the house and thought of all he and Jennifer had been through together. Major commitments, indeed.

"Yeah," he said again. "I think I'm getting an idea of where the story goes from here."

"Probably. Derm and Sheila are thinking about all this stuff, and they decide they've got to do the right thing. I mean, if they'd've asked me, I'd have told them come ahead, do the show, have a nice weekend, screw themselves silly, and think about all the rest of it when they get back, right? But who asks me?"

"So they told Marg and Phil?"

"Got it in one." Terry shook his head in exasperation. "I don't understand it. I mean, there's a sense of unreality that takes over when you're getting ready for any show, but those two were out to lunch completely. They seemed to have this romantic idea that Marg and Phil would be devastated and sit around crying their little hearts out while Sheila and Derm go off and do the show feeling guilty but noble, and then they'd come back and somehow everything would magically get worked out and they'd all live happily ever after.

"You might not believe this, but Derm actually said to me, he said, 'This is going to be very hard for Marg to accept. She's going to need a few days by herself to come to terms with it.' I mean, the guy's been living with the woman for ten years and he can say something like that? You know Marg, and I know Marg, and anybody that knows Marg knows that when she comes to terms with something she doesn't do it by herself. She does it all over the place, and it registers on the Richter Scale. If anybody knows that, it's Derm." Terry shook his head again. "I don't know. Must be the mid-life crisis or something." He looked up at Alan. "Is that what's going on here with you and Jennifer? This hotel caper — is that some expression of middle-aged *angst*? Is this what I've got to look forward to?"

"Listen, never mind the analysis, all right? What happened? When did they tell them?"

Terry didn't answer the question, but looked at Alan speculatively. "You'd do that, too, wouldn't you? Tell Jennifer?"

Alan mentally tried out a casual, "No, of course not," but decided he could not deliver it convincingly. "Yeah," he said, rather petulantly, "I suppose so."

"And Jennifer — of course, she wouldn't be having an affair in the first place, would she? But if she did, she'd probably tell you before she did it."

The image made Alan uncomfortable. "Finish the bloody story, Terry," he said. "When did Sheila and Derm break the news?"

"Yesterday. Or maybe the night before."

"Oh, boy. Great timing. And? . . . "

"Well, I gather that Marg started off by heaving

Derm's stuff out the bedroom window —jeans and boots and underwear showering down all over Gower Street. You remember he had all those old vinyl albums? Priceless stuff, they tell me. Originals. Out the window. The kids on the street were playing frisbee with The Beatles and the Stones.

"Apparently she hadn't been too happy about Derm doing this gig with Sheila in the first place, only she didn't say anything at the time because she didn't want to shag things up for you and Jennifer . . . " He glanced at Alan and hurried on: "Now, don't start feeling responsible. It's nothing to do with you. Marg knows that. Or she will when she cools down a little. .

"So she didn't say anything at the time, but she sure as hell made up for it once Derm broke the big news. She said some of it to me last night at The Ship — she said it to me, but everybody else in the place heard it, and so did anybody passing by on Duckworth street.

"The gist of it was that if Dermot wanted to take off with 'a skinny bitch with no tits and no talent' — I'm quoting here, you understand — Marg Delaney would not stand in his way, but he needn't think he was going to get any part of the house or custody of the kids or anything else . . . And a whole lot more in that line. My God, that woman's got a powerful voice on her."

"And Phil?"

"Pretty much the same kind of stuff, as near as I can make out, only maybe not quite so loud. Sheila and Derm didn't know what had hit them. Anyway, you can see why Sheila wasn't exactly ready to get aboard the bus on schedule and in character. Derm was running around trying to get his clothes back from the kids on Gower Street, and Sheila was trying to find somebody to take the cats because Phil said he was going to put the house up for sale and he wasn't going to look after them any more, and . . . you get the idea."

"Vividly. So why do you keep telling me not to worry?"

"Come on Alan, you know these people. They might be a bit flaky, but a show's a show, and they don't miss a performance as long as they're able to walk. And, anyway, they know how important this is to you and Jennifer; they're not going to let you down. They're going to drive out in Derm's car, once he finds the keys. Derm will drop Sheila on the road some place, not too far, and she'll call here and I'll . . . Oh. Right. The phone. Well, they'll figure something out. I told the people on the bus there was one more guest who'd apparently missed her flight, and I mentioned that some other guests would be arriving by car. They've seen that camper come in, and Simon will be arriving with Maid Marion, the Fearsome Feminist, so Derm's arrival will be nothing special.

"Listen, as far as the performance is concerned this is just a minor glitch. We've covered a lot worse than this on stage. If we need a bit more time to establish the plot, well, we can delay the murder a bit. That wouldn't make any difference. They'll be here for the drinks before dinner, believe me. Think about it. When did either one of them miss a free drink?"

"God, I hope you're right. Well, I guess I'd better get back inside." They began to walk along the driveway toward the front of the house. "What do I tell them, exactly?"

"All you need to do is repeat what I said: one guest appears to have missed her flight, and there's a couple more who are driving and haven't arrived yet. That's all. With all the coming and going nobody's going to think there's anything strange about it — unless you give the game away by going in there looking the way you do right now." Terry gave Alan a friendly punch on the arm. "You should see the face on you! Buck up, boy!

You're the big-time *hotelier* right? Get in there and follow the script. Knock 'em dead. Break a leg."

"Very funny."

They rounded the corner at the front of the house just as Simon's car drove up. Alan and Terry watched from behind a screen of leafless bushes as a young woman in a denim jacket and jeans swung out of the passenger seat and Simon extracted his long legs from the driver's side. The two were talking animatedly as they went to open the trunk.

"Ah, well," Terry said with a theatrical sigh. "Another dream shattered."

"What?"

"Oh, just confirmation that old Simon's definitely hetero. I'd always sort of hoped he might turn out to have . . . other interests. Mostly you can tell — or I can, anyway — but you never know with the clergy." Although Alan was determinedly open-minded about the fact that Terry was gay, this sort of conversation made him uncomfortable. Terry watched slyly for a reaction.

He was not entirely disappointed. "*Simon?*" Alan said incredulously. "You hoped that *Simon* . . . " He noticed how Terry was watching him, and changed to a bantering tone: "Maybe it's not as definite as you think. With the jean jacket and the construction boots, she could be . . . "

Terry laughed. "Come on, Alan, boy. You aren't *that* old. Even I can see that Simon's little friend is a knockout, or a stunner, or whatever archaic term your generation uses. There's no sublimation going on there. She's as female as they come, and more than most. The clothes just emphasize it — make her look like a female Indiana Jones. Beauty, sex and adventure, every adolescent boy's wet dream." He paused a moment, then added, "Every *straight* adolescent, that is. My fantasies didn't need

Maid Marion in them. I used to dream about Indiana himself when I was a lad."

"You're still a lad," said Alan.

"Maybe that's why I still fantasize about Indiana Jones."

Marion lifted a large hiking pack out of the trunk, leaving Simon to bring a smaller backpack, stretched to capacity with hard-covered books, and the two of them headed for the front door. "At least I don't have to carry her suitcase," Terry said.

Alan started forward to follow them to the house, then turned back. "Terry . . . "

"Yeah?"

"Thanks."

"Forget it. I am now going to go back and continue my campaign to charm the redoubtable Fait'. As me poor old father used to say, it always pays to be on good terms wit da cook." He delivered this quotation with full conviction, completely unabashed by the fact that Alan knew his father quite well, knew that the elder Mr. Byrne was no more than a year or two older than Alan himself, knew that he was a senior civil servant in a major department of the provincial government, and knew that he was most unlikely ever to have said anything remotely like the example of rough-hewn wisdom that his son had just attributed to him —and, if he had done so, would not have used the exaggerated Bonavista Bay accent that Terry had adopted for the occasion. Not for the first time, Alan's admiration for Terry's skills was tempered by an uneasy feeling that sometimes the younger man did not make a very clear distinction between himself and the characters he was playing.

As he turned back toward the kitchen, Terry added, "Do you think we could hire somebody to come in on Monday and haul all that luggage back out to the bus?"

Now, that was Terry Byrne being himself for sure, Alan thought.

III

FRIDAY AFTERNOON

*T*HE EVENING PROMISED TO TURN COOL ONCE THE FOG began to blow onshore, and Alan stopped by the library to set a fire in one of the two fireplaces. As he squatted on the hearth arranging pieces of birch, Jennifer came in. She put down the plates of biscuits she was carrying and put a hand comfortingly on the back of his head. "Terry told me about Sheila and Derm," she said. "He's going to go down to Hancocks' to call St. John's and see if he can find out what's happening. It'll be all right, Allie, you'll see. Put on a cardigan or something when you go to wash your hands, and we'll get things started."

By the time Alan got back to the library the guests were gathering. Faith was serving tea and coffee, and Jennifer was circulating with plates of biscuits and tiny sandwiches. Terry caught him at the door, and they stepped aside together, smiling and nodding as the Gilford sisters came down the stairs. "It's looking good, Alan," Terry whispered. "It seems they left town in Derm's car more or less when they expected, so they should be getting out here any time. Sheila will probably try to call . . . you're sure you didn't give them a back-up telephone number? Well, don't worry. They're good in a pinch. They'll come up with something, but it may delay them a little. Stall a bit if you can, but go ahead and start when you have to." He slipped away down the hall.

Alan entered the library, passing from one little

group of guests to another, telling Jennifer Terry's news when they met for a moment in the middle of the room. They waited as long as they dared, but finally, when everyone was beginning to refuse offers of more tea or sandwiches they had to begin, and they moved together to a position in front of the fireplace. They had rehearsed the movement and their speeches a dozen times in the same location, but as Jennifer put her cup on the mantel and turned to face the room, her mouth was suddenly dry.

"Ladies and gentlemen," she began, and waited a moment until the slight hum of conversation died down. "I'm sure we've met everyone, but just in case there is any doubt, I am Jennifer Foster, and this is Alan Davis. We are your hosts. And so is Faith Carter, who is pouring the tea and will be cooking us a magnificent dinner. Faith is from Cranmer's Cove, so if you have questions about the local area, you can ask her. Most of you have already met Terry Byrne, who drove the bus and brought in your luggage. Terry is from St. John's, and he will be joining us again shortly. If we can do anything to help make your stay more comfortable, please don't hesitate to ask any of us.

"I'm sure you will have no trouble finding your way around, but please feel free to explore. The main staircase leads up to a balcony that overlooks the hall on three sides. Some of the guest rooms open from the balcony, as well as a sitting room and the billiard room. The stairs go on up to the third floor, where the rest of the guest rooms are. There is a small elevator to the right of the main staircase for anyone who has difficulty with stairs. From the third floor a small staircase leads to the widows' walk on the roof. There are signs on the way up saying that guests use the widows' walk at their own risk: we've had it all restored and reinforced, and I am sure it is quite safe, but the insurance people insist on the signs. On a clear day there is a spectacular view from up there — the ocean on three sides — to the south, east, and north — and a view of the land back down the peninsula to the southwest, but it can be chilly. It's iceberg season, so if anyone is up there and sees an iceberg, I hope they'll tell the rest of us." Jennifer could see the guests looking around appraisingly, as they had been doing from the moment they arrived. From time to time she had wondered whether her own sense of the magnificence of the place came from the fact that she had seen it at its worst and had taken part in its transformation. Was she too close? How must it look to other people?

The library looked as it might have in 1900, with its high-backed leather furniture, now re-covered, its towering mahogany shelves, and a pair of polished wooden ladders that ran on an iron track suspended from the ceiling. Every volume had been removed and dusted, the leather bindings carefully dressed with a special oil provided by a book-fancying friend in St. John's. Jennifer's spirits lifted as she saw her own admiration reflected in the eyes of the guests. She carried on with greater confidence.

"As you know, you are our first guests and this is the real opening of Cranmer House. There will be an official opening a week from tomorrow for the dignitaries and the people who have been lending us money, but for us this is the real beginning, and we are very happy to share it with all of you. It is also the beginning of a special weekend for all of us, and we have reserved this time to get things started. Alan will take care of that part."

Alan cleared his throat and smiled nervously. "As Jennifer says, you are our first guests, but I hope that won't make you think of yourselves as guinea pigs. In fact, you're a select group, chosen from among the many people who wanted to be here for our first mystery weekend . . . " This was not strictly true. There had been fewer responses to their advertisements than they had hoped for, and there had not been a great deal of choice involved. Still, what else could he say? " . . . and because not all our rooms are ready for occupancy, there are fewer of you than we expect to be in attendance at future special weekends. This should mean that you will be able to have more personal attention, and possibly more opportunity to . . . ah . . . participate in events. We want everyone to have a wonderful time, so if there is anything we've forgotten, or anything you need, just let us know. One little problem has come up: we seem to have lost our telephone connection for the time being, and I'm afraid that if anyone has a cell-phone you'll find it won't work from here. But if anybody needs to make a call, just let us know and we'll see that you get to a working telephone."

The driver of the recreational vehicle that had broken the wire interrupted. "Have you informed the telephone company?"

"Yes," Alan said. He felt an urge to add something sarcastic along the lines of " . . . but only when I couldn't get in touch with the plumber," but suppressed it.

"In Ottawa, they'd be here within the hour, or I'd know the reason why!"

"I'm sure everyone knows how efficient things are in Ottawa," Alan said. Only the older couple from St. John's laughed. The driver of the van seemed about to take offence, but changed his mind and smiled placatingly. "Yes," he said. "Of course. I realize that it is a holiday week-end, and we *are* a bit out in the country, aren't we?"

Alan smiled in return and continued: "Now, I imagine everyone has already found the little brochure we left in each room, with basic information about everyone here, guests and staff. And if you've looked at it you've probably noticed that two guests who are mentioned there have not arrived as expected. Mrs. Dorothy Bates-Henderson, a Newfoundlander now living in Florida, was to be on the bus from the airport, but she seems to have missed her flight. Anyway, she didn't turn up. And Mr. Frank Lundrigan, an executive with the Abitibi-Price paper company, was expected to arrive by car from Grand Falls. We haven't heard from either of them. I suppose they may have tried to call, but can't get through." He carefully did not look at the driver of the RV. "Anyway, we hope one or both of them will turn up before dinner." Alan happened to be looking toward the Gilford sisters as he said this. He saw them exchange a significant look, and his heart seemed to miss a beat. Derm and Sheila would have to be doubly convincing when they arrived. He cleared his throat again.

"Now, everyone knows why this is a special weekend. Everyone here is a mystery fan, you all answered our advertisement, and we've exchanged letters with everyone. All the same, we felt we couldn't just plunge in without giving everyone a chance to talk about anything that isn't clear, and ask any questions they might have. Once we leave this room, 'the game's afoot' as Sherlock Holmes might say, and we'll all be part of a drama. In fact, we are all part of a drama right now, but this is the one time when we're allowed to acknowledge it."

One of the guests, a man in his sixties with white hair and a beard, took out a silver case, selected a small cigar, put it in his mouth and snapped the case shut. Jennifer turned at the sound. "I'm very sorry," she said. "But smoking is not allowed in the hotel. We've arranged a pleasant sitting area outside . . . "

The man frowned at her over his half-glasses. "I didn't think the Political Correctness thing had reached this far east. I thought Québec and Newfoundland were the last bastions of smokers' rights. Do you actually mean I can't smoke indoors?"

"Yes. I'm sorry."

"How about in my room?"

"I'm sorry, but smoking is not allowed in the guest rooms, either. The smoke detectors are very sensitive."

"Most hotels have rooms where you can smoke."

"This one hasn't," Jennifer said firmly, "but I am sure you will find the smoking area on the verandah very pleasant. It's glassed in."

He grunted and with an elaborate show of resignation put his cigar back in the case and the case back in his pocket. "Aren't you going to tell me that the place on the verandah has been provided for my 'comfort and convenience'? And aren't you going to thank me for not smoking?"

"I don't think so," said Jennifer.

Alan watched the exchange with interest. He hadn't thought of it before, but Sheila insisted on smoking all the time, no matter where she was, and had been banned from more than one St. John's restaurant as a result. He wondered to himself if she would accept the rule and smoke outside or make a scene, and decided that the scene was most likely — but a scene carried on in her character as Ms. Bates-Henderson, the rich Florida divorcée. Jennifer would be furious, but she'd probably lose.

Aloud, Alan went on with his talk. "I remember a teacher from when I was in high school who was the first person that I ever heard use the phrase 'the willing suspension of disbelief,' and I've never forgotten her. She made me realize for the first time what I was doing whenever I read a novel or went to a movie. I used to read a lot of science fiction, and even though I knew it was complete fantasy I acted as though the characters were real people, doing real things, and I made judgements about their thoughts and their motives. I knew I was doing it, but I wasn't really conscious of how it worked until I ran into that teacher.

"Well, as I said, we're all part of a drama here. From now on we'll treat everything that happens as reality, even though we know that some of it will be made up. But we want to take this last chance to sort out anything that may be bothering anybody, and to make sure everybody knows the ground rules.

"In a moment we're going to ask you each to introduce yourselves. I suppose those of you who came on the bus may have already got acquainted, but this is for everyone. As you know, everyone has had the opportunity to choose a character for the weekend. Some people have chosen to be themselves — the people they are in everyday life —and others have chosen to be somebody different. The important thing is that we all have to accept each other at face value. For the weekend, we all are who we say we are — the way we described ourselves for the brochure, and the way we introduce ourselves.

"Of course, that suspension of disbelief thing only works if the writer or the actors are skilful enough to keep us convinced. This weekend we're all involved in keeping each other convinced, and we all have to do our part. And I hope we're all going to have a lot of fun. Now, has anybody got any questions?"

The man who had taken out the cigar, a Mr. Browne who came from Toronto and described himself as a newspaper editor, half-raised a hand and spoke in a harsh, demanding voice. "I thought you mentioned ground rules. What are they?"

Alan suppressed a surge of irritation. Something about the man, quite apart from the abrasive manner, was making him uneasy. "I suppose there aren't any actual rules. We just expect people to act normally: to be themselves — or the people they've chosen to be. We do hope everyone will talk to each other about . . . whatever happens, because we want everybody to have a fair chance to follow what's going on, and we hope that nobody will do anything just to create confusion, but we'll just have to see how it goes.

"Any other questions?" No one else spoke. "Well, feel free to raise anything that might be bothering you. Maybe we can start the introductions off with our young friend Simon Tulk, who is the priest at St. George's Anglican church in Cranmer's Cove."

Simon knew he would be called on first, but he still reacted with surprise and confusion. By the time he had finished stammering and repeating himself, most of the company were convinced that he would figure in some way in the mystery they were expecting, probably as victim. One of the elderly women from British Columbia asked him a question about weekend services at St. George's; and she and several others seemed disappointed when he was able to answer without stuttering or hesitation.

Marion followed, not waiting for an invitation. She spoke briskly, as though anxious to get the introductions over. "I'm Marion Ivany. I'm a graduate student in Women's Studies at OISE, in Toronto. I'm a Newfoundlander, and I'm headed home to Mount Pearl to visit my family before starting fieldwork, and I am here for a few days to visit Simon. I don't actually read mysteries much — I don't have time to read anything that isn't connected with my work — but I am looking forward to the weekend." During this recitation she looked serious and almost forbidding, but as she finished she flashed Simon a dazzling smile. Jennifer found herself reflecting that authors are inclined to contrast the terms 'pretty' and 'beautiful' as though they were in some way incompatible. Marion Ivany seemed to demonstrate that it was possible to be both at once.

Several of the guests looked speculatively back and forth between the young clergyman in his 1950s sports clothing and the attractive young woman in denim and work boots, but no one said anything.

The man who had spoken up earlier did so again, also without invitation. He was in his mid-fifties, bald except for a fringe of white hair above his ears and a thicker curly patch on the back of his head. He had an untidy white beard and the dissipated look of a man in a sedentary occupation who eats and drinks too frequently and too well. He introduced himself as Sidney Browne, Managing Editor of a Toronto newspaper rather grandly called *The World* which, on the strength of a few subscriptions in Detroit and across the St. Lawrence in New York State, billed itself as "Canada's International Newspaper."

"I don't much like this word *fan*," Browne said, "but I've been a mystery *reader* for years," said. "I like the old-fashioned ones best. I don't care for these new ones where the main characters are women — with all due respect to Ms. Ivany —" he leered at Marion — "and they read more like a pathology text than a detective story.

"I spend most of my time in administration these days, but I still do the odd review — under a pseudonym, of course. I do food and plays, mostly, and since this promises a bit of both, I might just get a piece out of it. The regular reviewers don't like it, but they're not the Managing Editor. So you might see yourselves in *The World* one of these days." He laughed in a series of short barks, but no one joined in. Alan recalled that Browne had tried to negotiate a lower rate on the promise of a review, and was glad they had resisted. In any case, there seemed little doubt that one way or another Browne would have the newspaper pay for his weekend holiday in Newfoundland.

A feeling of irritation was left in the room, and Jennifer attempted to dispel it with a bright, enthusiastic tone as she introduced the next guests. "Perhaps we should hear now from Dr. and Mrs. MacEwen, who are both archaeologists, I understand. Such a fascinating profession!"

These, Alan noted, were the people from the big RV that had broken the telephone wire. The MacEwens were both in their mid-thirties, she more than a little overweight, nervous and self-effacing; he pudgy and not very tall, with reddish hair and an aura of what seemed to be somewhat forced cheerfulness. Mrs. MacEwen stood, clutching her hands together at her waist. Her speech was stilted by nervousness, and there was a faint touch of something Germanic in her voice, perhaps Dutch or Scandinavian. "I am . . . ah . . . Anna MacEwen, and this is my husband, Eric. *Doctor* MacEwen. He is an archaeologist . . . that is, we are both archaeologists. I am his assistant, you see. We have been touring the island in our recreational vehicle. I am very fond of mystery stories. We are very much looking forward to the weekend."

"You must have enjoyed travelling around in New-foundland," Alan said, "with all the archaeology sites sign-posted on the highways as tourist attractions. I haven't been driving on the Mainland lately; do they do that everywhere now, or is it only here?"

Mrs. MacEwen looked frightened and turned to her husband, who stood up and smiled around at the company in a manner that managed to be both expansive and ingratiating. He spoke with a Scottish burr — not the Highland lilt his name might suggest, but the precise, pedantic-sounding articulation of the Borders. "It's too early in the season, apparently, " he said. "There's no work going on yet. In any case, that is not our sort of thing at all."

"Yes," said his wife, "but I am sure it is very interesting to . . . ah . . . people who are . . . interested in it. Tourists and so on. Our field is Egypt. Tombs and . . . and pyramids."

She paused there, and her husband spoke again. "My wife has not told you the whole story. She did all the correspondence about this weekend, and she didn't tell me much about it. She may not have made everything entirely clear for everyone else, either. It is her birthday on Sunday . . . " there were murmurs and smiles, and Jennifer made a mental note to ask Faith to produce a cake and candles " . . . and to celebrate a minor professional success, I told her that we would spend this weekend in any way she chose. She chose to come here.

"It would not have been my own choice," Dr. MacEwen went on. The smiles disappeared and some of the listeners frowned in disapproval. He seemed to hurry to explain. "Mr. Davis has said that we are all mystery fans, but I am afraid I am not. My wife reads them avidly, but I have . . . never quite managed to get involved."

"You said they were silly," his wife said, in a small voice. Her manner made everyone aware that this was an unusual act of rebellion on her part.

"Did I?" said her husband. "Well, I certainly would not dare to say anything like that in this company, would I?" He looked around, as though expecting laughter or agreement, but no one reacted. "No, even though I was not — am not — a mystery fan, I had made the commitment, and Anna had made her choice. Since we had never been in Newfoundland before, we came in our recreational vehicle and have been seeing something of the province."

There was a moment's silence, then Alan said, "I'm sure we're all sorry to hear that you are not a mystery fan, Doctor MacEwen. But maybe you'll change your mind before the weekend is over. Happy birthday in advance, Mrs. MacEwen. You've chosen a great gift. Let's hope you've done your husband a favour at the same time."

MacEwen laughed as though this had been a particularly witty remark. "I hope so, too," he said. " But I am afraid she hasn't done the rest of you any favour by bringing me here. I would be no use at all at solving mysteries. I'll leave that to the rest of you, and just concentrate on not getting in the way, and trying not to do anything to lessen anyone's enjoyment of the . . . ah . . . entertainment."

Jennifer was somewhat taken aback by the admission of two guests that they had no interest in the main purpose of the weekend. She realized that she had unconsciously projected Simon's enthusiasm onto Marion, and she had expected everyone else to be avid mystery fans. She moved quickly on. "And we are very pleased," she said, her voice still artificially bright, "to have guests from our neighbouring province of Québec. Welcome to Newfoundland: *bienvenue á Terre Neuve, Madame et Monsieur Lapierre.*" Her sketchy French failed her at that point, and she added lamely, "Oh, and the baby, too."

The Lapierres, a rather ordinary-looking couple of about thirty, conferred quickly in whispers before Monsieur Lapierre stood up and beamed around at the company. "Hallo," he said. "Very happy to meet . . . I am Georges Lapierre, wife is Marie, and baby is Chantal."

"You didn't mention the baby in your letters," Alan said, trying not to sound aggrieved.

"Yes," said Lapierre, nodding in agreement. He looked fondly at the infant, sucking her thumb and gazing around owlishly from her mother's lap. "She is so small. And so beautiful."

After this declaration any further complaint would

have been impossible, but Alan was not ready to give up entirely. "I hope you will forgive me for saying so," he said, "but your accent doesn't sound French to me. Or at least not what we have been used to from Québecers . . . "

"Hah!" said Lapierre. "Is true. You have good ears, I think. Our mother's tongue, it is not French, is Bulgarian. In Bulgaria, name is Petrov. Giorgi Petrov. In English, is George Peters. Maybe George Stone, yes? But we come to Montréal, where is French language, so I am Georges Lapierre. In Bulgaria wife is Marya, so in Montréal is Marie." With his strong accent, the difference between the two was so slight as to be hardly noticeable. He smiled broadly at the assembly. "We are changing names," he added, in case anyone had missed the point. "Baby is Chantal Marie Lapierre. Good Canadian name."

Madame Lapierre spoke to him softly in a language no one else in the room even recognized, let alone understood. He answered her briefly and addressed the room again. "Marya is ask me explain. She is ashamed to speaking bad in English. I will say for her. She is happy and excitable to be here in great province of Newfoundland for mystery."

Marion turned to them with interest and spoke in French that sounded extremely fluent to the others in the room, although none of them was really capable of making such a judgement. Madame Petrov/Lapierre looked at her husband in distress, her eyes as wide as the baby's. "Marya is ashamed also she is speaking bad in French," he said. "Me, I speak bad, too. We are learning, but not so fast. Most of time we talk with people who speak same languages like us. I learn speaking good in English in Bulgaria, before we are coming here. But French? Both are speaking bad." In fact, Lapierre/Petrov had learned his spoken English from a

German engineer. His accent had intonations all its own; "v" and "w" sounds were particularly precarious

"It sounds as though you have some special feeling for Newfoundland . . . ?" said Jennifer encouragingly.

Lapierre translated quickly. His wife smiled happily and replied in her own language with enthusiasm. "Oh, yes," Lapierre said. "In old country, we are hearing much about this place. Before, when government is not allow any peoples to leave country, many are going for holiday to Cuba and are getting off airplane in Gander, staying in Canada. When changes come, we apply to come in Canada. We think maybe we go in Newfoundland, but immigration people they say, 'Go in Québec.' So we go. We are surprise Newfoundland is so far. But still we think, maybe sometime we are going here. Also, we are knowing Newfoundland is special place for mystery, so when we see advertisement, we must go. Is wery expensive, but we save money, borrow money, it does not matter. We must go."

Alan and Jennifer were both painfully conscious that the rates for their special weekends were high — and even at that they would need more guests to turn a profit — but they had not expected to have attention drawn to the prices quite so pointedly. Alan covered his embarrassment with a question. "You said that Newfoundland is a special place for mystery? I don't quite understand . . . "

"In old country we like very much books of murder mystery from England. Mrs. Agatha Christia, Mrs. Dorothy Sayer. Then we are reading special books. Life history for Mrs. Marble, and for Mister Hercules Porott. And who is writing these books? Lady in Newfoundland. In library. So when we are seeing adwertisement . . . "

Alan gave words to the question in everyone's mind. "You were able to read English well enough to? . . . "

"Oh, no," said Lapierre. "No. Marya is read these

books in German and also in Polish. I am reading in Russian. Soon, I hope, I will read in English. Also French." He looked around at the books lining the walls and turned to Jennifer. "You have these books in English? Perhaps also you are friends to this lady, who writes? Perhaps she vill wisit . . . will visit?"

"No, I'm sorry," said Jennifer, a bit uncertainly. If the books in question were available in all those languages, she did not like to admit that she had never heard of them. "We do have some mysteries, of course," — she indicated the only shelf that was bright with paperbacks — "In English. And certainly some are by Agatha Christia . . . I mean Christie, but I'm afraid we don't have the . . . the other books you mention. Not yet, that is . . . " Like others in the room, Jennifer had been feeling unconsciously patronizing about Lapierre's fractured English and his wife's apparent inability to speak it at all. His casual mention of competence in several other languages had left her painfully conscious that her own linguistic accomplishments were limited to English and a few words of school French. And there was the beautiful young Marion, apparently able to speak French so fluently and unselfconsciously . . .

Lapierre/Petrov had apparently been thinking along the same lines, and his next comment did not make Jennifer feel any better. "English peoples do not need to speak other language," he said. "Always when they have teaching for immigrant peoples, they say 'English as *Second* Language'. They are thinking all people are speaking only one, like them. Is not so. Most peoples must speak two, three, many language."

Jennifer decided to drop the subject. "And you are musicians, I understand?" she said, and immediately thought guiltily of her own childhood piano lessons that her mother had worked so hard to pay for.

"Musicians, yes." Lapierre nodded. "With Montréal

Symphony. Marya is oboe, I am bassoon. We are bringing instruments. Must practise each day."

"Oh, God," said Mr. Browne.

"Well, that is most interesting," said Jennifer, ignoring the interjection. "I'm sure we all look forward to hearing you play." She looked around and her eye lit on the older couple who had been sitting together near the fireplace, listening intently as the others spoke and occasionally exchanging whispered comments. "With so many visitors from other places, we are also happy to have Mr. and Mrs. Mullaly, from St. John's."

Mrs. Mullaly stood up, a solidly-built woman with blue-grey hair and glasses. "My name is Rosemary," she said, "and my husband is Gerard. Most people call me Rose and him Gerry. And I suppose we are from St. John's — we've been there nearly forty years, but we still think of ourselves as being from around the bay. Gerry's from Western Bay, and I belong to Ferryland." These distinctions meant nothing at all to the guests, but gave time for them to get used to her accent. "Gerry retired a few years ago. We raised four daughters and three sons, and they're all married now and having kids of their own, so I suppose I'm retired, too, except for babysitting.

"I'm like Mrs. MacEwen — I'm the big mystery reader in the family, and it was my idea to come on this weekend. Gerry reads them, too, but he pretends he doesn't. All the same, it's quite a thing for him to be here: he's usually off trouting on the twenty-fourth."

Her husband seemed content to leave it at that. Alan stepped in with a bit of local information: "The twenty-fourth of May is the traditional opening of the fly-fishing season in Newfoundland," he said. "They used to run a special train for trouters, but we haven't had a railway for a long time, now. People still flock into the country, though, even though the weather can sometimes be pretty bad."

"And what did you retire from, Mr. Mullaly?" Jennifer prompted.

"I was a policeman." Mullaly said. "Thirty-four years with the Constabulary."

"For the benefit of our visitors," Alan explained, "that's the Royal Newfoundland Constabulary. They're the municipal police force in St. John's and some other centres, and they were the last unarmed police force in the Americas, until a few years ago."

"We weren't 'Royal' when I joined," Mullaly said with a grin. "Just the plain old Newfoundland Constabulary. The 'Royal' part came later. And the guns came after I retired. I never carried one in all my years with the force and never felt the need to, thanks be to God."

The attention of the elderly Gilford sisters had been wandering as the introductions went on, but now they both leaned forward eagerly. "A policeman!" said one.

"A *retired* policeman," Mullaly said.

"Were you an Inspector?" said the other sister.

Mullaly grinned again. "I started as a Constable, but, yes, I did become an Inspector eventually."

"Then we must call you 'Inspector'!"

"Oh, yes! There's always an inspector, isn't there? Inspector Molloy. It's very exciting!"

"Mullaly," said the Inspector, but the Gilfords did not seem to notice.

"Doesn't seem fair," Mr. Browne growled from the other side of the room. "Even in a place like this, and with no guns, after thirty-odd years on the police force you must have investigated some murders. Seems to me you have an advantage over the rest of us."

"Well," said Inspector Mullaly, "we don't have a very high crime rate in Newfoundland, especially compared to Toronto, and we're glad of it. All the same, I have taken part in a few investigations that ended in a murder charge being laid, but I don't think anybody here has anything to worry about."

"Gerry always says that murder mysteries aren't very much like real-life murders," Mrs. Mullaly said. "And when he reads one, or we watch one on television, he's hopeless at figuring out who did it. He usually gets the wrong person."

Browne gave his barking laugh. "It seems that cops do that with real-life murders, too, and it's the taxpayers who have to foot the bill when somebody gets a few million for a false conviction." Inspector Mullaly's genial grin disappeared, and for a moment he looked haggard and old. Browne saw the advantage, and pressed on. "If they can't do it any other way, they put somebody in jail and then pay some convict who's already in there to say he heard them confess. They make a sham of the whole system."

"It's not just the police, remember," Mullaly said slowly. "The courts are part of it, too — the Crown prosecutors, the judges, the juries sometimes. It's supposed to be their job to see that innocent people don't get convicted. You know, we used to say that Crown prosecutors never win, and they never lose. The idea is, they're supposed to be there to see that the case against the accused person is presented fairly and honestly. It doesn't matter if the person is convicted or found not guilty, the prosecutor hasn't won or lost if they've done their job. But it *is* changing. I think maybe we're too much influenced by the American system.

"But I'd have to say you're right. False convictions have happened too often, and they shouldn't happen at all. And I have to admit that it starts with the police. They're the ones who make the arrest and make the case.

"But even so, I'd still say that real-life murder is

practically never like the mystery-story kind. The investigation isn't so much about 'who dunnit' as it is about putting together evidence that will stand up in court."

"Isn't that exactly the problem?" Browne said. "Wasn't that what the cops were doing with Milgaard, Morin, Marshal, and — didn't you have a couple of cases here in Newfoundland? The police 'made the case' in all those — only it was the wrong case."

"I said 'putting together' the evidence," Inspector Mullaly said, a bit impatiently, "not making it up. And if some policemen are incompetent, or they just don't care, well, it's the same in all professions. There are bad doctors and bad priests and bad teachers. I think most policemen try to do their jobs, just like everybody else. Usually, when somebody gets killed, what happened and who was responsible are pathetically obvious. Maybe that's why some policemen get trapped into making up their minds too soon."

Browne seemed ready to carry on with the argument, and Alan broke in. "I'm sure this is a discussion that could go on for a long time, but if we want to keep close to our schedule, I think we should move on. I don't think we meant to, but we have left . . . " he hesitated a little, even though he had been carefully schooled by Jennifer in how to refer to the Gilford sisters " . . . left the Misses Gilford until last." He turned to where they sat side by side at one end of a broad leather sofa. "You have come the farthest of any of our guests, from British Columbia, I believe."

Both appeared to be in their eighties and they were easily identified as sisters, although one was slightly taller and heavier, with white hair drawn back in a bun, the other slimmer and sharper-featured, with her hair coloured iron-grey and worn short. The taller sister got slowly to her feet, ignoring Alan's protest that it was unnecessary. "Yes," she said, "We are from British Columbia, although we were born in India." Her accent sounded English to everyone in the room except Jennifer. "Our father was an officer in the British Army there, and we came to Victoria as young girls with our parents, when he retired. I am Katherine Gilford, and this is my sister Alexandra. We are retired now ourselves, of course, but we were both teachers at St. Elfreda's." There was no need for her to explain that reference any further for most people in the room. St. Elfreda's private school for girls in Victoria was well and widely known in Canada, and its graduates were to be found in the Senate, the Supreme Court, the House of Commons, and on the faculty of universities across the country.

"I was Headmistress for twenty years; my sister was Games Mistress and taught Mathematics. From the time we first started there we have been known as 'Miss A' and 'Miss K'." Somehow her tone made clear that it was "K" and not "Kay", an initial and not a nickname, and must always be preceded by "Miss." "Cranmer House is delightful, and we are looking forward to an entertaining weekend." She turned to her sister. "Would you like to add anything, Lexa?"

Miss A, who was probably a year or two younger than her sister, stood up and looked severely around the library as she might once have looked at a roomful of unruly pupils. "I know what you are all up to," she said at last, "and I think the whole thing is perfectly disgusting. I am going to go to bed now, and if any of you have any sense left, you will do the same," and she strode out of the room without a backward glance.

There was a shocked silence. After a moment, Jennifer got up and started for the door, but Miss K, who was still standing, raised her hand to stop her. "No, thank you," she said. "I will go to her in a moment." Her voice broke on the last word, and she looked down, clearing her throat, and then, with an effort, raised her head to face the room. "I must apologize for my sister," she said, her voice still unsteady. "I have known for some time that her mind was . . . deteriorating, but until now it showed itself only in small ways — lapses that could be put down to mild eccentricity. I assure you, she has never done anything so . . . so irrational before. Or so public." She took another moment to compose herself, and everyone waited in silence.

"The doctor has told me that these incidents will . . . will become more frequent, and more intense, and last longer, but I had no idea . . . I knew that this would be our last . . . our last trip together, but had I thought that . . . " She drew herself up with an effort and turned to Jennifer. "We shall leave immediately, of course. If you would be kind enough to call for a taxi or something to take us back to St. John's, I should be very grateful. We shall stay in our room until the car arrives."

Jennifer put a hand on her arm. "Miss Gilford, please. You mustn't think of leaving. Now that you have told us, I'm sure we will all be prepared for any . . . incidents." She looked challengingly at Alan, Terry and the others in the room.

Typically, it was Simon who responded first. "Yes. Yes, of course," he said, and several other guests nodded and murmured agreement.

"You see?" Jennifer said. "I'm sure everything will be just fine. Your sister seems to be a delightful person who will make a real contribution to our weekend. I'm sure we will all be able to accommodate to her . . . difficulties. You go to her now and reassure her, and I'll be along in a moment to see if you need anything."

"Thank you," said Miss K. "You are very kind. You are all very kind. I can see that it would be difficult to leave now. Perhaps we will stay, at least until tomorrow." She left the room. The other guests looked at one another meaningfully. Lapierre apparently tried to explain to his wife what had just happened, and the Mullalys exchanged whispered comments.

"Well. I'm sure we will all do our best to help Miss K and Miss A," Jennifer said. "Now, we have finished the introductions — are there any more questions anyone would like to ask, or anything more we can tell you?" No one said anything.

"Remember," Alan said, "once we leave this room the game's afoot."

"I think we're as ready as we're ever going to be," said Mr. Browne. "Let's get on with it."

Jennifer slipped out of the room. "All right," said Alan. "We have a couple of hours now, when people can have a rest or perhaps go for a walk — the path along the cliffs is beautiful at this time of day. The breeze off the ocean can have a real chill in it, so a jacket or sweater would be a good idea. We have some winter jackets in the back porch, if anyone would like to borrow them. We'll gather here again around seven for sherry, and dinner will be at about seven-thirty. Remember that we are going to dress for dinner, so be sure to leave time to change."

Inspector Mullaly and Dr. MacEwen both looked startled and turned inquiringly to their respective wives, who had handled the correspondence. "If any of the men are interested," Alan added hastily, "we have a dress suit or two available, but of course, nobody is required . . . "

He happened to be looking at Rose Mullaly as he spoke. "The Constabulary has a very attractive dress uniform," she said.

"I don't see the point of mentioning that," her husband said, "since I didn't bring it with me."

"But then, you didn't pack for the trip, did you?" she asked blandly. Inspector Mullaly gave a wry grin and shook his head.

As the guests left the room, Terry crossed to where Alan was standing. He waited until they were alone, then said, "How're you doing?"

"Actually," said Alan, "I feel better than I did an hour ago. That was amazing. Every time somebody introduced themselves, everybody else figured they were a plant. They *all* sounded like actors, and the weird thing is that they're all pretty much being themselves. Only the MacEwens are pretending to be somebody they're not. If Sheila and Derm had been there in character they would have been about the most ordinary people in the crowd. But I'm getting damn worried that they aren't here yet. Have you got anything new?

"No, and I'm getting a bit worried too. All anybody in St. John's can say is the two of them started off, but they should be here by now. I suppose they could be having car trouble, but you'd think they'd call . . . oh, shit. Maybe they've been trying. Maybe they *will* arrive together. She could pretend she'd been hitch-hiking, and maybe they're cooking up something so the romantic connection will be established before they arrive. Hell, I don't know what to think."

"Well, I *was* feeling a bit better, but if you're worried then I'm more worried than ever. We've got a couple of hours now. Are you sure there's nobody else you can call?"

*   *   *

'A couple of hours' sounded like a lot of time, but it seemed to fill itself with activity. Jennifer comforted and reassured Miss K. Alan showed the MacEwens the path along the cliffs. A series of doleful-sounding scales on oboe and bassoon arose from the Lapierre's room, accompanied by gleeful, wordless and uninhibited singing from little Chantal. It had barely begun before roars of outrage came from Mr. Browne, so Alan and Terry assisted the musicians to move their instruments to the billiard-room, where the sound of their practice would not disturb other guests — or at least not bother Mr. Browne as much. Faith made time to drive down the road to make a phone call, and twenty minutes later one of her many brothers-in-law turned up in a van with a gleaming, futuristic high-chair that would have been at home on the bridge of the starship *Enterprise*, an elaborate crib that he and Terry installed in an unused pantry off the kitchen, and a huge array of soft toys. Faith was to be in charge of Chantal during dinner, and she made it quite clear that the baby would take precedence over the meal, the guests and her employers.

Miss A apparently had no recollection of her startling outburst in the library and once they were both back in their room was her usual lively self, impatient with her sister's solicitude. "For heaven's sake, Katherine," she said, "stop asking me if I want to lie down! Of course I don't. I'm having far too much fun. If you want to lie down for a while, go ahead. What do you think of our fellow guests?"

As usual, she didn't wait for Miss K's reply, but went right on. "I think they are a very interesting group and the whole thing is very exciting. Some of them must be actors, but some must be genuine guests, like us. Which do you think are actors, Kat? Of course there are the two who haven't arrived yet, or at least so Mr. Davis says — he could be pretending. Maybe they won't arrive at all — maybe the murder will take place off-stage, and we'll just be told about it. Oh, I hope not! That wouldn't be much fun, would it? Surely it will have to be one of the guests — screams in the night and that sort of thing. I've really no idea who is an actor and who isn't, but for the moment I think they must be that young clergyman and his girlfriend. I think he's overdoing it a bit, don't you?

And she's far too good-looking. So is he, for that matter. But it doesn't seem likely that we'd have a real police inspector, does it? Of course, he might not be an actor — he could be a real guest who is pretending to be a policeman. Do you think we should have pretended to be somebody else, Kat? We could have pretended to own a ranch, like that place near Kamloops where the Queen and Prince Philip stayed, with cattle and horses and cowboys. That would have been fun, wouldn't it?"

"But we couldn't . . . "

"Of course we could! We know how to ride. We had our own ponies in India. Do you remember that young fellow who used to take us riding every morning before it got too hot? What was his name, again?"

"Ranjit." said Miss K. Her voice was strange and seemed to be coming from far away, but Miss A didn't notice. "His name was Ranjit."

"Yes, that's it. Fancy you coming up with it just like that. His father was the *syce* — there, now I'm doing it. I haven't thought of that word for years, and it just popped out! But that's right, isn't it? His father was the *syce*, and looked after the horses, and the young fellow was being trained to take over the job."

"He didn't want to, though." Miss K's voice still sounded as though it were coming from a great distance.

"He didn't? But looking after horses was quite a responsible job for an Indian in those days."

"No. He wanted to be a doctor. Not an animal doctor, either. 'A people doctor,' he used to say. There were so many sick people in the villages."

"Did he really? How do you . . . oh, yes, I remember now. I remember how you and he used to talk all the time, and shut me out, during those last few months in India. I was very jealous, you know. I don't know now whether I was jealous of you because you spent so much time with him, or jealous of him because he took up so much of your attention, but I know that I was very jealous. I knew it was wrong, but I was jealous anyway. I suppose he wasn't so very much older than you were at the time."

"Two years," Miss K said. "Two years, four months, and a few days. He was fifteen that last summer, and I was thirteen."

"And I was ten. It was very difficult, you know. Ever since I could remember, everything was the same. There were Mother and Father, and some of the other officers and their wives, and our *Ayah*, and the Indians, and us. Oh, I suppose *Ayah* was an Indian, too, but I never think of her that way. And you and I were just little girls together, except that you were older. And then you began to change into a . . . a grown-up. It was most distressing. I wonder what became of that young fellow?"

"He was killed in the war. With a medical unit. He didn't manage to become a doctor, but he did get into a medical unit. Carrying stretchers, or something."

"For a long time, you wanted to be a nurse, didn't you Kat? Is that why, because whatsisname wanted to be a doctor? He was quite handsome, in an Indian sort of way. You didn't like me to mention him, I remember, but it's all right now, isn't it?"

There was no answer, and Miss A repeated her last question. "Isn't it, Kat?"

"What did you say, Lexa? I wasn't really listening, I'm afraid. I was miles away, thinking of something else. I'm sorry."

Miss A raised her voice, as though speaking to someone hard of hearing. "I said, 'It's all right to talk about him now, isn't it?'"

"Yes, Lexa, it's all right now."

"Good. I still think we should have pretended to be ranchers. All we'd have to do is talk about cows and buckaroos and things."

"I'm not really sure what a buckaroo is, exactly."

"It's a horse. The kind that jumps around when someone gets on it, but you have to stay on it, and then it calms down. We could talk about going for a ride on our buckaroos every morning. That would impress them. Oh, I wish we had done it this time, but next time we come to one of these things, we must be sure to pretend to be ranchers."

"Next . . . next time, Lexa? Yes. Yes, of course. We shall be anything you like."

*   *   *

The Mullalys took only a brief walk in the garden before going back to their room to relax. "All right," Mrs. Mullaly said, when the door closed, "you haven't said anything yet. What do you think?"

"What do you mean?"

"You know what I mean. I set this up, and it's costing us a fortune, and I feel responsible. What do you think of it so far?"

"Oh, for God's sake, Rose, you aren't responsible!" A mischievous grin crossed his face as he realized what he had said. "Never have been," he added. "No reason to start now."

"I don't know why I bother talking to you at all," his wife said.

"It's because I'm so smart. And I think everything is great, no matter what it cost." He patted her hand. "You wouldn't know this was the same place we drove by a few years ago. They've done a hell of a job of it, and you did the right thing to bring us here."

"The murder mystery should be fun. Do you believe that stuff about the two guests who didn't make it, or do you think it's part of the set-up?"

"I don't know. Anyway, I'm hopeless at mysteries. You said so yourself."

"Well, you are."

"Yes, but you don't have to tell a bunch of strangers, do you? It doesn't look good for a policeman, even if I am retired. That was pretty smart the way he slipped in the bit about the phones being out, though, wasn't it?"

"You think that's part of it?"

"Don't you?

She thought for a moment. "I don't know. Alan said that the big RV pulled a wire down . . . That would have to mean that the couple in it — the archaeologists — are actors. I suppose they could be . . . I just don't know. I suppose he could have arranged to have the wire come down . . . What do you think of the rest of them?"

"They seem like an interesting enough crowd, but I could do without Browne, no problem. And those two old dears from Victoria — they can't be real, can they?"

"Look on the bright side. They insist on calling you 'Inspector' don't they?"

"But they can't seem to get my name right."

"Yes. Jack Molloy will get a kick out of that."

"If anybody was foolish enough to tell him, he would."

"I might let it slip in conversation. I'm not responsible, remember."

"That young one — Marion — she's quite a dish, isn't she? No matter how she tries to disguise it. Did you really pack my dress uniform?"

"Oh, my God! You want to wear it to impress that young girl. You ought to be ashamed of yourself. At your age."

"I can remember a time when my uniform impressed the prettiest girl in St. John's."

"Oh, go on with you. It wasn't the uniform impressed me. It was because you always had a look about you that put me in mind of a puppy-dog left out in the rain."

"Who said I was talking about you?"

"Sure, you'd have to be. Nobody else would put up with you. I could have married Jack Molloy, you know."

"Yes, and where would you be now? Living in Mount Pearl."

"In a very nice house, though."

"Yes, but you'd be living with Jack Molloy."

"Well, there is that to it."

" Aren't you glad you married me instead?"

"Sometimes. But, you know, I can't get used to the idea of that young fella Simon. He looks like a priest and he sounds like a priest, and who else but a priest would wear clothes like that? And him with a girl. It doesn't seem right."

"Well, that's the way their crowd does things, I suppose." Inspector Mullaly edged toward the bath-room door before adding, "If he was one of ours, I suppose he'd have an altar boy with him," and he slipped into the bathroom and closed the door before his wife could react.

"That's a sin for you, Gerry Mullaly," she said to the door, slipping for a moment into the speech of her girlhood. "Wait till you comes out and you'll get a smack on the ear."

Her husband's voice was muffled by the closed door. "I'll stay in here all night."

"No you won't. You'll be too anxious to put on that fancy-dress uniform and get downstairs to make a show of yourself!"

*   *   *

When Alan and Jennifer finally went to their own small apartment to change, they did so in a rush. Jennifer was taken aback at the sight of her husband in his formal clothes He had always been strongly built, and the last eighteen months of heavy work had added muscle. His tuxedo jacket, borrowed from theatre friends, was slightly snug across the shoulders and chest. "Oh, my," she said, reaching out and squeezing one of his biceps in a parody of girlish admiration. "You look like a bouncer in a sleazy nightclub."

Alan grinned. "Are you sure?" he said, and traced the line of her collar-bone with a callused forefinger. "I thought I looked like a man with a lovely wife in a beautiful gown." Her own dress was borrowed from the same theatrical group, and she had been alarmed at how much back and shoulder it left bare, but Alan's gesture dispelled her misgivings. She hugged him tightly.

"Maybe you're right," she said. "How are you doing?"

"I'm okay. I'm worried as hell about Sheila and Derm, but I'm okay."

"What do you think of the guests?"

"They're not quite what I expected, but they're great, on the whole. Good characters. I don't like Browne much, though."

"I don't think anybody does. He's pretty obnoxious — as a guest, that is, but as a character in a murder mystery?"

"Well, yeah, he's okay that way, I guess, but there's something about him that puts me right off. Sheila ought to be able to get him involved in the plot up to his ears — if she ever arrives, that is. What do you make of the MacEwens?"

"Poor old Anna seems to have a bad case of low self-esteem, but he seems all right."

Alan snorted. "It's thanks to him that we've got no phones."

"You can't hold that against him. You guided him

down the driveway, after all. And he seems to be trying hard to be nice. It's funny that they're the only ones who have an assumed identity. Everybody else is pretty much who they are in real life."

"Yeah, they run some kind of second-hand shop in Ottawa, right? And now that you mention it, Terry says they've got that big camper stuffed full of old Newfoundland pine furniture. MacEwen didn't mention that when he talked about touring the province. They'll probably go back to Ottawa and boast about how they got all this great furniture from simple fisherpersons on the dole."

"We're in no position to talk about acquiring old furniture, considering what we got with this place."

"That's a totally different thing, Jen. We didn't swindle any poor sods out of their Granny's washstand. If we hadn't bought this place it would have just mouldered away. Cranmer wouldn't have spent any money on it. And we paid for every stick of furniture in it with sweat and calluses as well as money." He paused, then broke into a grin. "Borrowed money, a lot of it, I'll admit, but . . ."

"What do you think of the Lapierres?"

"Who knows what to think? I nearly had a fit when I saw the baby. But she's a cute little thing, isn't she?"

"She's got everybody wrapped around her little finger, especially Faith. And you, too, it seems. But what about the parents? I thought the weird English in their letters was because they were French-Canadian. Imagine them reading and speaking all those languages! We'll have to order those books they were talking about."

"I can't figure out the Gilford sisters at all," Alan said. "That business with the Alzheimer's or whatever it is, was that real, or are they putting us on?"

"Oh, I think it's genuine. Unless they're both excellent actors. I think the whole thing was a total surprise to

Miss K. I talked to her afterwards, and I think she was telling the truth. Her sister's mind has been going, and she's been telling herself that her it wasn't really too bad. It's very sad, really."

"Yeah. I guess she wouldn't have said they were going to leave if it wasn't genuine. Can you talk them into staying? Or is that a good idea? But we need the numbers — not to speak of their money. How bad is it, do you think? This whole thing is unpredictable, but if one of the guests is going around the bend . . . I wonder if Derm and Sheila can cope?"

"I think it'll be all right. I'll do what I can."

"I haven't had a chance to talk to Simon's girlfriend yet. She's a bit of a surprise, isn't she?"

"Oh, so you noticed?"

"I could hardly help it, could I? You know, Simon never said a word about what she looked like. Not once. Maybe *he* hasn't noticed. She sure as hell doesn't look anything like what I imagined."

"Oh, really? And what did you imagine?"

"Stocky, overweight, no make-up, steel-rimmed glasses, hair in a bun . . . "

"That, if I may say so, is a very old-fashioned image."

"I'm an old-fashioned guy. You talked to her, but I haven't. What's she like?"

"Apart from being a lot more attractive than I thought she'd be, I don't think she's nearly as daunting as she seemed when Simon was telling us about her."

"If somebody can string two sentences together without blushing and stuttering they count as assertive in Simon's book. So she isn't as fierce as we expected?"

"She's a bit spiky, but I had a conversation with her . . . oh, we should get going. I'll tell you about it later," and she rushed off to the kitchen and a last-minute consultation with Faith while Alan headed for the library

*   *   *

When Jennifer arrived the guests were all in the library and Alan was dispensing sherry. He had also produced a bottle of whisky, presumably under pressure from Mr. Browne, since Browne appeared to be the only one drinking it. She reflected for a moment on how short a time it had taken for her to dislike the man, but after a glance around the room her spirits lifted in spite of herself.

The scene was perfect. The stately old room had an air of permanence, as though the book-lined walls, tall windows, leather chairs, and polished reading desks had existed forever in their present form. It had been impressive earlier, at tea-time, but now the guests in their evening dress turned it into a setting for a period drama.

The Mullalys caught her eye first, standing near the fireplace. The Inspector's short, pale blue mess-jacket with cummerbund and black trousers with a blue stripe, along with his shock of curly grey hair, gave him a dashing nineteenth-century military air. A row of ribbons on his lapel completed the picture, even though some elementary arithmetic would show that Mullaly could never have seen active military service. The Inspector was clearly enjoying the effect himself, and as Jennifer watched, he turned his head to catch his own reflection in the small panes of a glass-fronted cabinet. Alan had told her of his earlier grumbles, and she smiled to herself. Mrs. Mullaly stood beside him, a solid St. John's matron looking forward to the evening with the gleeful anticipation of a girl. She had packed more than her husband's dress uniform, it appeared; her gown might have been bought for a Government House ball, dove-grey with dramatic highlights of deep red.

The Lapierres, over by a window, wore their evening dress with a workaday air that made it easy to imagine them side-by-side in the woodwind section of a symphony orchestra, interchangeable with the other musicians — except for the incongruous note of little Chantal's fuzzy pink sleepers against Lapierre's black jacket. She was perched in the crook of his right arm, her curly blonde head nodding sleepily against his neck as he gestured with the sherry glass in his left hand.

Jennifer had always been inclined to think that the uniform of black tie and dinner jacket robbed men of their individuality — made them all look alike — but she was rapidly revising this opinion. She glanced over to where Alan stood with Mr. Browne beside him holding out his glass for more whisky, and decided that although they were superficially alike — dressed identically, both balding and with light-coloured beards — their differences were even more pronounced. Jennifer had to stifle a giggle at the thought that Alan *did* look like a nightclub bouncer, but Browne wore his evening dress with the air of one who wears it all the time to whatever Toronto provides in the way of operas and first nights, not because it is required but because other men don't.

Jennifer felt the familiar catch in her throat as she caught sight of Simon, dramatic in his clerical black with the flash of white at the collar, but looking young and vulnerable, much more the curate than the vicar. He was talking to the Lapierres, and as Jennifer entered he glanced up and gave her a smile, but he had obviously been hoping it would be Marion. "She'd damn well better be good to him!" Jennifer thought, and surprised herself with her own ferocity. She moved casually toward them, not noticing that Browne was headed the same way.

As she arrived, she caught only the end of something Simon had just said about the bassoon. Browne, arriving at the same time, had caught the same words, and gave his too-loud bark of laughter. "Ah, yes, 'an ill wind that nobody blows good.'"

Georges Lapierre's brow wrinkled. "Bassoon is not good?"

Simon smiled nervously. "Oh, I'm sure Mr. Browne didn't mean that, Mr. . . . ah . . . Lapierre," he said. "It was a quotation. An American author. Mencken, wasn't it? A joke."

Lapierre turned to him. "Bassoon is *joke*?" he said. On his shoulder, little Chantal lifted her head sleepily. Mrs. Lapierre asked her husband a question in their own language, he replied briefly and she turned an indignant glare on Simon, who blushed. "In our language is many joke about bassoon," Lapierre said sternly. "All bad. You will say this American joke?" Browne looked from one to another with a broad grin.

Jennifer had seen it all before. Simon was forever intervening in the hope of avoiding unpleasantness and finding the hostility turned on himself, but he never seemed to learn. He gave another nervous smile. "It . . . ah . . . isn't easy to explain," he began, but it was obvious that he was going to try. "It rests on an English idiom . . . "

Lapierre looked surprised. "Mr. Browne is English?"

"No," said Simon, equally surprised. "That is, I don't know. I don't think . . . " He turned for help to Browne, who had no intention of giving any.

All three Lapierres were watching Simon intently. Jennifer decided it was time to play the hostess. "Yes, it is difficult," she said. "Probably it would be best to wait until you have enough time to discuss it thoroughly." She touched Chantal's tiny hand. "The baby is looking beautiful. In fact, everyone is." The little group turned obediently to survey the room. The McEwens were closest, and perhaps not the best example.

Anna MacEwen was nervous and ill at ease, slightly frumpish in a badly-chosen high-waisted gown with a long pleated skirt, all in an unsuitable green. She and her husband stood alone, but even so she kept turning to him for reassurance. She had not mentioned the matter of dressing for dinner to her husband, and he had not taken up Alan's offer of evening dress but looked very much the professor of archaeology in a tweed jacket with leather patches on the elbows, grey flannel trousers and a woolen tie. Somehow his attire accentuated the formality of the others rather than detracting from it. Anna MacEwen might have been uncomfortable, but her husband was smiling broadly, if somewhat artificially, resting for a moment between bouts of hearty small-talk with other guests.

The Gilford sisters sat primly where they had been at tea-time, Miss A animated and cheerful, Miss K watching her with a mixture of pleasure and apprehension. Life had handed them the role of elderly spinsters, but Jennifer could not decide whether — Miss A's problems apart —they were playing it simply as themselves or were engaged in skilful parody. Surely no two real-life women of their age at the turn of the twenty-first century would wear quite so much pale mauve, dusty rose and trailing lace. If they smelled of lavender when she got closer, she decided, she would know it was parody.

Relieved at his rescue, Simon gave Jennifer a grateful smile. He had gone home to the rectory to change, and had come directly to the library when he returned. He looked hopefully around the room. "Marion isn't down yet . . . ?" he said, and blushed.

If it were any other woman, Jennifer might have thought she was delaying over her make-up until she could make an entrance, but she knew that Marion had been out exploring while Simon had gone to change, and clattered in through the kitchen only a few minutes ago, while Jennifer was talking to Faith.

Earlier, when Jennifer had shown her to her room, the younger woman had dumped her two back-packs on the floor and turned to face her. "It's really nice of you to let me stay here," she said, "and let Simon off the hook. He would have died if he had to tell me I couldn't stay at the rectory." Jennifer had allowed herself to be drawn into the belief that Marion had been completely fooled by the arrangement. She was so bemused by this revelation that it was some time before she realized that the weekend's arrangements had let Marion off the hook as well.

Marion nudged one of her back-packs with the toe of a dusty boot. "Simon told me I should bring a dress for dinner," she said. Suddenly she smiled broadly and give a slight giggle. "I always have trouble quoting him to anybody. As soon as I say, 'Simon says . . . ' I have to laugh." Just as abruptly, she turned serious again. "He's really fond of you two, you know, and he really *really* wants things to go right for you this weekend. I don't wear dresses usually, you know, so I had to get one. I didn't have time before, but I left an hour early for the airport and I stopped in at this second-hand place on Bloor Street. You know, all the rich bi . . . women take their clothes there when they're through with them." This was all said in a sudden, confiding burst. As Alan had noted earlier, Jennifer's impressions of Marion had been formed from Simon's descriptions and she was surprised to find the young woman less sure of herself and more vulnerable than the image they had built up.

Marion nudged her back-pack again. "There was only one dress in the place that was my size and it was way too expensive, so I was going to have to forget the whole thing, but the woman in the shop said I had to try it on, so I did. Then she said I *had* to take it, and when I said it was too expensive she said it was on sale, only she hadn't got around to changing the price, and anyway, I could have it for half the sale price. And she'd give me some shoes to go with it. So I took it. I hope it's okay. Simon *really* likes you, you know."

Jennifer hoped it would be okay, too, for Simon's sake. She looked at Marion's boots, and was glad about the shoes.

Simon was still looking hopefully around the room. "She'll be along in a minute. Don't worry," Jennifer told him. If the library had been the stage set of her imagination, at that moment the lights near the doorway would have brightened almost imperceptibly. As it was, the level of animation in the room increased a notch, and all heads turned toward the doorway as Marion came in.

The dress was definitely okay. An improbable dark-blue shot with green, it had been made for a wealthy Torontonian who had undoubtedly hoped it would do for her what it was doing for Marion Ivany now. Jennifer found herself parodying John F. Kennedy: "ask not what the dress can do for you . . . " She could imagine how much of a discount the woman in the second-hand store had given, and could fully understand why she had given it. Although its original owner would never have known, it was the sort of dress that could be crammed into a backpack for days and still come out looking marvellous. And the shoes were exactly right.

Inspector Mullaly gave Marion a look of open admiration, then said something to his wife. Mrs. Mullaly replied without taking her eyes away from the young woman, then turned her gaze on Simon with an expectant smile. Simon's face lit up and he started forward. The Gilford sisters stood up, as though a signal had been given that some new stage of the action could begin.

Simon proudly led Marion across to the sherry, and then to join the MacEwens. Alan came and stood beside

Jennifer, smiling at the guests. It was only when he turned his face away from the room that she could see the strain. "Christ, Jen, they aren't here!" he whispered. "This was a crucial time. They were supposed to be getting things going, setting it all up, now and during dinner! What the hell are we going to *do*?'

"They'll come, Allie, I'm sure they will," said Jennifer. But she was not sure at all.

Alan moved to the centre of the room and raised his voice. "Excuse me, ladies and gentlemen," he said. "I hope you are all enjoying yourselves and getting to know one another. You've probably noticed that our two missing guests are still not here. Or not here yet. As I mentioned earlier, Mrs. Bates-Henderson was to be on the bus with the rest of you from the airport, but she didn't turn up. And Mr. Lundrigan was to arrive by car from Grand Falls, but he hasn't arrived, either. We've delayed a little, but dinner can't wait forever. And I'm sure we can't wait too much longer for our dinner. We'll just have to go ahead without them, and they'll just have to catch up when they arrive." There was a small murmur of low-voiced conversation. Was this part of the script, or were there really missing guests? Alan paused for a moment and then went on.

"Faith has prepared us a magnificent meal, and we'll be moving into the dining room in a few minutes. In the meantime, if anyone would like another drop of . . . " He was interrupted by a stifled exclamation and the sound of a sherry glass hitting the polished wood floor. Everyone turned to where the Gilford sisters stood, Miss K half supporting Miss A by the arm.

"Lexa, what is it?" she said in genuine alarm. "What's the matter?"

Miss A was staring at the window. "A face!" she said. "A horrible, grinning face, staring in at me! I just looked up, and there it was!"

Alan shot a glance at Jennifer, and she replied with a tiny shrug. Most of the guests had a knowing, calculating look; Mr. Browne snorted contemptuously. Jennifer picked up the largest pieces of the broken glass and slipped out to the kitchen for paper towels and a dustpan.

The sun would not set for another hour or two, but a bank of heavy black cloud had built up in the west, and fog was beginning to drift in from the south. The library windows were shaded by the broad verandah, and the whole side of the house was shaded by overgrown bushes, dense even without their leaves. The lights were on, and the glass of the tall windows showed mostly reflections of the room and its occupants; little of the outside was visible. Alan put his face close to one of the panes and shaded his eyes to look out. "Nothing there now," he said. "Jennifer will ask Terry to take a look around outside. Miss Gilford, perhaps you'd like to sit down for a few minutes?" He put another small glass in her hand, and picked up the decanter. "I'm sure there's nothing to worry about."

Five minutes later Terry entered and spoke briefly to Alan, shaking his head as he did so. He wore a crisp, starched white jacket for serving at the table, and Jennifer was glad she had talked him out of the tailed butler's coat he had wanted to wear. He moved to the doorway and, with his voice pitched exactly to the room, announced that dinner would be served in the dining room, if the guests would care to follow him.

On the announcement, a small group moved toward the door, Miss A among the first. As she stepped into the hallway she looked to her right, gasped and tottered. "It's him!" she said, her hand at her throat.

"It's *he*," Miss K muttered quietly.

"Oh, for heaven's sake, Kat!" her sister whispered,

then, rising to the occasion, raised her voice again. "The face at the window!"

The small group behind her crowded forward into the hall, and Jennifer hurried after them. Browne splashed more whisky into his glass and followed. Some of the others had not noticed the commotion, and remained in conversation by the fireplace, finishing their sherry. The Lapierres were taking Chantal to the kitchen.

The apparition was disappointing. Just inside the large front doors stood a boy in a worn black leather jacket, jeans, and baseball cap on backwards, at first glance just another sturdy youth of sixteen or so, with several prominent pimples and the wispy beginnings of what would one day be a moustache. But there was something that did not quite fit the image, and after moment a keen observer might notice that his posture and expression suggested a much younger child.

Jennifer slipped through the little knot of guests. "Oh, Ernie!" she exclaimed in exasperation. "What are you doing here?"

The intruder ducked his head and gave her a disarming, gap-toothed grin. "Um a ee oo," he said.

Jennifer crossed her arms and glared at him severely. "Didn't I tell you not to come and see me today? Or tomorrow? Or the next day? Didn't I?"

The boy wriggled uncomfortably. "Um a ee a ee-poo," he said, in an injured tone, thrusting out his lower lip.

"You came to see the people? But didn't I tell you not to? Didn't I tell you not to come while the guests were here?"

He swung his head away with an exaggerated pout, refusing to answer, but after a moment turned back toward her with the beginnings of mischievous, confiding smile. "Ee um oo a immo," he said.

"Yes, Ernie, I thought that was probably you. You know it's not polite to look through windows! And you frightened Miss Gilford. Now, aren't you ashamed of yourself?"

Ernie was clearly used to being scolded. Jennifer's severe tone, far from intimidating him, seemed to reassure him. He tried to look ashamed, but without much success; he was much more occupied with staring past her in open-mouthed curiosity at the little group of guests.

Browne gave his barking laugh. "I've got to hand it to you people," he said. "You've really covered the clichés. We've got the big-city journalist, the dumb Irish cop — and a Newfie to boot —" several of the guests looked nervously around, but Inspector and Mrs. Mullaly were still in the library "— a couple of nutty old maids — " a look of resigned exasperation from Miss K and an indignant in-drawing of breath from Miss A "— the vicar and his popsy, only she's a women's libber, too — " Simon's flash of anger gave way almost immediately to apprehension, followed by relief as he looked over his shoulder to where Marion was still in conversation with the Mullalys in the library, unaware of any insult. Miss A was by this time about to begin a withering retort, but Browne's abrasive voice drowned her out: " . . . and now the village idiot. Terrific. What's next?"

Jennifer turned sharply toward him, her eyes widening in anger. "Ernie," she said coldly, "is my friend." Behind her, Ernie beamed and nodded emphatically. "He does a lot of jobs for me, and he is a great help." She spoke clearly and deliberately, her English girls'-school accent very much in evidence. "He has a developmental disability," — Ernie drew himself up, looking solemn and important, and nodded again — " . . . and he has a speech impediment that we have been working on together. I expected to be very busy this weekend, so I asked him not to come and visit me, but perhaps he misunderstood."

She turned back to the boy in the doorway. "Now, Ernie," she said, "you can see that we are very busy tonight. I haven't got any jobs for you right now, and I haven't time for a talk. You run along now, and come back in a couple of days. Will you do that?"

Ernie had been startled by Miss A's reaction when he looked through the window, but after regaining his courage he had intended to creep into the hallway and have a look at the guests through the library door. He had certainly not expected a whole group of them to be looking at him. He backed up a step and reached behind him for the door handle. During Jennifer's earlier speech, he had perceived that its sharpness had been directed toward the bulky man with the bald head and beard. As he opened the door he scowled fiercely in Browne's direction and raised his free hand to point at him. "Omp ike ip!" he said emphatically, and slipped out, leaving the inner door open and banging the outer one shut behind him.

Browne gave another laugh and took a gulp of his drink. "What'd he say?" he inquired of the room at large.

Miss K, at his elbow, looked up at him. "I believe he said that he didn't like you," she said placidly. She turned to her sister and went on in the same pleasant tone, "I've noticed before how people with that sort of disability can be remarkably perceptive in some ways. Come along, Lexa, I am really looking forward to dinner." The two elderly women moved toward the dining room door, where Terry was standing.

"He wasn't horrible at all," Miss K went on as they walked.

"Who wasn't?"

"That young Ernie fellow."

"Of course he wasn't. Who said he was?"

"You did, in fact. 'A horrible, grinning face,' you said."

"Did I? Oh yes, perhaps I did. Well, he *was* grinning, and he did startle me. And once everyone was looking at me, I could hardly say 'a foolishly grinning face', could I? I mean, this is supposed to be a mystery, after all. Grinning faces at windows have to be horrible in a mystery."

By this time the sisters were being shown to their seats at the dining room table by Terry, but Miss A's voice was still audible in the hall. "Who do you suppose that annoying fat man meant by 'a big-city journalist'?" No one looked at Mr. Browne as they moved toward the dining room.

IV

FRIDAY EVENING

*T*HE DINNER WAS, AS PROMISED, MAGNIFICENT. FAITH'S home-grown skills as a cook had been honed by some intense instruction from a master chef in St. John's — who had also, incidentally, learned a few things from her — and she had been planning the opening dinner for months. It began with a small serving of Newfoundland pea soup, followed by a choice between cod *au gratin* and, for the adventurous, pan-fried cod tongues. Jennifer and Alan took pains to explain that the cod had been legally caught, but no one seemed to pay any attention. The main course offered another choice, between moose *bourgignon* and salmon fillet with a tart partridge-berry sauce. Appropriate wines accompanied each course, including Newfoundland berry wines, and things would wind down with coffee, tea, bake-apple liqueur and a choice of desserts leading on to Newman's port and cheese.

Jennifer had expected trouble when Faith was told that Marion was a vegetarian who did not even eat fish, something that Simon had not bothered to mention — or perhaps had not noticed — but the difficulty didn't arise. One of Faith's teen-aged daughters had also given up animal products, and Faith put together a very attractive vegetable plate and promised to do something fancy with tofu for the next day. Somehow Jennifer had expected that Marion would not drink alcohol, either, but she had taken a glass of sherry in the library, and allowed Terry, who was doing most of the serving, to fill her wine glass at the table.

This was to be the time when Terry, Sheila and Derm were to have worked hardest, setting things up for the crime that was to occur overnight or on the next day. Without the other two there was little Terry could do, and Alan and Jennifer could do nothing to help. The conversation, left to itself, revolved around the food until well into the main course, when Mr. Browne found a red wine he liked, forced Terry to leave a bottle in front of him, and began trying to stir up the other guests. He started with the Gilford sisters. "St. Elfreda's has a reputation as a pretty strict school," he said. "Did you use the cane a lot?"

"D'you know," Miss K replied, "that question seemed to be a source of great fascination for men of . . . about your age. When I was headmistress I used to get some very strange letters. Some were just disgusting, but others were quite amusing. We often had a good laugh at some of them, didn't we, Lexa?"

"Oh, but Katherine," said Miss A earnestly, "I'm sure Mr. Browne didn't . . . "

"Certainly not. I wouldn't suggest for a moment . . . "

"Of course, they usually didn't sign their real names . . . "

Browne was unsettled by the fact that instead of responding to his needling, the sisters spoke to one another, and seemed to finish each others' sentences in their heads. He turned his attention on the MacEwens. "And you two are archaeologists, you say? I guess you don't ask archaeologists 'what's new?' do you? What do you say? 'What's old?'" He laughed loudly at his own joke, but no one joined him. Anna MacEwen turned a panicky look toward her husband, who had been engaged in conversation with Jennifer and had not heard Browne's attempt at humour.

"'What's old?'" she repeated, trying hard to smile. "That's very funny, isn't it, Eric?"

"It *was*, I suppose, the first time somebody said it," Dr. MacEwen said, and laughed loudly himself, to show he meant no offence. "They say the same thing to antique dealers."

Browne was not deterred. "You work in Egypt, I think you said? That must be quite expensive."

"I'm afraid it is," said Anna MacEwen. "We need rather a large crew . . . "

"And I suppose the Canadian taxpayer picks up the tab?" Browne said. "Is there anything left to dig up in Egypt?"

Anna bent her head over her plate and her husband looked toward the door to the kitchen, hoping that Faith or Terry would come in with more food or wine. To their relief, Mr. Browne turned his attention to the Petrov/Lapierres who had been whispering busily to one another in several languages as the dinner progressed. "Speaking of drains on the Canadian taxpayer," Browne said, "How are you enjoying life in this country?"

"Oh, yes," Georges Lapierre said, gesturing broadly at the table. "Enjoy very much. We are not eating mooses before this time." This was not quite the reply Mr. Browne had expected. After a momentary pause and a whispered comment from his wife, Lapierre added: "Marya ask, soon we are singing songs?"

"Songs?"

"In Bulgaria, always for holiday there are songs. This is holiday weekend, yes? But what is holiday, please? Always people are saying, 'twenty-fourth-of-May' but Monday is only twenty first. Still we do not know what is holiday."

"I think it is the official birthday of the Queen," Miss

A. "When we were in school we used to chant, 'The twenty-fourth of May / is the Queen's birth day . . . ' " She paused for a moment and frowned in concentration. "Actually, I think we said 'the *King's* birthday'. We had a king then, didn't we, Katherine?"

"Yes," said Miss K. "Yes, we did."

"I thought so," Miss A said. "So we would chant 'The twenty-fourth of May / is the *King's* birthday . . .' that doesn't sound right. Do you suppose we said 'the Queen's birthday' and meant Queen Victoria, Katherine?"

"I really don't know, Lexa. I don't remember."

"Well, anyway, we'd finish up " . . . If you don't give us a holiday / we'll all run away.' And they'd give us a half-holiday, as I recall. Does anybody have half-holidays now?"

"Ah," said Lapierre. "Now I am understanding. Is half of holiday. When is other half, please?" His wife whispered urgently again and he added, "And Marya want to know, when will come songs?"

Other conversations stopped while the assembly considered the question. "I suppose we could sing *God Save the Queen*," Miss A suggested.

Lapierre whispered to his wife, who smiled brightly. "This is holiday song?" Lapierre asked. "We do not hear this song in Québec."

Mr. Browne contemplated the hazards of a conversation involving Miss A, Georges Lapierre, Québec, the Queen and the holiday, and decided to look elsewhere for entertainment. He settled on Simon. "And your church, Mr Tulk," he said, "seems to want the taxpayers to cough up the money to keep you from going bankrupt because you've had to pay off all the Indians who went to your residential schools — or pay the lawyers who help you not to pay the Indians. Does that mean we'll be paying your salary soon?"

Simon went pale and stammered, and finally shook his head helplessly, obviously feeling the full weight of guilt on behalf of the Anglican Church. Mrs. Mullaly could see that both Jennifer and Marion were about to spring to Simon's defense, and she raised her voice to continue a conversation she had been having with Marion before everyone's attention had been distracted. "As I was saying," she said, "neither of us ever got to university when we were young, but since he retired Gerry's been taking courses. At least he did as long as the University offered them free to retired people. I don't know what he'll do now that they've changed the policy."

Marion took this, correctly, as a signal that they should ignore Mr. Browne. "Did you ever take courses yourself, Rose?" she asked.

Inspector Mullaly cut in from across the table. "No, she never would, but she should have. She worked harder than I did on the ones I took — read all the books before I did, went to the library, had me tell her all about the lectures. She'd have written the term papers if I'd let her. As it was, she criticized everything I wrote. If she'd taken the exams, she'd've got better marks than I did."

"But didn't you ever *want* to take the courses yourself?" Marion persisted.

"No, girl. It didn't seem right, somehow, going to university at my age."

"But it was all right for your husband?"

"Oh, well, it's different for a man, isn't it?"

"Is it? What sort of courses did you and your husband take?"

"Oh, all kinds. Things he was interested in but didn't ever have a chance to learn about. Philosophy, Psychology, Anthropology, anything. I think I liked the Anthropology best."

Browne took advantage of the pause in the conversation to attempt to re-open his earlier argument with

Inspector Mullaly. "So, Inspector, in spite of all your university courses and all the evidence to the contrary, you still feel that the police do a good job of catching murderers?"

"I didn't say that. What I did say is that most real murders aren't mysteries. And most mysteries aren't much like real murders."

"I thought we were not to talk about that sort of thing," said Miss A.

"It's all right," Alan said. It was the first thing he had said since dinner began, and Jennifer was disturbed by his tone. They had agreed that they would both limit themselves to one glass of wine with dinner, but Alan had emptied his glass several times, and was not eating much. His words were slightly slurred.

"That's right," said Mr. Browne. "We aren't going to break any ground rules." He poured himself more wine. "You're going to have to explain yourself, Inspector."

"I don't have to do anything," Mullaly said, and pointedly addressed his reply to the table at large. "What I've been trying to say is that mystery stories make a big thing of the old 'means, opportunity and motive' stuff, and motive is pretty important."

"And that doesn't apply to real-life murders?" Browne put in, trying to keep control.

"Not to most of them. When the police are called in, the means and the opportunity are usually pretty obvious, and so is the perpetrator, most of the time. As for the motive . . . well, if the person who did the murder can explain it at all — and often they can't — it isn't usually an explanation that makes any sense to reasonable people.

"Remember that most murderers and victims know each other — they're related, or they're married; or they live in the same house, or they've been friends. In those cases, the motive is probably all tangled up with things that have happened over a long period of time — maybe some petty annoyance that has got bigger and bigger in the mind of the person involved —but it would sound pretty foolish to anybody else. Mystery writers, though, have to try to come up with motives their readers will understand — something that will make a good story."

Terry had just made a round of the table with the wine bottles, and he paused in the kitchen door to catch Alan's eye. He mimed holding a telephone to his ear, then pointed in the direction of the Hancocks' house and went out.

Simon had been listening to Inspector Mullaly in fascination. "Do you subscribe to the idea that we could all be murderers in the right — or I suppose I should say the wrong — circumstances?" he asked.

"I know a lot of so-called experts say that," the ex-policeman replied slowly, "but I don't think I agree. At least not the way most people think of it. I mean, when most people think of murder, they're thinking of novels they've read, or movies and television programmes they've seen, and the scattered real one that gets a lot of media attention, and those are mostly the ones that have a motive people can understand: financial gain, or some sort of sexual satisfaction, or getting back at somebody. We use to call them the 'three Rs' — rape, robbery and revenge. Then when Registered Retirement Savings Plans were being advertised all over the place, some smart guy added another — self protection. That's when somebody kills somebody else to protect themselves — like, they might be caught doing a robbery, and kill the witness so they can't be identified. Or maybe somebody commits a rape, and then kills the victim in a panic, hoping to hide what he's done. I guess killing somebody in self-defense would fall into the same category, but we were just thinking about murder. Anyway, there were all these television ads for RRSPs, so we started talking

about 'RRRSPs'. Rape, robbery, revenge, and self-pro-
tection. It was a sort of joke."

"So policemen make jokes about murder?" Browne
said.

"Yes. Don't journalists?" Mullaly retained his affable
tone, but the hostility was evident.

"I don't quite see the connection yet," Simon said.

"Oh. Sorry," said Inspector Mullaly. "You see, most
people can *understand* those kinds of motives. They
know emotions like that can be very strong — especially
the last one, which is fear, when you come right down to
it — and they know that anybody can be capable of doing
pretty awful things under strong emotions, so maybe
that's why when the experts say we can all commit
murder, people believe them. But I don't think it's true,
really. Or at least not under ordinary conditions.

"And, you know, when you think about it, there's
nothing strange about these kind of distinctions. People
make them all the time, but they don't do it consciously.
Like, every once in a while the media describe some
killing as 'senseless.' Doesn't that imply that some murders are sensible? What they really mean is that some
murders are the kind where ordinary people can understand the motives, and others aren't. So when people
hear on the news about a 'senseless' killing, they're
frightened by it, but they don't think they could have
done something like that themselves."

"I've always sort of hoped that was true, and it's
comforting to hear a policeman say it," Simon said. "But
what you call — what is it? RRSPs? — they aren't the
usual kind of murder anyway, I think you said?"

"No, they're not. Most murders seem to be sudden,
spur-of-the-moment kind of things. After they've happened, the killers seem to be as confused as everybody
else. Alcohol is a big factor — that and drugs. Something
flares up, somebody loses control for a minute, some-

body gets killed, and everybody is left wondering how it happened, including the person who did it.

"Most of the time, it comes as a surprise to the killer as much as it must have been to the victim. Maybe that kind of thing *can* happen to anybody. I don't know . . . "

Browne had wanted an argument: he had not meant to provide the Inspector with a platform, and he looked around the table for a way of taking charge again. His eye lit on Marion.

"Well, now, Ms. Ivany," he said. His tone suggested that she had been waiting in line for him to notice her, and he stressed the "Ms." so that it sounded like something from *Gone With the Wind*. "I understand you're a graduate student?"

Marion looked up. "Yes. I'm working on a doctorate at OISE."

Simon, who was seated on the other side of the table, smiled around at the guests. "The Ontario Institute for Studies in Education," he explained.

Although the explanation had been meant for everyone, Browne treated as though it had been addressed to him alone. "Yeah, yeah," he said dismissively, "I know." He turned back to Marion. "What kind of a doctorate? What in?"

"Women's Studies."

"Women's Studies?" Browne put on an exaggerated look of astonishment. "You mean they give people PhDs in *that* now?"

Marion took a sip of wine and dabbed her lips with a napkin. "No," she said levelly. "No, they don't give them. You have to earn them."

Browne grinned. He was impervious to slights, and this was more the sort of person-to-person exchange he had been looking for. "But all these things — Women's Studies, Canadian Studies — in the States they've even got *Black* Studies, whatever the hell that is — can you really do a PhD in that kind of thing? I mean, doesn't a doctorate involve all kinds of rigorous theories and things? . . . "

Marion interrupted, raising her voice slightly. "I think you'll find, Mr. Browne, that disciplinary boundaries are not nearly as clear as they used to be. There are many theoretical perspectives that cut across . . . "

"Oh, yeah. I bet there are. And what 'theoretical perspective'" — he gave the words a mocking emphasis — "do you follow?"

"For my thesis research I am using a Marxist-Feminist framework . . . "

Browne gave a single bark of laughter. "Don't tell me old Karl was a closet women's libber! Or maybe it's Groucho you've got in mind?"

Georges Lapierre, the former Giorgi Petrov, had been following the conversation intently, his head swivelling from one to the other like a spectator at a tennis-match, his brow furrowed in concentration. The mention of Marion's theoretical perspective gave him an opening. "Is finish, Marx," he said.

Miss A looked up from her plate in astonishment. "Finnish?" she said. "Oh, I don't think so . . . "

"Yes, yes, yes," said Lapierre eagerly. "Marx, Lenin, Stalin — all finish."

"Really?" said Miss A. "Are you sure? All of them? I had always understood that Marx was German, and surely Lenin was Russian? And wasn't Stalin a Georgian or something, Katherine?"

Lapierre nodded vigorously in agreement. "Yes. Is true. Russia, Georgia — all of Soviet Union — Germania of the east, all places — all finish, Marx."

Miss A looked inquiringly at her sister, who gave a slight, ladylike shrug. Browne's grin widened. "Karl Marx, the Finnish Feminist. What do you say, Miz Ivany?

Aren't you going have to drop old Karl? Even the Russians can't stomach him any more."

Marion sighed. "There is a distinction to be made between Marx's sociological theories and the policies of . . ."

"Yeah, yeah. I know," Browne said again, with a dismissive wave of his hand. "The last bastion of Marxism: in Canadian universities, paid for with our money. Anyway, tell me, now that we've got your 'theoretical perspective' sorted out, what's the topic? What are you writing about?"

Simon gave an anxious clergyman's smile, including the whole company. "Well," he said, perhaps we should . . . " He paused, searching for something to suggest, but he had not thought that far ahead.

Marion ignored him, still gazing levelly across the table at Browne. "It's an analysis of the class position and exploitation of female sex workers in Toronto and Montréal."

Simon's forced smile faded, and he picked up his knife and fork again. Browne gave a whoop of laughter. "*What* kind of workers?"

"Sex workers," she said again.

"Dear me!" said Mrs. MacEwen. "What on earth? . . . "

Marion turned toward her, her tone noticeably more friendly than the one she had used with Browne. "It's a term we use to include prostitutes, strippers, table-dancers, porn-film and peep-show performers, massage parlour and escort-service workers . . . "

"Good heavens!" Mrs. MacEwen said faintly. "Really?"

"Yes. We refer to it as 'the sex industry', and it's structured like any other industry, with owners and managers and investors . . . and workers."

"But you said *female* . . . ah . . . sex workers," Miss A said, horrified but fascinated.

"Yes."

"But surely those are all . . . "

"No," Marion said. "Not at all. The majority are women, certainly, but there are males in each of those categories. The customers are almost all men, though, but not entirely. I'm concentrating on the female workers because, just as in any other line of work, they suffer the greatest exploitation."

Browne was still chortling and shaking his head. "Oh, this is great stuff. *Das Kapital* meets the Happy Hooker. Sex workers of the world unite: you have nothing to lose but your chains — and whips and black leather underpants! What are you going to do, organize a union?"

"I'd prefer a society where that kind of exploitation didn't exist at all," Marion said. "But that would mean the elimination of the patriarchal system, and since that doesn't seem likely in the near future, a union might not be a bad idea."

Browne was enjoying himself immensely. "Well, Reverend," he said to Simon, "what do you think of all this — your lady friend consorting with hookers?"

Simon, taken unawares, blushed and stammered. Jennifer silently willed him to produce a devastating retort, but Simon remained Simon and none was forthcoming. After an awkward moment, Mrs. Mullaly intervened.

"It seems to me that there are plenty of good precedents in the Bible," she said. "At least there are in the Catholic version."

"What?" said Simon, startled. "I . . . "

"Didn't Our Lord sometimes prefer the company of prostitutes to . . . " she smiled sweetly at Mr. Browne " . . . to more respectable people? Like policemen and priests . . . and even journalists, maybe, if they had them then?"

Browne had no immediate response, and the others waited to see how he would react. With no one speaking, noises could be heard from the front hall — scuffling, a male voice, loud but incomprehensible, then a tearful female cry: "Please, Steve! You can't go in there! Please don't!"

All eyes turned to the doorway between the dining room and the front hall, and Alan and Jennifer got to their feet as Faith and Steve appeared there, she tugging ineffectually at his sleeve. Steve was as tall as Alan, but thinner. His dark hair was matted and uncombed, and he had not shaved for several days. He was wearing a stained coverall that hung loosely on his lanky frame, and a small, bright-red tool-box dangled from his right hand. They stood there for a moment in tableau, Steve staring glassily back at the guests, until he shook Faith's hand off his sleeve and began to plod forward, breathing heavily through a slack mouth, walking with exaggerated care, his eyes fixed on a doorway at the back of the room, beside the swinging door to the kitchen.

Alan moved to intercept him. "Steve!" he said with false joviality. "What are you doing here?"

The combination of his local accent and his advanced state of drunkenness made Steve's reply unintelligible to most of the guests, but Alan understood him clearly. "Goin' down d'fuckin' basement." One of the oddities of the old house was that stairs led down to the large basement from a door in the back wall of the dining room. Other stairs led off the hall, and from the rear entry porch, but Steve had chosen the dining room.

"Steve, you don't want to go down the basement!" Alan moved in front of him. "Listen, why not go into the kitchen? Faith will give you a cup of tea and a bite to eat."

"Don't want to eat. Goin' down d'fuckin' basement. Take out d'fuckin' panel box."

Alan was now walking backwards as Steve continued his dogged advance. "You can't do that, Steve! Look, we've got all the guests here. You can't! . . ."

"Won't pay me my fuckin' money, take out d'fuckin' panel box!"

By now, Steve's back was to the guests at the table. He attempted to push past Alan, there was a confused flurry of movement that no one saw very clearly, and he suddenly staggered back, blood streaming from his nose. He looked at the guests in vague astonishment, as though seeing them for the first time, raised his left hand to his nose, then looked at it with the same air of innocent surprise. "Blood," he said.

Suddenly, and shockingly, he began to cry. He put his hand to his eyes, smearing his face with blood and tears, and his thin body shook with racking sobs. "Sorry," he said to the room at large. "Sorry. Too mush a drink," and he turned toward the hall door, the tool box still dangling from his right hand.

Alan put an arm around his shoulders, and began to lead him toward the door. Jennifer, who had been frozen by her chair, half-way between sitting and standing, came up on Steve's other side, and between them they half-steered and half-supported him out into the hall. Faith was still there, leaning against a wall, distraught and in tears.

"How on earth did he get here?" Jennifer asked. "I hope he didn't drive. Faith, you take him home. Terry and I will take care of dessert and coffee, and the washing up." She darted into the little toilet-and-wash-basin cubicle under the stairs and came back with a damp washcloth. While Jennifer wiped his face, Steve stood obediently still. Apart from the fact that she had to reach up to wipe his face, he looked like a small boy being attended to by his mother after a playground accident, his thin shoulders heaving from time to time with great sighs in the aftermath of his sobs. She put the washcloth into his free left hand and his hand to his nose. "Just hold it there," she said. "It's nearly stopped now."

While Jennifer was busy with Steve, Faith wiped her eyes and walked determinedly into the dining room. Ignoring the other guests, she went directly to Marya Lapierre. "I'm sorry," she said, "but you'll have to look after the baby. I've got to take care of —" she flapped her hand toward the hallway — "of that," and she turned abruptly and walked back into the hall. Marya stared after her, wide-eyed in panic, until her husband provided a quick translation and she rushed through the door to the kitchen and into the pantry where little Chantel lay sleeping, peacefully oblivious.

Alan led Steve outside, and assisted him to sit down on the stairs, where he sat hunched over, holding the washcloth to his nose and mumbling incoherent apologies.

Back in the kitchen, Faith was hurriedly setting out dessert bowls, cups and saucers. "I'll just get this ready," she said, "then I'll take him home. I'm real sorry about all this, Jennifer, I am so. Steve'll be sorry, too, when he sobers up."

"Don't worry about it," Jennifer said. "Just look after him. We'll manage. It's heartbreaking to hear him cry like that."

"Ah, he always cries when he's drinkin'," said Faith. She dabbed angrily at her eyes. "Gets to me every time, though. I'll be in for breakfast. You go on in and talk to your guests. He'll be all right on the porch for a few minutes, till I gets the desserts ready."

"I'm sorry Alan hit him like that. I don't know what got into him. He's never done anything like that before."

"Ah, that's nothin', sure. He often gets bet up when he's drunk. Serve him right most of the time. But I feels sorry for him, all the same."

Out in the hall, Terry drew Alan aside into the library and flicked on a lamp. "I see Steve showed up," he said. "Listen, Alan, we've got some big trouble."

Alan slumped into a chair. "They're not coming, right? They'd be here by now. What happened?"

"You don't really want to know," Terry said. "Listen, I've got an idea . . . "

"I want to know," Alan said. "I've got a right to know."

Although he was not drunk — certainly not by comparison with Steve — Alan had had more to drink than was advisable. Terry didn't argue. "Well, they got to Clarenville. Apparently they'd been squabbling a bit along the way — you understand I'm putting this together from three versions. I called Marge — you can see how desperate I was — and I called Phil, and I called the hospital in Clarenville and talked to Derm."

"The hospital?"

"Yeah. He's in there."

"Oh, great. Wonderful. Where's Sheila?"

"Look, maybe I'd better just tell you what happened, right?"

"Okay. Go ahead."

"Okay. So they're squabbling away down the highway, and by the time they got to Clarenville they weren't speaking to each other. Derm parked in the strip mall — you know, the place with the big square parking lot, where the Co-op is. He pulled up and got out of the car. I think Sheila had the idea that he was going to phone Marg. Maybe he was.

"The Mounties say Sheila got behind the wheel and tried to run him down, but I don't believe that. You know how she drives. I think she was just planning to take off and leave him, but she can't drive a standard. Can't drive an automatic worth a damn either, come to that. Anyhow, she went through the front window of the Co-op. Fortunately nobody was hurt. Except Derm. She kind of clipped him on the way through the window.

"So she jumps out of the car and rushes over to Derm, who's lying there in all the broken glass, and she kneels down and pulls his head onto her lap and she's crying and yelling that she didn't mean to hurt him and she loves him and she's willing to die for him, and he's yelling 'Leave me alone you crazy bitch,' and everybody in the parking lot is standing around like a Greek chorus saying, 'Don't move him, don't move him.'

"Then some guy puts his hand on Sheila's shoulder, and goes, 'He's in shock. He doesn't know what he's saying,' and Derm looks up at him and says, 'I'm not in shock, you fucking idiot! I know exactly what I'm saying,' and Sheila hollers, 'Take your hands off me!' and the guy jumps back and falls down and cuts himself on the broken glass, and everybody goes back to yelling at each other and saying 'Don't move him.' It must have made a great scene. You could do it on stage, but it'd have to be in a movie to do it justice."

"I don't give a shit about the scene. What happened next?"

Terry looked surprised and offended that anyone could treat such a dramatic scene so lightly, but he realized that Alan was under strain and he continued. "Well, the Mounties showed up, of course, and of course they thought they just had an ordinary accident; they don't know anything about Sheila. And I guess she'd got herself a bit worked up, so she's in the lock-up: assault with a dangerous weapon — that's Derm's car, and it's dangerous even without Sheila behind the wheel — assault causing grievous bodily harm; using abusive language — I believe that one, for sure — resisting arrest, assault on a police officer, and a few others I can't remember. She must have pissed them right off."

"And Derm?"

"In hospital with a broken leg and what they call minor cuts and abrasions. I talked to him on the phone, and he seems okay, only he can't walk. And they won't give him his clothes back."

Alan stood up wearily. "Well, that's it. I'll go and tell Jennifer."

At that moment, Jennifer walked into the library. "Tell me what?"

"Terry can tell you the whole story later, but the short version is that Derm and Sheila won't be here. It's all over. We're finished."

Terry drew a sheaf of papers from an inside pocket. "Listen," he said. "I was afraid they weren't going to get here, so I started putting down a few ideas before I went over to the Hancocks'. We can still do it if we can get Simon and Maid Marion to play ball. It won't be as good as what we had planned, but we can still swing a murder, maybe tomorrow afternoon. We might have to kill you, Jennifer, and maybe we could make Simon the murderer. He'd like that."

Alan rubbed his eyes and massaged his forehead. "Terry, I really appreciate what you're trying to do. You've done more than your share already, and I want you to know that I'm grateful for it, but we can't salvage it now. There's this whole business with Steve — he's not going to go away, you know. He's going to sleep for a couple of hours, then drink some more and be back here again. One of the Gilford sisters has gone around the bend and the two of them are going to take off tomorrow, and Browne is antagonizing everybody . . . I hate that guy. He gives me the creeps. It's all falling apart. I just haven't got the strength . . . "

"Come on, Alan," Terry said. "Pull yourself together. We can do this."

Alan shook his head. "I really don't know what made us think we could run a hotel at all, let alone manage a murder mystery on the opening night. You were right, Terry, it must have been some sort of mid-life thing. But I can see now that it could never work."

"Hey, wait a minute," Terry said. "You can't just throw it all away like that. Jennifer is part of this. You've been equal partners all along. What do you say, Jennifer?"

Jennifer's face was pale and strained. "Yes, we have been equal partners. Alan, we've put everything we've got into this place, and I don't have to tell you what we owe. We need this weekend. We need the money. Nobody will lend us any more until we start showing some coming in. The invitations have all gone out for the opening next weekend, and we've been taking reservations, and we're already filled up for the next mystery weekend on July First . . . "

"Listen," said Terry. "You don't have to pay me. At least not right away. I can get by until you . . . "

"Thanks, Terry," said Alan. "I really appreciate it." He turned to Jennifer "Jen, I just can't do it. There's all kinds of things going on here, things I need to talk to you about, but I can't . . . Maybe all the preparations were too much for me, but I really haven't got the strength to keep going."

"All right," said Jennifer, her voice shaking. "If Alan says he can't go on with it, then that's all there is to it. We have to do it together or not at all."

"Right," said Alan. "I'll go and tell the guests." He squeezed Terry's arm. "Thanks for everything. I'm sorry it didn't work out."

They watched him move out into the hall, walking slowly, his shoulders slumped.

"Funny," Jennifer said. "I was just in there, and they're all talking a mile a minute. I think most of them believe that Steve was part of the entertainment."

"There you are!" said Terry. "They don't know what to think. We can set up anything we like and they'll buy it. Go after him, Jennifer, tell him we can do it!"

"No, Terry . . . and thanks, by the way, for trying, and for all you've done. But I think Alan's really lost it. You weren't in there to see what he did to Steve, but I don't think he's in any state to be going on with this. If he says it's over, then it's over. We'll sort out the pieces later." She walked out of the library.

Back in the dining room, Alan did not sit down, but stood behind his chair. His face was pale, and there was a smear of blood on his white shirt-front. The guests, who had been talking animatedly, fell silent one by one, and looked in his direction.

"Ladies and gentlemen," he said. "I'm very sorry about this . . . unpleasantness. As you might have gathered, Steve is Faith's husband, and he's an electrician. He did a lot of work for us when we were renovating the place, and he did an excellent job as long as he was sober. Unfortunately, he has a serious alcohol problem. We had to bring in another electrician to finish the work, and to re-do some of the things Steve did when he was falling off the wagon. When he gets drunk, Steve still believes that we owe him money for the contract. That's what all this was about. When he sobers up, he'll be all right." Alan's own voice gave evidence that he, too, had had a little too much wine.

No one spoke for a moment. Georges Lapierre broke the silence. "Before she go upstairs with baby, Marya tell me, 'Is very sad. He cry. Hit him in nose is wrong to do!' "

"Yes. Well, I'm sorry about that, but I couldn't let him go downstairs. In his condition he could have

112

electrocuted himself, set the place on fire . . . I had to stop him." Judging from his expression, Georges Lapierre remained unconvinced.

"There is something else I must tell you," Alan went on. "I am sorry to say that we have to cancel the mystery weekend."

To his surprise, the guests did not react, but continued to look at him expectantly. "As some of you might have guessed, the two people who have not arrived — Mrs. Henderson-Bates and Mr. Lundrigan — were to have been actors. They were the ones who were supposed to set up and carry out our mystery. Unfortunately, they have been . . . unavoidably detained. They won't be here, and without them, we can't go through with our plans.

"Naturally, we will refund your advance payments, and there will be no charge for the weekend if you choose to stay until Monday. If you prefer to leave, we will help in any way we can to make arrangements, beginning tomorrow morning." Alan was not sure how he and Jennifer would finance all this, but he felt he had to say it. There was still no response from the guests.

"Now, in spite of everything that has happened — and *hasn't* happened — I think you will agree that we've had a very fine meal. And it's not over yet. We'll have coffee, tea and dessert shortly: in the meantime, you may want to stretch your legs a little. The fog has come in, so we don't recommend the cliff trail — it could be dangerous — and you wouldn't be able to see anything from the widow's walk on top of the house — but the garden is completely safe. And if you walk out along the driveway, the house looks fascinatingly spooky and mysterious in a low fog like this. I'd really recommend that you walk out down the driveway and look back.

"We'll take a break for a half an hour or so. Jennifer and Terry and I will set out the dessert and the beverages in here, and you may take whatever you like into the lounge or the library. Now, if you are going outside, you'll need a sweater or a jacket. As I mentioned before, there are a few winter jackets in the back porch. It's definitely a bit chilly, but I think you'll enjoy the fog. It's going to be really dark out there, so we've also got a few flashlights in the kitchen that you can borrow if you like.

"And let me say once again how sorry I am that we will not be able to go ahead with the mystery weekend. We were looking forward to it as much as you were, I am sure, but we simply can't go ahead without our actors." He turned, walked into the hall and out the front door.

Miss A looked around the table brightly. "Cascara bark is a very efficient laxative," she said. "In British Columbia, the Indians used to call it 'shittum stick'." She laughed heartily and pointed at Simon. "That young man could use a good laxative, I think."

Miss K looked nervously around the table, but none of the guests would meet her eye. Simon blushed bright red. There was a slight buzz of conversation for a few minutes, and the guests began to stand up and move out to the hall. Mr. Browne re-filled his wine-glass, and strolled to the front door with it in his hand.

V

FRIDAY NIGHT AND SATURDAY MORNING

*W*HEN FAITH FINISHED IN THE KITCHEN AND WENT OUT
to collect Steve, he was gone. Whether he had left on
purpose or just wandered off, he was nowhere to be
found around the house or the grounds. The stained
washcloth lay on the stairs beside the red tool-box he
had been carrying. On Jennifer's urging Faith drove out
to look for him on the road, but didn't find him. She
went home to tell her daughters to call one of their aunts
immediately if their father showed up there, then came
back to Cranmer House to begin clearing up the kitchen
and organizing the tea and coffee. Jennifer joined her,
and Terry went outside for a smoke. The guests strolled
in the garden or on the verandah, or poked about in the
library. Alan had disappeared.

It was a little less than an hour after the dinner broke
up that Dr. MacEwen raised the alarm, rushing into the
house through the front door. "Alan!" he called. "Jennifer! Come quickly. Someone's hurt!"

He was pale and agitated, clearly frightened. Several
of the other guests appeared from the library or the
lounge, and Alan came out of the washroom cubicle
under the stairs, unconsciously smoothing a band-aid he
had just applied above his right eyebrow.

"You'd better come quickly," Dr. MacEwen repeated. "Someone's hurt — or fallen or collapsed, or

something!" They headed for the door, but he stopped suddenly. "We'll need a flashlight," he said, and Alan darted into the kitchen. Georges Lapierre emerged from the library and was immediately caught up in the excitement. He ran out with them, and Dr. MacEwen led the way around the east side of the house, along the driveway to the rear parking area. About halfway along, Alan's flashlight beam picked out the form of Sidney Browne, lying face-down on the gravel, the fringe of hair at the back of his head matted with blood. "Oh, my God!" MacEwen exclaimed. "I didn't realize . . . I was just going to walk around the house to the back and get something from the camper and I actually tripped over him, but I couldn't see . . . Who is it?"

"It's Browne," said Alan, who was kneeling by the prostrate body. "God, I can't tell if he's breathing! I don't think he is!" Browne made a faint gagging sound as Alan put a finger tentatively on his neck, then lapsed again into stillness. Alan started and drew his hand back. "I think he's alive. Or . . . " he looked up in horror " . . . or maybe he just died!"

Lapierre pointed at Dr. MacEwen excitedly. "You are doctor!" he cried. "You must help him!"

"I'm not that kind of doctor," MacEwen said, backing away. After a moment, he bent and picked something up from the grass at the edge of the drive. "This must be the weapon," he said, holding up a strange, club-shaped object. "Somebody must have come up behind and hit him with this." He held the object out to Lapierre, who took it and tilted it toward the light from a curtained window above them, dulled to a soft glow by the fog. "Is heavy," he said.

"If that really is a weapon," said a voice behind them, "then you shouldn't be handling it like that." Inspector Mullaly had followed them out. Lapierre dropped the object as though it had burned him. Mullaly glanced at

Browne, whose upper body was still framed in the beam of Alan's flashlight. "That looks serious," he said. "We'd better get police and medical help right away. And we'd better not move him. We'll get a couple of blankets over him, just in case he's still alive."

Alan was still kneeling by the body, transfixed. "Come on, boy," Mullaly said. "Snap out of it. We'll have to go to your neighbours' to call. Get going. MacEwen, you stay with him. Don't move around, and don't touch anything. Lapierre, you come with us: you can get some blankets from Jennifer and bring them back." No one seemed to resent his taking charge; they all meekly did as they were told. Alan got slowly to his feet, and Inspector Mullaly took his arm and hurried him toward the front of the house.

At the corner of the verandah they met Rose Mullaly, Madame Lapierre, and Miss K, who were headed in the opposite direction. Behind them, Jennifer, Faith and Terry were hurrying to catch up. Inspector Mullaly spoke to his wife, but his words were clearly meant for them all. "I don't think you should go down there, Rose. Mr. Browne's been hurt. I don't think you can do anything for him. We'll get some help here as soon as possible." The women and Terry retreated to the verandah, Jennifer and Georges Lapierre went in search of blankets, and Alan went for his car keys.

There was no hospital in Cranmer's Cove, and no nursing station, but there was an ambulance service operated by the Cooper brothers, Walter and Chesley, who had training as paramedics. They were both notably taciturn, but when Alan explained the need for help, Ches volunteered that Corporal Cameron of the RCMP had just been in to visit them. "He just left here. Can't be far past your place. I'll give him a call on the radio. He should get there as quick as we do."

Ches was right. Corporal Cameron was only a short

distance past Cranmer House when he got the message, and he turned back immediately, not bothering with siren or lights, arriving just as Alan and Inspector Mullaly returned from making their phone call. Time spent waiting for police or ambulances usually seems frustratingly long, but in this case the little group on the verandah found the arrival of the police cruiser improbably rapid.

Corporal Cameron did not, however, match the speed of his arrival. He got out of the cruiser slowly and plodded toward the front steps. Jennifer did not know him well but she had met him once or twice, and his laborious movements did not fit her image of him at all. The people on the verandah were still directing him around to the side of the house when the ambulance arrived, and he had to plod back to his car to move it. By the time he had clambered out of it again, Walt and Ches had backed their ambulance into the narrow driveway and were wheeling their stretcher over the gravel toward the centre of activity, so that police and paramedics arrived on the scene almost together.

Cameron's powerful flashlight picked out Browne sprawled on the driveway. Lapierre and MacEwen had covered him as best they could, but his head was still exposed and the blood glistened in the light. Simon had not been in evidence after the dinner had ended, and everyone had thought he had gone home, but he was kneeling by the body in an attitude of prayer. He stood up, his clerical trousers grey with dust from the knees down.

The brothers stopped, waiting for the policeman to make the first move. "Take the blankets off him and everybody stand back," Corporal Cameron said. He produced a small camera from the pocket of his tunic and rapidly took several pictures from different angles. The blue-white light of the flash created a dazzling cavity in the fog, leaving a brilliant after-image that made the darkness more intense. No one spoke. The Mountie was breathing heavily through his mouth, and his speech was barely intelligible. The comparison with Steve was inevitable. "Good God," Alan thought. "Cameron can't be drunk, too, can he?"

"Okay," Corporal Cameron said to the ambulance attendants, and gave way to a paroxysm of coughing.

"Can somebody hold a light on him?" one of the brothers asked. Alan shone his flashlight on the figure sprawled on the ground. The brothers maneuvered their stretcher parallel to the body and collapsed it down to its lowest level, then spread a sheet of stout fabric beside him. One of them placed Browne's arms, which were flung out and bent at the elbows, down by his sides. The other knelt by his head, slipped a brace around his neck and fastened its velcro straps, then pressed a large gauze dressing to the wounded area. Alan noticed that both Cooper brothers were wearing surgical gloves, but he could not remember when they had put them on. Together, unceremoniously but expertly, the brothers rolled Browne onto his back on the sheet.

Since he had been lying face-down, the blood had flowed forward to saturate his beard and fringe of white hair, making a ghastly frame for his pale, slack face. His dinner jacket and trousers were grey with dust, and a patch of it showed where his forehead had struck the gravel. His mouth hung open, and a dental plate protruded loosely. A half-smoked little cigar lay wetly on the gravel where his head had been, and a smudge of black on his cheek showed where the cigar had burned the skin before it went out. He had apparently been carrying one of the Cranmer House flashlights, had dropped it when he was struck, and then fallen forward on top of it. It lay on the driveway, half pushed into the gravel, still gleaming weakly.

The watchers barely had time to register these details before one of the ambulance attendants deftly removed the denture and tucked it into Browne's top pocket. The two of them used the sheet to half-lift and half slide his limp body onto the stretcher. They stood up and raised the stretcher in one motion and started for the ambulance, moving out of the pool of light. Their speech might be slow and deliberate, but the brothers did their jobs with professional speed and skill.

Everyone had been standing still, watching in silence, but the sudden removal of Mr. Browne seemed to release them, and they all began to move and talk at once.

"Shut up!" Corporal Cameron snapped. The witnesses were shocked into silence again and the policeman seemed startled by his own vehemence. "I can't hear myself think," he added, sounding almost apologetic. "Now, who found him?"

"I did," said Dr. MacEwen.

"Name?"

"Eric MacEwen."

Corporal Cameron tried to hold his flashlight while writing in his notebook, but after a moment he put the notebook and pen back in his pocket. "I'll take your statement in the house," he said. "Now, did somebody mention a weapon? Is that it, there?" He shone the beam of his flashlight on the object, which was lying where Lapierre had dropped it.

"It could be the weapon," Inspector Mullaly said. "Probably is. But I think you should know that it has been moved."

"And you are? . . . "

"Gerard Mullaly. RNC, retired." At times there was a certain tension between the RCMP, who did most of the rural policing, and the Royal Newfoundland Constabulary, who handled St. John's and a few other urban centres. Inspector Mullaly wanted the Mountie to know sooner rather than later that he had a retired member of the Constabulary on his hands.

"Ah," Corporal Cameron said. "That's the dress uniform, isn't it?" He didn't wait for an answer. "How do you know the weapon's been moved?" Then, in recognition of the other's seniority, he added, "Sir?"

Mullaly explained succinctly. Cameron plodded back to his cruiser for equipment and with the inspector's help and Dr. MacEwen's advice marked the approximate original location of the supposed weapon. Browne's position was already marked by a patch of bloody gravel. Cameron used a large, clear-plastic bag to pick up and contain the heavy object Dr. MacEwen had found, used another bag for the flashlight that Browne had been carrying, picked up the wet cigar butt with tweezers and dropped it into a smaller container, and finished by enclosing the whole area in a rough rectangle of yellow plastic tape stretched between trees and shrubbery. "I'll go over it again in daylight. Everybody should stay away from his area," he said, and they all went indoors. The guests were in the library, where Faith, Jennifer and Terry were serving tea. No one seemed to want dessert or after-dinner drinks. Simon was in earnest conversation with Marion, his trousers still dusty from the gravel drive.

In the light, the reason for Corporal Cameron's heavy movements and hoarse breathing became clear. His eyes were bloodshot and watery, his sinuses were congested and his nose was completely blocked, his voice was hoarse and he was racked from time to time by heavy coughing. It was apparent that every bone in his body hurt: he moved as though his clothing were made of lead. Just looking at him gave Jennifer a sympathetic headache.

"My God, boy," Inspector Mullaly said, "you're in no state to be working. You should be home in bed."

"Tell me about it." said the Mountie, trying vainly to blow his nose. His nasal passages were so congested that his speech was hardly intelligible. "That's where I was going when I got the call from Ches. I've got one constable in hospital with this bloody 'flu or whatever it is, and one at home, flat on her back. It's the holiday weekend, and we need everybody we can get on the highway. We've got an ambulance out of commission — that's what I was doing here, seeing if I could get Ches and Walt to station themselves nearer the trans-Canada until the weekend's over. And to top it all off, the drug squad's got information about a shipment coming into Trinity Bay, so every possible replacement is out there with binoculars. I'm it. There's nobody else."

"I'd be glad to help if there's anything I can do."

"Thanks. I appreciate the offer, sir." Cameron could not think of a tactful way to say what he felt Mullaly should already know — that if he was to be a witness, it was better that he had no connection with the investigation. For his part, Inspector Mullaly was unable to imagine any way of behaving at a crime scene other than as an investigator. Cameron had an inkling of the dilemma, and added, "Maybe you could draw me up a list of everybody who's been here this evening. I'm going to have to take statements from them all."

Jennifer joined them. "Hello, Corporal," she said. "I'm Jennifer Foster. We met at . . . "

"Yes, I remember," the policeman said. "Look, I'm going to have to interview everybody in the house. Where would be a good place to do it?"

"How about the dining room? It's fairly private, and we've cleared the table. The lights can be turned up."

"That'll be fine. Do you think you could let me have a cup of tea and maybe three or four aspirins?"

"Yes, of course," said Jennifer.

Cameron turned and raised his voice, addressing the room at large. "Ladies and gentlemen," he said. "I am Corporal Cameron of the Royal Canadian Mounted Police." With his congested nose it came out as something like 'I ab Gorboral Gaberud,' but everyone seemed to understand, even Georges Lapierre, who seemed disturbed and intimidated by the uniform, unable to take his eyes off the holster on the Mountie's belt. "As you probably know, there has been what appears to be a very serious assault here tonight, and we don't know much yet about how it happened. I'm afraid I'm going to have to interview you each individually. I apologize for having to keep you up, but I am asking you all to stay here, in this room, until I call for you. I'll be as quick as I can, but it will probably take some time." No one said anything. "I'd like to have a word first with the management and staff," Cameron added.

Alan, Terry and Faith joined the little group around the Mountie. "Okay," Cameron said. "Is everybody here? Everybody who's been here this evening?"

"Let's see," said Jennifer. She scanned the room. "Miss A isn't here. And I don't see Ms. MacEwen or Ms. Lapierre . . . And there's somebody else missing . . . Oh, dear! I was looking for Mr. Browne!"

"Well, we know where he is, I guess," Terry said.

When asked, Miss K explained that Miss A was in their room. "She's probably reading an Agatha Christie she picked up in the library. She . . . " Miss K hesitated for a moment, then squared her shoulders and finished the sentence firmly. "She's read them all before, but she doesn't always remember. I will go and get her."

"Could I go?" said Jennifer.

"No, thank you. I can explain things." Miss K left the library to go upstairs.

Georges Lapierre explained that his wife was upstairs with the baby. "Cannot leave her alone. If Marya come down, I must stay." He said this with some trepidation and seemed relieved when Cameron nodded in agreement.

Dr. MacEwen was still pale and agitated, and showed none of the amiable jocularity he had projected earlier. He said that his wife had gone to bed. "She is very upset. She expected a nice, tidy murder mystery, not . . . this sort of thing. She is very sensitive. All that blood . . . "

"But she didn't see Mr. Browne, did she?" Terry asked.

"No. But she did see Mr. Davis and that electrician fellow, and that upset her. And I described Mr. Browne when I came in."

"Must have been some description," said Terry.

"What's all this about her expecting a murder?" Corporal Cameron said. "And Mr. Davis and an electrician?"

Faith intervened. "Steve was here. He was drunk."

Cameron had had dealings with Steve in the line of duty. "I heard he'd been drinking again. When was he here? Where was Browne?"

Among them, they explained. "So when did he disappear?" the Mountie asked.

"He wasn't there when I went out after dinner," Alan said, "so he was gone off the steps before Browne went out."

"And what about Mrs . . . ." he glanced at his notebook "Mrs. MacEwen expecting a murder?"

Alan and Jennifer began to explain, Cameron listening with a growing expression of incredulity and suspicion. "All right," he said finally. "I'll get a fuller explanation when I take the statements. Dr. MacEwen, would you ask your wife to come down, please?

"Now, was anybody else here?" Faith explained about her brother-in-law, and Jennifer explained about

Ernie. "Okay," said Corporal Cameron, and sighed again. "Well, I'd better get at it. Maybe I could start with you, Ms. Foster, and I'll take you next, Mr. Davis, then the rest of the staff, Mr. Byrne and Ms. Carter. Inspector Mullaly, if you wouldn't mind, you could send people in as I need them. These are going to have to be formal statements, with signatures, so I'll just take a minute to get the forms from my car."

Cameron did his best to speed up the process, but there were twelve people to be interviewed, and it was nearly two a.m. before he finished. After her interview, Jennifer checked with the guests again, and told Faith to go home as soon as she had given her statement. Then she excused herself and went to the small apartment off the kitchen that she and Alan shared.

The guests, all gathered in the library, talked excitedly.

"I really don't know what to make of all this," Rose Mullaly said. "I really don't."

"I think it's bloody clever!" said Miss A, with great enthusiasm.

"Lexa!" her sister said. By now, whenever Miss A spoke, people were uncertain how to react. Sometimes it was difficult to distinguish between blunt pronouncements that went on to be astute and keen-witted, and those that were produced by a spasm of irrationality.

"Ah . . . what do you think is clever, Miss Gilford?" Simon asked guardedly.

"The whole thing!" Miss A said. "These are very competent actors."

"I'm afraid I don't understand."

"We all came for a mystery, didn't we?" There were nods and sounds of agreement. "Then Mr. Davis told us all that nonsense about 'suspension of disbelief' and said we mustn't talk about the mystery until it happened, and when it did we were to pretend it was real. Then he told us it wasn't going to happen at all. That it was all off. And *then* there was a murder!"

"Yes," said Simon, "but . . . "

"Don't you see? We've got a mystery, and we don't have to pretend. Whether it is real or not is *part* of it! Was Mr. Browne an actor, or was he really an obnoxious newspaper editor and did somebody really bash his head in?" The crime sounded doubly violent when described this way by an elderly lady, but she seemed to relish the description. "And either way, who did it? We don't have to 'suspend disbelief' or anything like that, we can talk about it any way we want."

"He did seem to go out of his way to make everyone dislike him," Mrs. Mullaly said, thoughtfully.

"There's no doubt in the world it was real," said her husband. "No doubt at all. I saw him lying there in the driveway."

"You are thinking Corporal of Mountain Politzia is real?" Georges Lapierre said. "Hah! Why he is arriving so quick? Why he does not point gun and say, 'Freeze, asshole'? Why he is polite, saying 'please' and 'thank you' and not hitting people? Why he is alone and not bringing other politzia to push people and punch them? Why he sits in dining room talking to people and writing? No. He is actor."

It occurred to Inspector Mullaly that Lapierre's image of policemen had been formed by American cop shows on television and their Canadian imitators, presumably combined with direct experience in his homeland, but he could not help but take the description personally. "I suppose you think all his coughing and wheezing is an act, too?" he asked. The question came out rather more aggressively than he had intended, but Lapierre did not seem to take offence.

"No. Actor is sick, but Corporal is actor. Mr. Browne is also actor. Mr. Davis is pretend actors not to come, then he is pretend to killing Mr. Browne so we have mystery weekend after all."

"You see?" said Miss A. "When we watch Inspector Morse on television, Katherine is always annoyed with me because whenever he takes an interest in a woman, I say that she is involved in the murder. Katherine thinks I'm cheating, because I am using clues that are not part of the story. And she's right, in a way. I'm not 'suspending disbelief'. But now, *everything* is part of the story. So I think it's brilliant — if it's real, that is. I mean, if it's *not* real. Well, you know what I mean."

"Mr. Davis and Mr. Browne were arguing on the verandah just after dinner," Miss K said. "I overheard them."

"Terry argue, too, with Mr. Browne also," Lapierre said excitedly. "Saying rude words very loud. I am hearing this."

Terry looked exasperated, then shrugged. "Okay, we did have a bit of an argument. He was drunk and damned rude. I told him what I thought of him, that's all." He looked around challengingly, but no one said anything.

"Why did Alan have a band-aid over his eye?" said Marion after a moment. "It wasn't there during dinner, was it? When did he get hurt, and how?"

"Jennifer asked him that earlier," Rose Mullaly said. "He said he had gone out to the parking area, where he'd been raking gravel before we all arrived, and in the dark he stepped on the rake and it flipped up and hit him."

Lapierre's face registered disbelief.

Inspector Mullaly turned to Simon. "You live right here in Cranmer's Cove, or so they say, and you're a friend of the family. You must know . . ."

"But I *don't*," Simon said. "They made a point of not telling me about the . . . the murder or whatever, so I would be — both Marion and I would be — on the same footing as the other guests. I don't know what's happening, but I can't believe that Alan . . . "

"But he *would* say that, wouldn't he?" Miss A said gleefully to the rest of the company. "Whether he knows what's going on or not, wouldn't he say exactly the same thing? Oh, it's so exciting! We can't all be actors, but any of us *could* be. And if it's real, one of us must be a real murderer!"

The Inspector turned to Terry. "How about you? You must know about the plans for whatever was supposed to happen."

"I do, as a matter of fact. I *am* an actor, although I've done a lot of other jobs, including waiter and bell-boy, to keep myself alive. I'm from St. Johns's, and there were two other actors who were supposed to be here, and the three of us were going to collaborate on the 'murder' but the others didn't arrive, just as Alan said. I went down the road to make some phone calls during dinner, and I got the news that the others wouldn't be arriving. I tried to get Alan to go ahead with a makeshift script, but he wouldn't do it. He didn't think we could carry it off without the other two, and he canceled the whole thing." There was a hint of wounded professional pride in the last sentence.

Inspector Mullaly turned to his wife to claim vindication, but Miss A interrupted. "He's just repeating what Mr. Davis already said. Isn't that exactly what he would say either way — if if the whole thing was real, or if the two missing actors were really a fiction, and if Mr. Browne was really a plant?"

"Mr. Browne is *plant*?" Georges Lapierre said. "We are watching on television, film where people are plant. They are coming from other galaxy in space ship. Are extra-cholesterols. No. Is wrong. Are estraterresterols. Looking like ordinary people, talking American English, but are plant. Have green eye. Must wear compact lens to change colour. When they die, from inside their clothing comes leaves. Marya is frightful all night, cannot sleep, and I am frightful, too." He looked sternly around at the other guests. "Is good story for television late at night, for making people frightful, but cannot be real. Alan tell us before, he is reading scientific frictions. Mystery must seem to be real. If he makes story where Mr. Browne is plant, it is not good!"

"I didn't mean *that*," Miss A said impatiently. "A 'plant' means . . . it means somebody who isn't really who they say they are. They have them all the time in mysteries and private eye stories."

"What kind of eye?" Lapierre said doubtfully.

Alan had come into the room while the discussion was going on. "I can assure you that Mr. Browne was *not* a plant, Miss Gilford. Someone really attacked him savagely, and I would very much like to know who. Terry, Corporal Cameron is talking to Faith right now, and he'd like to see you next."

"I understand this now," Lapierre said to the group. "Plant is actor."

"Well, yes, more or less," Alan said.

"So Mr. Browne *is* plant."

"No! He was *not* a plant . . . not an actor!"

Lapierre looked sceptical. "Why you have band-age on head?"

Alan sighed and explained again about stepping on the rake in the dark. "I had just washed off the blood and I was putting the band-aid on when Dr. MacEwen came in to tell us about Browne."

"What colour is blood?"

"Oh, for God's sake!"

"Is green?"

"Of course not! My blood is red, like anybody else's."

Lapierre seemed convinced that Alan was attempt-

129

ing to introduce elements of science fiction, and was not pleased..

"Did anyone see the weapon?" Rose Mullaly asked.

"Lapierre and I saw it outside," Dr. MacEwen said, "But it was dark out there."

"It's some sort of sculpture, isn't it?" Marion said. "I saw it through the plastic bag Corporal Cameron had it in."

"It's got blood on it," Miss A said. "Red blood. Probably hair, too."

"Lexa, for goodness' sake!" said Miss K.

"But, Katherine, murder weapons *always* have blood and hair on them. Skin, too, sometimes. And sometimes *tissue*. They call those little paper handkerchiefs 'tissues', and it sounds quite innocent, but somehow the singular sounds really grisly, doesn't it?" She repeated the word with relish: "*Tissue*." Her sister turned away, shaking her head.

"Marion's right," said Alan. "It's a human figure, about two feet high, made of brass or something — some kind of metal, anyway. It's hollow, but it's pretty heavy. The house was full of stuff like that when we took it over. It must have come from Africa or South America or someplace when the Cranmers were at their height. Their ships carried salt fish all over the world, and they brought back all sorts of things. There's another one around somewhere."

"Another?" said Mrs. Mullaly. "Really?"

"Yes, there's a pair of them. One looks as though it's supposed to be a European, maybe a sea-captain or something and the other is a man in some kind of Native dress. I think the one in the bag is the European. It was probably in the little entrance porch, just inside the front door."

"Would the other one be there?"

"Probably," Alan said. "I'll go and look." He was

back in a moment without the figure. "Doesn't seem to be there. Funny, I thought they were both in the porch."

"Were they together?" Dr. MacEwen asked. "Why wouldn't it be there?"

"We use them to prop doors open, so they're often in the entrance porch, one for the outer door and one for the inner — but we haven't needed them much yet this year. The weather hasn't warmed up yet."

"So where is other one?" Lapierre asked suspiciously.

"Could be anyplace, I guess," Alan said. "We've been doing a lot of painting and varnishing in preparation for this weekend — it could have been used as a door-stop almost anywhere. I'll have a look around. It'll turn up."

*   *   *

Later, as the gathering began to break up, Marion walked with Simon to the front door. "Oh, dear," said Simon. "It's really late, isn't it? Everybody will be wondering where I am."

"But you live alone, don't you?"

"Well, yes, of course. But everybody in the Cove will know that my car hasn't been there most of the day. And somebody is sure to see me coming home, no matter how late it is, and by morning everybody will be talking about it."

"Are you coming back for breakfast?"

"I thought I would, yes."

Marion gave a completely uncharacteristic giggle. "It's hardly worth going back, is it?"

"Oh, they'd *really* talk if I didn't come home at all!"

The implication that if it were not for his parishioners' gossip, he would consider not going home was very daring for Simon, and Marion noted it with a mixture of excitement and alarm. "What on earth is going on here,

Simon?" she asked. "You said that Jennifer and Alan were a very nice couple, and they seemed that way at first, but I do have to wonder. All that business with Faith's husband, and he was crying and Faith was crying . . ."

"Yes, it's amazing, isn't it?" Simon said. "I knew they would do something dramatic, but I never thought . . . They've turned out to be amazingly good actors, haven't they?" He paused, then added smugly: " . . . and I think we've been keeping up our part very well."

"Do you actually think all this was planned?"

"Of course. You know they didn't tell me exactly what was going to happen because they wanted us — you and me — to react just like everybody else. I know Terry's an actor, of course — and he's a friend of Jennifer and Alan's; he's been around the hotel before. But they had to hire somebody to drive the bus and wait on the table and all that, and I know that Terry can't make his whole living by acting, and he has to take jobs as a waiter or whatever else he can get, so I suppose this was ideal for him. I expected that at least one of the other guests would be an actor, too, but I had no idea it would be Mr. Browne. I don't think he's from St. John's. I wonder where they found him?"

"I can't believe . . . "

"It was clever of them to pretend that they had to cancel, wasn't it? I thought at first they'd gone too far — been too convincing, and that everybody would want to leave, but then Corporal Cameron said that everyone had to stay. I really don't know how they got him to come. And he was so sick, poor fellow. He's a very nice man, too, you know. I expect he did it as a favour to Alan and Jennifer, but he certainly worked hard at it. I'm surprised the Mounties would allow something like that. And I had to pretend to pray for Mr. Browne. I didn't quite like doing it, but I suppose Alan and Jennifer didn't really think about it. It wouldn't have seemed right if I didn't."

Marion looked at Simon appraisingly, her expression unreadable. She sighed. "It's cold out here," she said.

"Yes," said Simon. "It is. You'd better go back in." He gave her a hasty kiss on the cheek, almost touching her lips, and hurried down the stairs. "Goodnight. I'll see you in the morning."

Marion sighed again and went back inside.

*   *   *

Upstairs, Miss K collapsed into a soft chair by their bedroom window while her sister bustled around excitedly, unable to keep still. "Imagine, Kat!" she said. "Here we are, guests in a big country house, and the telephones aren't working, and a murder has taken place, and nobody knows who did it! Oh, it's so exciting! I'm so glad we came!"

"Well, I find it exhausting," Miss K said. "I can hardly keep my eyes open. Did that sniffling policeman really have to take so long to question everyone? And I couldn't understand half of what he said. I've never seen a person with such a stuffed-up nose. Even the girls were never that bad."

"Mr. Browne must have been an actor all along. I didn't expect that, but I'm rather glad of it, all the same, because that means he must have been acting when he was so unpleasant earlier. Who do you think did it, Kat?"

"I have no idea," Miss K said, "and I don't care. All I want to do is go to bed."

"I won't be able to sleep at all, I'm sure," Miss A said, "but I shall keep thinking. Oh, I hope we can figure it out first!"

* * *

Back in their room, Inspector Mullaly sat down heavily in the armchair and his wife dropped onto the bed with a sigh. "Well," she said, "what did you think of that? I think Miss A is right — it *is* bloody clever."

"You don't think it was all an act, do you?"

"Come on, Gerry! What else could it be? Or do you really believe they could bring us all here on the promise of a murder mystery, and then a real one would happen?"

"Listen, I was out there. I saw Browne lying there on the driveway. That was real! He really did get hit on the head."

"That's what I mean when I say that it's clever. It's got you fooled."

"Or you."

Rose Mullaly slipped off her shoes and began to unbutton her dress. "Whatever else it is, it's exhausting. I thought we'd never get out of there."

"Police work always takes time. I used to tell you that when I was working. Maybe now you believe me."

Rose stood up and gave her husband a little hug. "I know you worked hard, Gerry. Too hard, sometimes." She thought for a moment. "And I think Jennifer and Alan are working too hard to make this whole thing seem authentic. If they keep this up, they'll wear us all out. What time is it, anyway?"

"There was a time when this wouldn't seem late, but I guess it's well past our bedtime these days. And you're just plain wrong if you think Alan and Jennifer planned whatever happened out there on the driveway."

"Maybe."

* * *

Alan made his way exhaustedly to the private apartment

and into the bedroom. Jennifer's bedside light was on, and she was sitting up with a book in her lap. He slumped into a chair beside the bed. "Whoosh!" he said. "You're lucky you got away when you did. You know, as Cameron interviewed them, they didn't go to bed. They came right back into the library, and told everybody about the interview. It took him forever to get through them all, but they didn't seem to mind. Was it only last night I was telling you not to worry, and everything would be okay? Seems like a week ago."

Jennifer looked up from her book but said nothing. Alan leaned over to untie his shoes. "Jenny," he said, "what are we going to do? I can't handle this. All those bloody idiots think it's part of the act. The whole thing — Ernie coming in, and then Steve, and Browne getting bashed on the head . . . It doesn't matter what I say to them, they just think what a great actor I am. They're having a whale of a time. Probably all up there right now, reading over their notes and counting suspects. With me at the top of the list. Nobody seems worried that it could happen again, but somebody clocked Browne, and it must have been somebody . . . "

Jennifer took off her glasses to look at him and cleared her throat. Her voice was tense. "Alan, some of them were saying that you had a fight with Mr. Browne out on the verandah, just before . . . before he . . . "

Alan looked at his feet, then stood up and turned partly away from her. "Not a fight . . . "

"An argument, then. Shouting at each other. Is that true?"

"Well, he was shouting. Or talking pretty loud, anyway. I was . . . " He moved farther away from the bed and the light so that his face was in shadow. "Jenny, there is more to that whole thing than you know about. I was going to tell you about it tonight, before all this . . . "

"You knew him, didn't you?" she said. "Before to-day, I mean. Someplace else?"

Alan nodded. Jennifer continued to look at him levelly. "I could tell there was something. The way you looked when he was behaving so rudely at dinner . . . "

"Yeah. I had no more idea who he was than you did when he wrote for a reservation. I mean, Sidney Browne, journalist, with an address in Etobicoke? How many Sidney Brownes must there be, for God's sake? And I didn't recognize him when he came in. I only began to get an inkling at dinner, but I didn't want to believe it. He had a pretty good idea who I was, but he wasn't sure. He said he made up his mind after that . . . scuffle I had with Steve . . .

"Look, Jenny, this is hard for me, all right? It's a part of my life I'd just as soon forget about. And I had — well, maybe not forgotten about it, but at least put it behind me. Until Browne showed up." He remained standing in the shadow, and leaned back against the wall. "I've been going to tell you about it a hundred times, but . . . well, I just didn't, that's all.

"But I was going to, tonight. When Browne brought it all back, before all this other stuff happened, I'd made up my mind to tell you the whole thing, when we could be alone. I mentioned it when we were in the library with Terry, remember? " He gave a bitter little laugh. "Of course, now all those amateur detectives know about it, so . . . "

"They know? What do you mean?"

Alan pushed himself away from the wall with a twitch of his shoulders and moved restlessly around the room. "It isn't easy for me to talk about. It would have been bad enough if I could have picked the time and place. Which I should have done long ago — I know that. You had a right to know about it, but I just . . . Well, enough of that.

Now's the time, whether either one of us likes it or not. I just wish I'd done it earlier, that's all."

He went back to the chair and sat down on it backwards, straddling the seat, hitching it sideways so that the light from the bedside lamp would not shine on his face and crossing his arms on the back. "I know it's late, but can you bear with me a while? Let me tell this my own way?"

"I'll try."

"Okay. Here goes. You know what I've told you about myself from before we met — dropped out of the University of Toronto, got involved in theatre, got into set design and construction, came to St. John's when the theatre scene was booming . . . and you know the rest."

"Yes."

"Well, that's the way it was, only there's a couple of years left out. And that's the hard part." He took a deep breath and exhaled slowly, puffing out his cheeks. "It started off the way I told you. I come in to the U of T from Oshawa, right? A nice 'fifties family — Dad works in the car plant, mom keeps house, and their only son is going to be an engineer, and have a better job and a bigger house and a nicer car than Dad had.

"Only I get a trendy young professor for first-year English who knew what was happening, man, you know? Also, I had to take something called a Religious Knowledge Option. I guess it was a left-over from when everybody had to take religion. All the first-year students had to take one of these things, one hour a week. They didn't have to have anything to do with religion — the professors just talked about anything they wanted. And I got this hip young American sociologist. He was the first guy I ever saw with long hair. We all thought he was gay, at first, only we didn't call it that then. Well . . . you know all that stuff. The sixties were beginning to happen, right? You went through the same kind of thing in London.

"So pretty soon I'm skipping my Physics and Chemistry classes, and I'm hanging out in the coffee houses in Yorkville, and I didn't want to be an engineer any more. First I was going to major in English. Then maybe sociology, then anthropology. The old search for relevance, right?"

"Alan." Jennifer said, "you don't have to . . ."

"Okay, okay, I know. Look, I'm not putting it down, I'm just trying to . . . put a bit of distance in here.

"All right, so there I am. There's all kinds of alternate theatre stuff around, all very 'with it', as we used to say, and I get into it. A bit of acting, a bit of writing, and pretty soon I'm not even pretending to be a university student any more.

"So, this other guy and I, we write a play. All very relevant and intense. Four characters. Set in a prison." Alan gave a grunt of bitter laughter. "Talk about foreshadowing! Of course, it was an American prison. For all our social consciousness, we were still pretty colonized. The characters were American draft-dodgers. Anyway, we've got the play, and I'm going to direct and stage-manage and do the lights and all that, and my friend and a couple of other guys are going to act.

"We did it in a coffee house, of course. Walls all painted flat black — you know — a couple of black cubes for the set, lighting just a couple of stark white spots and one that projects a shadow of bars across one side of the set.

"And it wasn't bad, either, the set or the play. One of the reviews said, *What it lacks in polish it more than makes up for in sincerity.* I treasured that. Wasn't hip to pay much attention to a review in an establishment paper, but it meant a lot to me, all the same.

"Browne was a reporter for the third-rate, low-rent

newspaper, and he had his own column about three times a week, called 'The Straight Goods', believe it or not. Back then, 'straight' didn't mean 'not gay' like it does now, it meant . . . well, you know what it meant. He wrote under the name of S. Melville Browne. I always thought it was hyphenated — like Melville-hyphen-Browne, but I guess it wasn't. And I guess the 'S' was for 'Sidney,' but nobody knew that. Anyway, he was just as bigoted and reactionary as he is now — or *was* — only not as slick. He made his reputation attacking the — I'm not sure whether anybody was calling it 'the countercul-ture' yet, but whatever it was called, he milked it for all it was worth. Titillated the straights in the suburbs with all kinds of sanctimonious bullshit about hippies and the breakdown of civilization as we know it.

"So our little play was getting a bit of attention, and of course S. Melville Browne had to check it out.

"Now, there was a scene toward the end with the three prisoner characters, and one of them's managed to get hold of a joint, and they share it around. The audience knows that something bad is going to happen to the central character — it turns out he gets killed by the fourth character, the guard — and they also know that one of his two buddies has set him up. And there they are sharing what's going to be this guy's last joint, like a sacrament, and talking about brotherhood and freedom and stuff. All very symbolic. It's embarrassing to have to admit it now, but the guy's initials were 'J.C.' And the smoke was really dramatic in the white spot-lights.

"We discussed that scene over and over before the play went on, and we all agreed. It had to be, like, *real*, man. Anything else would be a violation of artistic integrity.

"S. Melville Browne thought the play was the shits, of course. *Gives a new meaning to the term 'theatre of the absurd*' was one of his better lines. But that scene was perfect for the kind of thing he did. I can quote him practically word for word: *The only whiff of realism comes when one of these unbelievable characters lights up what is supposed to be a marijuana cigarette. Of course, it might have been somebody in the audience burning an old mattress, but we don't think so. Isn't that sort of thing illegal?*

"This is in a morning paper, right? And of course nobody we knew would admit to reading anything like 'The Straight Goods,' but by that afternoon everybody is talking about it. We discussed it, and all of us — people who ran the coffee house, actors, me — we all agreed. No compromise.

"So that night the place is packed. Standing room only, and everybody's looking around to see if the guy next to them is a narc. Well, they get to that scene, everybody's waiting for the cops to storm up on the stage, tension is at a peak, they light up the joint, and . . . nothing happens. The rest of the play is almost an anticlimax."

Alan was speaking slowly, with frequent pauses. For the most part, he kept his eyes down, watching his feet pushing his shoes around on the carpet, lifting and dropping them aimlessly. From time to time he would look up at Jennifer expectantly, as though for some sign of support or encouragement. She met his eye when he looked at her, but otherwise remained impassive. He breathed deeply again, and went doggedly on.

"So the following morning Browne's column comes out again, and he isn't letting go: *My spies tell me that after a mention in this space on Tuesday, that hippy play up in Yorkville is breaking all attendance records. They're also breaking the law. Maybe the people who should be interested in that sort of thing can't get tickets.*

"So we go through the whole thing again — do we use the joint or not? — and this time it takes us even less time to decide. We're making a statement here, and all the heads are slapping us on the back and saying 'right on' and stuff, and we can't back down now. So we go ahead, and again nothing happens.

"We were coming to what was supposed to be the end of our run, but we were still playing to packed houses, so we start to talk about holding over. We had a bit of trouble with the idea — some of us thought it sounded too 'establishment' — you know, 'Held Over by Popular Demand' like a stripper at the Victory Burlesque — but it was an attractive idea all the same — but some of us thought we should get out while we were still ahead. Anyway, we still had a couple of nights to go in the normal run, so we didn't decide right away.

"Browne's column comes out in the Saturday morning paper, and this time he's pulled out all the stops. He wanted to *make* news, not just report it, and he was pissed off because he was being ignored. So he gave it the full treatment, right in the opening paragraph." Alan assumed a loud, preaching tone that sounded rather like Mr. Browne at dinner: "*The other day on Bloor Street I watched a policeman going down a row of illegally parked cars, putting tickets under windshield wipers. If one of them had been mine I'd have been annoyed, but not at the policeman. He was just doing the job that our taxes pay him to do. But some of us find it hard to understand how it is that a couple of blocks away in Yorkville, three grungy, long-haired hippies stand up every night in front of a crowd of people, many of them barely old enough to have a driver's licence, and smoke a substance that is prohibited by the Criminal Code of Canada. Are Toronto's finest so worn out from catching jaywalkers and parking violators that they haven't got the energy to enforce the laws that are supposed to protect our children from the menace of drugs?*" It was clear that Browne's articles were burned on Alan's memory.

"Well, that did it. I've got to give the cops credit; they

really didn't want to bust us — one of them even showed up for the performance in uniform, for God's sake. All we'd've had to do was roll up a bit of oregano or something with some Drum tobacco, and we'd have been okay. But of course we didn't. We talked a lot about the theatre of real life, and we went ahead, and we got busted. The audience kicked up a bit of a fuss, and when the dust settled six of us were under arrest — the three actors, the manager of the coffee house, me, and a guy from the audience who'd yelled 'pig' a bit too loud when the bust was going on.

"It was when they started sorting out the actual charges that things started to get really . . . interesting. The cops were mad. Browne had made them look stupid, and they were getting flak from the politicians, and we hadn't helped any by going ahead with the performance right under their noses. They had to do something to save face, but they didn't want Browne to get credit for forcing them into it. At the same time, they didn't want the thing to become a *cause célèbre*, either, with people marching around with signs and raising money for the defence of the Yorkville Six, or some damn thing.

"So, first of all, they let some of their media friends know that the bust was part of 'an on-going investigation,' and that Browne had nearly screwed it up with his ill-timed comments. That put him in his place. Then they laid out their scenario.

"See, I was stage-managing and all that stuff, so I had to make sure the guys had the joint for the performance — that they didn't forget it or toke it up backstage or something — so I kept a stash in my pocket and made sure they had it when it was needed. I was also handling the money, and every once in a while I'd take a few bucks out of the box-office receipts for expenses.

"Well, that was perfect as far as the cops were concerned. They didn't press charges against the coffee house guy, or the noisy guy from the audience, or two of the actors who hadn't actually touched the joint before the bust took place. The guy who took the joint out and lit it, they charged with simple possession. And they hit me with trafficking. The way they set it up, everybody else was just misguided and naive, and I was the bad guy, using the situation to promote drug use for my own profit.

"My parents were devastated. They didn't understand at all, but they did the best they knew how. Dad tried to get me a big-time lawyer, which he couldn't afford, but I wouldn't cooperate and went with Legal Aid. Browne was pissed off because the cops had hijacked his story, and he wanted everybody to know that he was responsible for bringing this wicked criminal to justice, so he reported the trial as though I was a mass murderer. A few heads demonstrated in front of the Courthouse, and somebody painted slogans on Browne's car, and that brought the rest of the media in . . . I mean, it was the old theatre of real life stuff we talked so much about, and I was playing the lead.

"It didn't last long. I . . . " Alan's voice broke and he paused, swallowing hard and looking at Jennifer in agonized appeal. "Jenny, they gave me *two years!*"

Jennifer made a move to get out of the bed and come to him, and at the same moment Alan heaved himself out of the chair, stumbled for a moment over his shoes, then sat heavily on the edge of the bed, bending over awkwardly to bury his head on Jennifer's shoulder. She embraced him and stroked his hair, pressing her cheek against his.

After a moment Alan pushed himself back to a sitting position and rubbed his eyes. "Jenny, I'm not going to tell you about being in jail. Maybe I will some day . . . some of it . . . if I can. I was barely twenty years old." His voice caught again, but he cleared his throat sharply and continued. "I thought I knew just about everything, and I didn't know anything at all.

"But I learned fast. Crash course in survival, you might call it. Found out pretty quick that peace and love weren't always . . .

"I was young, and I guess I looked pretty good to some of those guys who'd been in for a few years, but I was big, and I'd worked at labouring jobs for a couple of summers, so I was pretty strong. So I made it. Not exactly unscathed, but I made it. Had to serve the full two years and a couple of months extra because of a few..ah . . . incidents in which people got hurt. It all went on my record, but I figured that was better than . . . than the alternative. I learned how to handle them. And they learned to leave me alone. That's why when Steve tried to push past me . . .

"Browne must have been keeping track, because when I came out he did a column re-hashing the case and reminding people of his own heroic role. Said he was a bit worried because I had a record of violence in prison, and might be out for revenge." Alan gave a wry shake of his head. "Just the kind of thing a guy needs when he gets out of jail, right? Though I've got to admit that sometimes when things got bad inside, I used to think about going after him.

"But nothing was further from my mind when I got out. I didn't go back to Toronto. Went out to Vancouver for a while, and then to Ottawa. I was already pretty good with my hands, and I'd spent a lot of time in the carpentry shop for a year or so, so I got into cabinet-making, and . . . well, you know the rest.

"So you can see why . . . I mean, I had no idea who the guy was when he arrived. Never crossed my mind. I was too busy trying to figure out what we were going to do without Sheila and Derm and everything. He made me uneasy, but I could see that he did that to everybody else, too. But at dinner I began to get a feeling . . . that was when I started thinking that we couldn't go on with the whole thing.

"Then, after dinner, when everybody was supposed to wander around for a while and then have dessert and go to bed, and I was off the hook for a while, I just went out onto the verandah to be by myself for a minute. So I'm standing there looking out into the fog, trying to get myself together a bit, and my head's just about coming off with all the stuff whirling around in it, and Browne comes up behind me and says, 'Well, well. Rick Davis. Who'd have thought?' — you know, in that obnoxious tone he was using at dinner."

Since Alan had ended their embrace, Jennifer had been holding his hand tightly. Now she released it and looked at him in puzzlement.

" 'Rick'?" she said.

"Oh. Yeah. I didn't mention that, did I? You know my first name is really Richard. Well, that's what I went by — Ricky when I was small and Rick when I got older. I was Rick and Richard all through the trial and everything, so when I got out, I just started using my second name, that's all. And, of course, that's partly why Browne wasn't sure when he made the reservation and that. It's a bit of a stretch from Alan Davis the Newfoundland hotel-keeper to Rick Davis, Toronto drug dealer and violent jailbird."

"But he made the stretch"

"Yeah. Not at first, but eventually he did. He must have heard I was in Newfoundland — or out east someplace, anyway. He wasn't sure at first — we've both changed a bit — but I guess he got surer as the dinner went on . . . So he comes up behind me and says, 'I see you're still a stickler for realism in the theatre, Rick. I could have sworn that was real blood on that fellow's face a few minutes ago.' You can imagine how I felt, with everything else that was going on.

"I don't know what I said back, but we got into a bit of a . . . discussion, you might say. And we said a lot of things. At one point I was stupid enough to kind of ask him not to write about it, you know? I mean, I could just see the kind of thing he'd have in his column, and what it could do to us. I guess I wasn't as sure it was all over as I thought. But you can imagine what he said. I was trying to keep my voice down, and he was being as big a loud-mouth as he'd been at dinner. He was enjoying himself, the bastard!"

"You said the other people — the guests — that they know about all this, too? How . . . "

Alan shook his head and rubbed a hand down over his face. "Yeah. Well, Browne and I were having our little conversation on the verandah, just off to the right, as you come out the door. And apparently one of the Gilford sisters — the sane one — came out right behind us. Now, if you come up behind a couple of people you hardly know, and they're having an argument, what do you do? I mean, normally you shuffle your feet or clear your throat or something, right? Let 'em know you're there, and then go away and leave them alone, right? Especially if you're a nice old lady from Victoria.

"But not if you're a character in a murder mystery, you don't. Then, what you do is, you keep quiet and stay behind the corner of the entry-way, there, and listen to the whole business. They were all doing that kind of thing, watching everybody and listening, expecting something to happen . . . " He shook his head again in frustration.

"Anyway, apparently that's what she did. Stayed there out of sight, listening until I got fed up and stamped off in one direction, and I guess Browne went in the other. And, of course, as soon as the news about

Browne got around, she told her fellow sleuths what she'd heard. And when the Mountie interviewed her, she told him all about it. I can just imagine it." Alan assumed an exaggerated old-woman voice that did not sound anything like Miss K. " 'Yes, Corporal, and then Mr. Browne said . . . ' My God, I wonder if she quoted him word for word? He was using some pretty heavy language. So was I, come to think of it. I bet she repeated it to try to shock poor old Cameron. They've all got the poor bugger pegged as the dumb local Bobby in some Agatha Christie whodunnit, you know. They're going to drive him nuts as well as me."

Jennifer had been sitting up with the bedclothes around her waist, and she suddenly realized that the room was chilly. She pulled the blankets up around her shoulders and shuddered.

"Did you tell Corporal Cameron about it?" she said.

"Well, not at first. I mean, I didn't see any need to. And I didn't want to have to explain all that stuff . . . "

"But you did eventually?"

"Yeah. Well, I had to, didn't I? I mean, after he talked to the old lady he came and asked me about it, so what else could I do?"

"So he thinks you were hiding it when he interviewed you?"

"I guess he does." Alan got up from the bed, picked up his shoes and moved across the room to put them into the closet. "That wasn't the end of it, either. After the Mountie had gone I figured they'd finally go to bed, but they were still hanging around in dressing gowns and things, having the time of their lives. Miss A had rounded up Inspector Mullaly and a couple of the others and they started questioning me!

"It didn't matter what I said to them. I mean, I explained the whole thing, told them that the Mountie was a real cop, and Browne had really got bashed on the head, and the actors hadn't showed up, and the Mystery Weekend was off —" he waved his hand — " . . . didn't faze them a bit — except for Mullaly. He knows Browne really got it. The rest of them just figured, 'Hey, what a clever plot!' and 'What a great actor this guy is!'

"And then Inspector Mullaly starts saying, 'But Miss Gilford *did* hear you having an argument with Mr. Browne before the crime was committed?' and stuff like that. So I told them. Not the whole story, the way I've told it to you, but enough to give them the gist of it. I mean, I just wanted them to shut up and let me get to bed. I didn't have the strength to do anything else. So I guess Mullaly thinks I did it, too, only he knows it was real."

"Alan," Jennifer said, "how did you get that cut over your eye?"

Alan had turned to the closet and was taking off his dinner-jacket, but at her question he turned back to look at her in astonishment.

"Jenny," he said, "I told you about that! After I left Browne I went out back . . . "

"You didn't say anything about leaving Mr. Browne."

He was still standing in the closet door with his jacket half off. "Well, no," he said. "Not then. Not with all the others around. But I told you how I went out back, and stepped on that bloody rake, and . . . " He stopped, incredulous. "Jenny, you do believe me, don't you? Surely to God you don't think? . . . "

"I don't know what to think, Alan." Her voice shook a little, and she cleared her throat. "I really don't." She paused and hunched the blankets higher around her shoulders.

"When you . . . " She paused again and stared for a moment at the bedclothes covering her knees, then began again. "Alan, you know how I hate violence, can't stand to watch it in the movies, or on television. Well, I thought we both felt that way.

"Do you know that I have never before, ever, in real life seen one person hit another with a fist like that? And he was *bleeding*! And he *cried*! And it wasn't just anybody getting hit, it was poor silly old Steve, who's his own worst enemy, and whose wife is somebody I talk to every day. And it wasn't some thug who hit him, it was *you*!

"Alan, we've been together for more than twenty years, and I thought we knew each other as well as any two people ever could. I didn't think you could do a thing like that. And now you tell me . . .

"I don't know you at all. I don't even know your right *name*!" She leaned her head foward on her knees, crying.

Alan put a hand on her back, but she shrugged it off. "It isn't exactly easy, for me, either, you know," he said. Jennifer didn't reply. "Maybe I should go and sleep in one of the unfinished rooms." Jennifer still did not answer. He took his pyjamas from behind his pillow and went out the door.

VI

SATURDAY

*O*N SATURDAY MORNING CRANMER HOUSE CAME AWAKE slowly. Faith arrived shortly after seven o'clock with her two teen-aged daughters and went immediately to the Lapierre's room. She told the tired parents to sleep a little longer while she took little Chantal to the kitchen where with much hilarity the two girls changed the baby's diaper, bathed her in the sink, sat her in the highchair, gave her kitchen utensils to play with, and began to supply her with unsuitable foods while they helped their mother prepare for the guests' breakfast. Jennifer had not slept well; she had already been for a walk before coming into the kitchen to help, where she found that Faith and her daughters had things well in hand. The girls were tall and slender, in contrast to their stocky mother, and as boisterous as any teens when Jennifer was not present. When she was there they would chatter softly to each other, their mother and the baby, but became tongue-tied and shy when Jennifer spoke to them. They were not twins, but were only a year apart in age, and looked alike. Jennifer knew that one was Debbie and the other Michelle, but she could never quite remember which was which.

As Jennifer took over some of the kitchen activities, they quietly and efficiently ranged through the public areas of the hotel, tidying, dusting, polishing and vacuuming.

Steve had not come home, Faith reported. His battered old pick-up truck was missing and so was he. "I expect he's gone to the cabin," she said. "He'll sober up, and then he'll be too ashamed to come home — 'til he runs out of food. He does it every time. I could strangle him sometimes. But I worries about him when he's out there drunk and all alone."

"Yes," said Jennifer. "I'm sure you do. Shouldn't somebody go after him?"

Faith shook her head. "He'd only run off into the woods. He'll come home when he's ready. It's when he comes home right away, before he's sobered up properly, that I really worries, because he's liable to take off drinkin' again. He can't help hisself."

Corporal Cameron came by at eight o'clock, bleary-eyed and coughing, to examine the scene he had enclosed in yellow tape the night before. He asked about Steve, heard Faith's account, refused coffee and left, saying he had a great many things to attend to and would be back later.

Simon came in at about eight-thirty, in casual clothes. "Marion down yet?" he asked, attempting a tone as casual as his clothing.

"Not yet," Jennifer said. "But she might be up and studying. I thought I heard some movement in her room. Why don't you go and see?"

Simon ignored the suggestion and began to make overtures to the baby, which included outlandish faces and sounds. The two teenagers watched with wide, inquiring eyes, but said nothing. By nine, the guests began drifting into the dining room, where Faith and Jennifer had set out a hearty breakfast in chafing dishes. Simon joined the first group to arrive, and the girls, directed by their mother, slipped up the back stairs to make beds, tidy and lay out new towels in the rooms belonging to guests who appeared in the dining room.

Faith seemed determined to see that the newly-devised routines of the hotel would continue to operate smoothly, no matter what else might be happening.

The ice in the container by the orange juice was in chunks rather than cubes. "It's from an iceberg," Jennifer explained. "One grounded near here last year, and some pieces came ashore. We kept some in our freezer."

"But isn't it salty?" Miss K asked, eyeing the ice doubtfully.

"No, it isn't," Jennifer said. "Once you wash off the salt water it's been floating in, it's completely fresh."

"And it's probably the oldest thing you'll ever touch," said Inspector Mullaly. Several of the guests were intrigued, and wanted to hear more. "Well," Mullaly said, "it's a piece of the Greenland ice-cap. The cap is a huge glacier, and each year snow falls on it and presses down on the snow underneath, and the snow lower down gradually turns to ice. The whole glacier moves slowly out over the ocean, and each year pieces break off. They become icebergs, floating in the water.

"They might hang around Greenland for a year or two, and then get blown offshore and end up in the Labrador Current and drift down to us. What you're drinking could have fallen on Greenland five thousand years ago, or more."

"Good heavens," said Miss K. "Is it safe to drink something that old?"

"It's probably safer than anything else you might drink. Think what the earth was like back then. No industrial pollution, no PCBs, none of the things we worry about now. It's probably the purest water we'll ever see.

"You'll notice that it pops and fizzes a bit in your glass. That's because the air bubbles trapped in it are under pressure, compressed by the weight of snow and ice above them."

The guests who arrived first passed some of this information along to the others, and Inspector Mullaly was called upon to repeat himself several times.

Mrs. MacEwen was red-eyed and strained-looking, and had little to say, leaving it to her husband to explain that she had hardly managed to sleep at all. "She can't stand any more of this nonsense," he announced. "I've taken our suitcases out to our vehicle. We are leaving as soon as we've had breakfast,"

"But didn't Corporal Cameron ask us to stay?" Inspector Mullaly asked. "A crime was committed last night, and we were all here. He can't let us leave until he knows what happened."

"Oh, but that was all an act. He wasn't a real policeman."

Inspector Mullaly gave a slight smile. "Opinion seems to be divided on that point. In any case, you were out there last night. You found the body, and you didn't seem to have any doubt that it was all real."

"Well, I have to admit that it shook me up. It took me by surprise, after Alan had said it was all off, but I've had time to think about it and I've changed my mind. It had to be an act. The idea that a fake murder could be cancelled and then a real one happen is ridiculous. But the whole thing is much too gruesome, and it has upset Anna. Even if it was all real, Cameron couldn't keep us here against our will, could he?"

"Well, maybe not in theory," said the Inspector, "But it depends on how much he wants us around. If somebody took off, he could decide they're a material witness and get a warrant to bring them back, or just bring 'em back and sort out the legality later. And to drive out of here you'd have to either take down that yellow tape he put up, or drive through it. That's an offense all by itself. How far do you think you would get in that big van of yours before Corporal Cameron would have you pulled over? Of course, that's if he really is a Mountie. If it's just an act . . . "

"I'd forgotten about the tape," MacEwen said slowly. "And you believe it's all real?"

"I do, yes."

After a few moments' consideration Dr. MacEwen turned to his wife. "Maybe we should stay, Anna. For a while, anyway. You can go up to our room and lie down again as soon as you've had a bite to eat."

"Oh, Eric! Do you really think . . . ?"

"I think it is best," said Dr. MacEwen firmly. "You needn't have anything to do with any of it. I'll go and get our suitcases again after I've had my breakfast."

"I suppose we shall have to stay, too," said Miss K.

"Of course we are going to stay, Katherine!" her sister said indignantly. "What on earth are you thinking of? I wouldn't leave now for the world!" She helped herself to breakfast and sat down. "Now, Inspector, who are our suspects? I can only think of one."

"Really?" said Simon. "Who is that?"

Miss A looked around before replying in a confidential near-whisper. "Mr. Davis, of course. He showed he could be violent with that drunk fellow, and Katherine heard him arguing with Mr. Browne after dinner, and they had some sort of old quarrel from long ago, and he has that band-aid on his forehead . . . "

"I don't see what that could have to do with it," Simon said, "seeing that Mr. Browne was hit from behind." He paused for a moment, then added, "He was, wasn't he? Hit from behind, I mean?"

"Well," said Miss A, "They had an argument. Suppose they continued it after they were out of Katherine's hearing. Suppose Mr. Browne hit him. Punched him and knocked him down, and then walked off. So Mr. Davis gets up, takes the sculpture from the front hall, runs after him and bashes him on the head from behind.

Then he hears Dr. MacEwen coming, so he drops the sculpture and runs around the house, in the back door, and into the washroom, where he notices that he has a cut over his eye, and he sticks on a band-aid. Or maybe he already knew he had a cut and went in there to put a patch on it."

Miss K rolled her eyes and shook her head, but said nothing.

"Good heavens!" said Simon. "That's very convincing. But I would accept it only if it was an act. I simply don't believe that Alan could do such a thing in real life."

"Makes no difference," said Miss A airily. "What do you say, Inspector? My analysis has all the things you talked about — an old animosity, alcohol, a sudden flare-up of temper . . . "

The Inspector sighed. "Yes." he said, "I suppose I did say all that. But with all due respect, I'd have to say that you are doing exactly what Browne said the police and the courts did in all these false convictions — seizing on one explanation of events and excluding all others. Apart from your sister's testimony about overhearing an argument, everything you've said is pure speculation. The next step would be to go and search for evidence that supports your story, and that's the way false convictions happen. Maybe you've got it right, but a proper investigation has to start by standing back and looking at all possibilities."

"What other possibilities are there?" Miss A said, rather belligerently.

"Well, for a start, I think pretty well everybody disliked Mr. Browne. As Rose said last night, he seemed to go out of his way to antagonize people. Miss K heard him quarrelling with Alan, and Mr. Lapierre says he heard him quarrelling with Terry, but he might have gone around quarrelling with everybody. He could have made some remarks to Lapierre about the bassoon, or to

Marion about her thesis, or to Simon about . . . about his relationship with . . . " Marion and Rose Mullaly entered the room at that moment, and the Inspector finished in a rush: "Sure, he could have started needling me again about police work, and *I* could have hit him!"

"And did you?" asked his wife.

"Of course not. But there is no reason why anybody should accept my word for it — except you, Rose: I expect you to believe me."

"Maybe I do," she said, "and maybe not. When it comes to mysteries, you can't trust anybody."

"Well, you ought to believe me. But there's no reason anybody else should accept anyone's word. We had all been drinking, probably more than we usually do. Lots of things could have happened out there. If that sculpture was standing in the entrance porch, any of us could have picked it up and gone after him. And if whoever did it hasn't confessed by now, they're not going to until they're forced."

"That is all very well," said Miss A, " but as you said yourself, Mr. Browne did seem to make an effort to be unpleasant to everyone. He could have been setting things up so that there would be several suspects. Anyway, I imagine new clues will turn up."

In the momentary silence that followed, Dr. MacEwen looked up from his plate. "Oh, I found the other one, by the way," he said.

"The other one?"

"The other sculpture that Alan was talking about last night. I found it. It's in the back porch, off the kitchen. I noticed it when I was taking the suitcases out."

"Could we have a look at it, do you think?" Rose Mullaly said.

"I don't see why not," Dr. MacEwen said. "I'll go and get it."

His wife stood up shakily. "I don't feel very well, Eric," she said. "I really don't want to see any more . . . "

"But this isn't the weapon!" Miss A exclaimed. "It won't have any tissue on it, or anything like that."

"I don't care," said Mrs. MacEwen. "I don't want to see it. I don't want to see anything to do with . . . all this . . . "

Miss A sniffed impatiently. "I don't understand why you came here at all, or how you can be a mystery reader."

"It's not the same when you're reading. Not the same at all."

"You go on upstairs, Anna," MacEwen said. "I'll get the sculpture, and later on I'll bring you some tea and toast."

The Lapierres came in, blinking and yawning, somewhat surprised to be about to have breakfast without Chantal, whom they had left in the kitchen, her smiling face smeared with blueberry jam, happily banging a large spoon on the tray of the highchair and shouting for more bacon while Faith and her daughters — including the vegetarian — encouraged her with delighted laughter.

Madame Lapierre said "Good bye" shyly to the room at large, and then corrected it to an even shyer "Good day" after a few hasty words in their own language from her husband.

"You were outside last night, weren't you?" Miss A asked.

"Yes," Lapierre said. "We walk in fog, walk on . . . " he searched for the word 'verandah' but did not find it " . . . on front of house, but is cold. We come inside . . . "

"Did you quarrel with Mr. Browne?"

"This means . . . fighting?"

"Well, not physically. More . . . arguing. Disagreeing."

"Yes," said Lapierre. "No. Mr. Browne is not nice man. We do not wish to talk with him. But we hear him talk with Terry. Terry is speak loud, say rude words. I tell this already last night."

"The only people who are going to admit quarrelling with Browne are ones somebody overheard," Inspector Mullaly said.

"Yes," said Miss A, eagerly, "but they'll have to spill their guts on Monday morning!"

"Lexa!" Miss K exclaimed. "What on earth are you saying?"

Miss A was defensive. "Well, that's what they always say in American mysteries. 'Spill their guts' — it means they tell everything." She thought for a moment. "I don't quite see why they put it that way. It doesn't really make much sense, when you think about it. But that's what they always say. It's very colourful, don't you think? 'Spill their . . . ' "

"Lexa!" Miss K said sharply, very much the older sister. "That is quite enough. It is a thoroughly disgusting and ridiculous expression, and there is no need to keep repeating it."

Miss A subsided, but mouthed the words silently to herself.

The Lapierres were conferring rapidly in their own language. "Please," Georges said, "What is 'guts'?"

"Alan didn't mention his own quarrel until Miss K did," said Marion thoughtfully, ignoring the question. "I don't think he even told Corporal Cameron about it until later. I wonder if Terry . . . "

Dr. MacEwen came back and placed the second sculpture on the table, a dark metal figurine about two feet high, depicting an African-looking man wearing a toga-like garment and holding a pair of rods or sticks crossed in front of his chest. The figure's hair, or perhaps a head-dress, rose above the head in a tapering swirl, so that the whole figure seemed to swell outward and downward, slimmer at the top and becoming thicker and blockier about the legs and feet, but the shape was nonetheless graceful. The man was standing on a patch of grass and small plants, rendered very realistically in the metal.

"I feel very badly about handling the other one last night," Dr. MacEwen said, addressing Inspector Mullaly. "It was there on the lawn, and I just . . ."

"I don't think there's much to worry about," said the Inspector. "If these things have been knocking around the house and being used for door-stops, they've probably got a half a dozen peoples' fingerprints on them, so yours and Lapierre's won't make much difference. It's sort of a textured surface, anyway — at least this one is — not great for prints. If the Mounties are lucky enough to find anything they'd have to get comparison prints from a lot of people. And even if the perpetrator's prints were on the thing it would only be useful later on, for an extra bit of evidence in court. They're going to have to find him — or her — some other way. "

Alan came in the door from the kitchen. "Oh," he said. "Where did that come from?"

"It was in the back porch," Dr. MacEwen replied, "lying under those shelves down to the right of the door."

"Funny. I thought I looked there last night when I didn't find it in the front porch. Must have missed it. I guess none of us were at our best last night."

Miss A put out her hand to the figurine. "Careful," said Dr. MacEwen. "It's hollow, but it's quite heavy."

She gave him a slightly condescending smile, picked it up easily with one hand and held it out at arm's length for a moment, then swung it back and forth at her side.

"When I was games mistress, we used to use Indian Clubs," she said.

"We were both born in India, you know," Miss K added. "We came to Canada as young girls, and we could not understand all the references to Indians and Indian things that had nothing to do with India."

"They were made of wood, and we used to do exercises with them," Miss A said, raising and lowering the figure. "I don't suppose they call them that any more."

"I think most progressive people call them 'First Nations'," said Marion.

"First Nations clubs?"

"No, I mean the people. People who used to be called 'Indians' are called 'First Nations' now."

"But what do they call Indian Clubs?" Miss A persisted. She transferred the figure to her other hand and raised it to shoulder height.

"I don't think they use them anymore," Marion said. "They didn't have anything like that when we had Phys. Ed. in school."

"P.T., we used to call it," said Miss A. "Physical Training." She held the figure by its head-dress in both hands and swung it up and down in a chopping motion. "The weight is mostly in the lower half, just like an Indian Club, but this is heavier. If you hit somebody with this, it would do a lot of damage." The watchers backed away slightly. Abruptly, she put the figure back on the table. "We used to have medicine balls, too. I don't suppose they have them anymore, either."

Rose Mullaly came forward. "Could I have a look?" She stroked the figure's shoulder. "I think it's bronze," she said. "Bronze darkens like this — a kind of greenish black." She turned to Alan. "And you say that the other one — the one Corporal Cameron took away — is like this?"

"Yes. They seem to be a pair — or at least we've always treated them that way. The other one looks like a European, with a tall hat, and a short skirt or tunic. We always thought he looked a bit like a sea-captain, somehow — maybe like the pictures of John Cabot, or somebody. But otherwise it's pretty much like that one — the same size and so on. You'd almost think they were made deliberately to show the similarities between the two men. As Miss A says, you could give a person a nasty clout with either one of them."

"In fact, it seems that somebody did," said Mrs. Mullaly

The fog had burned off early, and the sun shone in a brilliant blue sky. As they finished breakfast, several of the guests took cups of tea or coffee onto the part of the verandah that faced south, toward the driveway and the road, shielded by the house from the cool northeasterly breeze. Rose Mullaly headed for the library.

Miss A had come to breakfast in stout walking shoes; she now put on a jacket and announced her intention to go for a walk. As she went down the broad front steps, she fixed Georges Lapierre with a penetrating stare. "You had better watch your step!" she said, and strode off down the driveway.

"Oh, dear," said Miss K, watching her go.

"Don't worry, Miss Gilford," Jennifer said. "Miss A said she was going to walk down to the vill . . . to the Cove. Faith's daughters are headed home in a few minutes: they know everybody around here. In fact, they're related to most of them, one way or another. They'll pass the word, and everybody will keep an eye out for Miss A. She'll be in somebody's sight all the time, and she'll be perfectly safe."

"Is kind lady," said Georges Lapierre. At first it seemed as though he was referring to Jennifer, but he was looking at Miss A's retreating back. "Telling me watch steps. In Montréal, I must watch steps always. Is many dog. Big dog." He put a hand on the bannister and raised one foot after the other to inspect his soles, looking pleased with the result. "In Montréal, always I am cleaning shoes," he added, then called cheerfully after Miss A, "Watching steps!" Either she did not hear what he said or else she had forgotten whatever she had meant by the original admonition: she looked up from her examination of a shrubbery and waved gaily before striding off again.

Dr. MacEwen seemed to have been waiting for Miss A to leave. As she reached the end of the driveway he turned to Miss K. "Miss Gilford, I'm sorry to have to ask this question, but were you with your sister all the time last night?"

"What on earth do you mean?"

"She's remarkably strong and fit for . . . for a person of her age . . . "

"Yes?" Miss K would never say 'and so what?' but it was implied.

"That figurine is quite heavy, but she handled it as though it was nothing. It occurred to me then that she could easily have struck Mr. Browne with the other one."

"What a perfectly dreadful thing to say! What possible reason could she have to do such a thing?"

"Most of the time she is very sharp-witted, but she *has* been having some . . . ah . . . moments of irrationality, as you explained to us. If she were to have a sudden flash of . . . well, she wouldn't necessarily remember anything afterwards . . . " Dr. MacEwen fumbled a little, hesitant to put his suspicions into words.

"I'm sure she did nothing of the kind." Miss K's voice wavered a little. "I believe that yesterday you told us that you had no intention of involving yourself in things to do with the mystery weekend, but what you are doing now seems remarkably like it, and I find it most distasteful." She paused, but noticed that the others were watching the exchange closely. "For the others present I will say that, in fact, I was not with Alexandra all the time last night. As you can see, she is much more active than I am. She walked about while I stayed on the verandah. But I am absolutely sure that she did nothing wrong."

Marion put a comforting hand on the elderly woman's shoulder, but Miss K pulled away from her impatiently. Dr. MacEwen did not reply. The other guests looked thoughtful, and avoided meeting Miss K's eye.

Alan had found that Jennifer had little to say to him, and guests tended to stop talking when he was around. He wandered around to the garden on the west side of the house, where he found Terry seated on a bench with his usual breakfast of cigarettes and coffee. "This gets weirder and weirder," Alan said. "Most of the guests are trying to figure out who cold-cocked Browne last night. Half of them think it was part of the act, and the rest don't seem to care. I think they think it was me, either way."

"Well, you *are* the best suspect, after all."

"Me? Why me? Nobody liked him."

"Most of us only met him last night. You knew him before, and hated him. You had an argument with him just before . . . "

"So did you! Lapierre overheard you. And you must have squabbled with him after I did. He came up behind me on the verandah almost as soon as I got outside after dinner, and it must have been another half hour or so before MacEwen found him. Anything could have happened in that time."

"How long was he lying there?"

"I don't know," Alan admitted. "But you must have been yelling at him after he was talking to me. And other people must have seen him or talked to him. Maybe Cameron knows. Lapierre says you shouted 'rude words' at him. What brought that on?"

"Oh, he was just being a prick."

"He was doing that all evening. What did he do specifically to get your back up?"

Terry stood up in exasperation, spilling some of his coffee over his fingers. "He propositioned me, all right?"

"Propositioned you? Browne? But he's about as . . . as homophobic as you can get! Or at least he used to be when he was writing his column back in the sixties."

"That's not unheard of, especially in guys his age."

"But surely . . . "

"He put his hand on my bum and suggested that we could go up to his room, and I should bring along another bottle of that red wine. Is that good enough for you?"

"My God, I can't believe it! But I thought you . . . " Alan hesitated.

Terry dropped his cigarette on the path and threw the dregs of his coffee into the bushes. "Yes?" he said in a dangerously soft tone. "You thought . . . what, exactly?"

"Well, I mean, I thought . . . Alan stammered.

"Goddamn you, Alan," Terry burst out, "I know what you were going to say. You were going to say, 'But I thought you were gay,' weren't you? As though that would make it all right for that flabby old bastard to come on to me! You're a real asshole, do you know that?"

"Listen, Terry, I didn't mean . . . "

"Oh, I know what you meant. And you listen for a change. Suppose it was little Miss Fancypants — Maid Marion — telling you that old dork had fondled her pretty little ass and laid a crude proposition on her. What would you say? 'Oh, I thought you were heterosexual. I can't see why that should bother you.' Is that what you'd say? No fucking way you would! But with gays it's okay. We're such sex-mad perverts we're ready to jump into bed with anything, even an old shit like Browne!"

"Terry, I'm sorry. Really, I didn't mean . . . "

"So what *did* you mean, just out of curiosity?"

"I just meant that . . . Well, I thought . . . I thought you people handled that kind of thing better than the rest of us."

Terry looked at Alan for several seconds in disbelief before his anger gave way to a gust of laughter and he collapsed back down on the bench. "Oh, that's a gem, that is," he gasped when he had caught his breath. "I hope you don't mind being quoted from one end of the gay community to the other, because I'm going to have to pass that one on. 'I thought you people handled that sort of thing better . . . ' " he leaned back again, laughing helplessly.

Alan was not entirely sure what he had said that was so funny, and he did not much like the idea of being quoted as a buffoon, but he was glad Terry seemed less angry. "Terry, I'm sorry. I really am. I really didn't intend . . . "

"You're still an asshole," said Terry, trying to stifle a giggle, "but you're a *well-meaning* asshole."

"Thanks. I suppose. Okay, so that's what Lapierre heard. Browne propositions you, and you jump all over him."

"Well, no, not quite. At first I was quite moderate. I just told him to piss off and keep his hands to himself. In ordinary conversational tones, pretty much."

"So what made you yell at him?"

"No matter what a dork he was, Browne had a pretty sharp eye. He'd seen me on stage, in Toronto, in a piece I did at Tarragon Theatre a couple of years ago. Him recognizing me was kind of complimentary, in a back-handed sort of way, but he didn't get around to mentioning it until I told him to piss off, and then he said that he had lots of pull on the Toronto theatre scene, and if I wasn't a good boy he could see that I never worked there again. That's when I lost my cool."

"Did you lose it enough to clobber him with that sculpture?"

"No. How about you?"

"No."

"I'll believe your story if you'll believe mine."

This did not seem to Alan to be a particularly satisfactory conclusion, but he could think of no way to improve on it. As he turned away, Terry began to chuckle to himself, repeating "But I thought you people . . ."

* * *

Everyone turned up for lunch except Anna MacEwen, but the conversation was stilted. With Alan present, Miss A did not want to return to her speculations about his guilt, and with the Gilford sisters present no one wanted to make reference to the question Dr. MacEwen had raised about Miss A. Jennifer was in the kitchen helping Faith when the doorbell rang. She left it for Alan to deal with, but it was Miss A who popped her head through the swinging doors from the dining room. "Oh, Ms. Foster," she said, "that young policeman is here. He'd like to speak to you." Her voice was bright and excited. She was obviously enjoying herself.

Jennifer found Corporal Cameron standing on the front porch. His voice was still hoarse and congested, and he looked as though he was running a fever. "Good morning, Ms. Foster. I wonder if you'd mind stepping outside with me for a minute? I'd like to ask you to give me a hand with something."

Puzzled, Jennifer went with him down the stairs and out onto the drive, expecting the Mountie to turn toward the area where Browne was found. "It's about this retarded kid," the policeman said. He nodded toward the bottom of the driveway just as Ernie shot into view bent low over the handlebars of his bicycle, made a hand-signal, swerved into the entrance and braked suddenly, slewing the back wheel around in a circle and throwing up a shower of gravel. "I wanted to ask him a few questions, but it's kind of hard. I can't get him to hold still, and anyhow I can't understand what he says. I'm not sure he can understand me, either, with this flu or whatever it is I've got. I know he comes up here a lot, and you've sort of befriended him, so I said your name a couple of times and pointed up the hill, hoping he'd get curious and come up. I figured you might be able to interpret for me — or for both of us."

Ernie caught sight of Jennifer and began to peddle up the drive toward them. "But if you are going to question him," Jennifer said, "shouldn't his mother be present?"

"Apparently Lydia's at work. They're processing crab down at the fish plant."

"Well, in that case, shouldn't you wait until she gets home?"

Ernie pedalled past them emitting a noise like motorcycle engine, and made another skidding turn at the top of the drive where Cameron's car was parked. Jennifer sighed. She and Alan had asked him a dozen times not to churn up the gravel, but he never seemed to remember. She and the Mountie watched as he began to pedal down the far side of the driveway loop.

"Look, Ms. Foster, I don't need to remind you that something pretty serious happened here last night. According to my information that kid was on the premises. He could have seen something or heard something that would help us find out just what went on. Maybe he didn't see anything, and maybe he couldn't remember if he did, but I need to get whatever information I can. Now, I can go into the plant and drag Lydia out and scare her half to death and make her lose an hour's pay, or I can talk to him here and you can help me. It's your call." Ernie braked again dramatically as he reached the exit onto the road, and looked carefully both ways.

"I see," said Jennifer. "But you will talk to her?"

"I will if it's necessary. Right now I'm gathering information."

"All right. I'll do what I can."

"What would you say his mental age is?" Cameron asked.

"I don't think that kind of measurement means anything much," Jennifer said, "except maybe for school work. In some ways he's like a five year old, and in some ways he's like a normal teenager, and everything in between. Sometimes he can be amazingly sharp, and then there'll be some little thing that seems so simple and he just doesn't seem to be able to understand it." She paused to think about what she had said, then added: "I don't really know much about that sort of thing."

"Neither do I." The policeman looked down to the entrance, where Ernie had reappeared. He had turned his bicycle upside down and was squatting beside it, spinning the back wheel. "He seems to get along pretty well, though, doesn't he?"

"Yes, he does, on the whole. His mother's really a remarkable woman. His father was drowned when he was small, and she's brought him up by herself, pretty much — with a lot of help from her family, of course. She's got sisters and brothers and cousins all over the area. I imagine you've seen how he rides that bicycle on the roads — always wears his helmet, and makes all the hand signals and everything just the way we were taught back in England when I was a girl. His mother drummed that into him, and all sorts of other safety things. He's almost the only youngster in town who can swim really well. When she's working his other relatives keep an eye on him, but you just can't be watching all the time."

"Do you think he's better off than he'd be in an institution? Do the other kids give him a hard time?"

Jennifer did not answer immediately. Why was the policeman asking questions like this? "I don't know what an institution would be like, really," she said at last. "But I don't think it would be good for Ernie. I'm sure he is better off here with his family. The other youngsters tease him sometimes, but they tease everybody . . . if somebody's overweight or wears glasses . . . they can find something to tease everybody about, and they can be merciless at times. But they sort of protect him, too. He's different, but he's one of them in a sort of a way. It helps that he's been integrated into the school all along; that's one advantage of having a big regional school — they've got a special class with just a few kids with learning problems. And in a little place like Cranmer's Cove everybody has known everybody else all their lives.

"Last winter, a group from the high school at Clarenville came up for a basketball game, and some of them started making fun of Ernie. The kids from Cranmer's Cove put a stop to that in a hurry. Although on another day, they'd be making fun of him themselves — but that's different. It's like family."

Cameron was still watching Ernie. He cleared his throat. "Anyway, I need to ask him some questions. Can you get him up here?"

"He probably wants to come up and talk to me, but he'll be a bit shy because you're here. And I told him to stay away from the house while the guests are here." She called out: "Hi, Ernie! Are you going to come up and see me?"

The boy slowly righted his bicycle and began to walk up the driveway, pushing it.

"You told him to stay away, eh?" Cameron asked. "Why?"

"Well, this is our opening, you know. It's the first time we've had guests, and there is a lot to do. And he takes up a lot of time and attention when he's here."

"But he came anyway?"

"Yes. He's always curious. If anything unusual is going on he wants to be in on it. He didn't do any harm, he just wanted to see the guests."

Ernie stopped several feet away and stood looking at them. "Hi, Ernie," Jennifer said again. "This is Corporal Cameron."

"I owe," said Ernie. He pointed a forefinger with thumb upward at the holster on Cameron's belt and made shooting noises, then looked at Cameron with a sly grin.

"He wants to ask you some questions, Ernie, all right?"

The boy nodded warily.

"Hi, Ernie," Cameron said. "Thanks for coming up here. You were here last night, weren't you?"

Ernie looked away with the beginnings of a pout. "It's all right, Ernie," Jennifer said. "He knows you haven't done anything wrong. You came up to see the guests, and you came into the hall, and then I asked you to go home and you did. Isn't that right?"

Ernie nodded again. "Yif," he said.

"But you didn't go home, did you?" Cameron asked.

The boy hung his head, then shook it.

"Where did you go?"

"Own a orp," said Ernie, still looking at the ground.

Cameron looked at Jennifer. "He says he went down

to the government wharf. The kids hang around down there." It occurred to her after she'd said it that Cameron probably knew more than she did about how the young people of Cranmer's Cove spent their time.

"And you came back up here again later, didn't you? After it got dark?" Cameron asked.

Jennifer turned to the policeman in surprise. Ernie noticed the movement and looked at her anxiously, backing away a step or two. "It's all right, Ernie," she said again. "I'm not cross at you. Did you come back here?"

He hung his head again with a guilty expression. "Yif."

"What did you do?"

"Ook im a immo."

"He says he looked in the windows," said Jennifer. "He did that earlier, before he came into the hall."

"Yes," said the Mountie, "I heard about that. Ernie, did you see any of the people when they came out of the house after dinner? When it was dark?"

"Yif."

"Did any of them speak to you?"

By this time Ernie had forgotten to feel guilty or intimidated, and answered readily. "Yif. Ba' man."

"*Batman*?" said Cameron. With his congested nose, it came out as something like 'badbad,' which the other two did not understand at all. Jennifer looked puzzled and Ernie took another cautious step backwards.

"Do you mean a *bad* man?" Jennifer asked him.

"Yif."

"Any idea who he means?" Cameron said.

"Mr. Browne said some things earlier when Ernie was in the hall, and Ernie took a dislike to him. That must be it." She was beginning to wish she had insisted on waiting for his mother to get home.

Cameron continued to concentrate on the boy. "Was he a tall man with a beard?"

"Yif." He scowled.

"What did he say to you?"

Ernie's eyes widened with indignation. "O ne ut op!"

Cameron turned to Jennifer. "He says the man told him to . . . ah . . . eff off," she said.

"O!" Ernie said, shaking his head with great emphasis. "O ne *uck* op!"

"Yes, I know, Ernie," Jennifer said, "but that isn't a very nice word. We don't need to repeat it." She felt strangely hypocritical. There had been a time in her life when she had used the word in question with fashionable frequency, and still did occasionally when she was with certain old friends, and here she was acting like a Sunday school teacher. But somehow it didn't seem right for Ernie to be using it, and the idea of repeating it for the policeman was oddly embarrassing.

Ernie regarded her sulkily and muttered, "*Uck* op," with a stubborn frown.

"What did you do?" Cameron asked him.

The boy's expression changed in a flash to a triumphant grin. "Eep a iff owa ip!" he said enthusiastically.

"Oh, Ernie!" Jennifer exclaimed, shaken. "You mustn't say things like that!"

Ernie was pleased with the effect he had created. "I um ay ap," he said. Then, mimicking Jennifer's shocked tone, "Oh, Erwie!"

He parodied her expression and inflection so skilfully that in spite of the rising tension of the last few minutes the two adults both laughed spontaneously. Ernie was delighted. He leaped on his bicycle and rode in a wide circle around them, repeating the phrase several times.

The laughter ended as quickly as it had begun. "What did he say?" Cameron asked.

"He said, 'My mum says that,' then he imitated me saying 'Oh, Ernie!'" She spoke quickly and nervously.

"Yes," Cameron said. "I caught that. But what did he say before?"

"Oh," said Jennifer, "that was when he was saying that Mr. Browne had told him . . ."

"Ms. Foster," Cameron said, "I know you're worried about the boy. And please be assured that I will speak to his mother if it becomes necessary. But you must understand that if he has anything to tell us about this business I've got to hear it. I hardly need to tell you that this is a very serious matter. Now, what was it he said? Do you want me to ask him again?"

"No," said Jennifer.

"All right. I asked him, 'What did you do?' and he said? . . ."

"He said, 'I beat the piss out of him.'" Jennifer paused for a moment, then added in a rush, "It doesn't mean anything! The other boys encourage him to say things like that. They let him watch these horrible, violent videos, and they . . ."

"All right, now just take it easy."

Ernie had stopped riding in circles, and was watching their conversation with a self-satisfied smile. "What did you do to the man?" Cameron asked him.

"It ip!" the boy said proudly.

The policeman needed no interpretation. "You hit the bad man?"

"Yif! It ip!"

Jennifer drew in her breath, but the policeman waved a hand to silence her. "What did you hit him with?"

"Fiss!" Ernie said, with a fair imitation of a karate punch.

"You see?" said Jennifer with a faint note of relief. "He doesn't . . ."

Cameron ignored her. "Where did you hit him, Ernie?"

Ernie scowled fiercely. "Imma fafe!"

"You hit him in the face. Did you do anything else?"

"Yif."

"What did you do?"

Ernie placed his hands in the position of holding a machine gun. "Oot ip!" he said, and imitated a rattle of shots. "Us ike am-o!"

The policeman understood the gesture, but turned to Jennifer for a translation of the last part.

"He said he shot him. 'Just like Rambo'." Her voice was flat. Ernie nodded affirmation and made more karate gestures.

"You see what I mean," Jennifer said with a pleading note. "They all act out these dreadful movies, and the other boys egg him on . . . " her voice trailed away as she realized that her explanation was not doing much to allay whatever suspicions the Mountie might have.

"Do you think he knows the difference between fantasy and reality?" Cameron asked her.

"Of course he does. Now, Ernie, you didn't do any of those things, did you? It's just a story, isn't it? You didn't do anything to that man?"

"Did so!" said Ernie, clearly. "Eep a iff owa ip!" and he gave them both a sunny, innocent smile.

Corporal Cameron smiled back. "Thanks, Ernie. And thank you, too, Ms. Foster. I think that will be all I need for the moment. And don't worry, I will be calling on his mother. I'll tell her about your concern for his rights." He turned to go.

"Oh, but surely you don't think . . . "

The policeman turned back, interrupting her. "I'm just collecting information, Ms. Foster. It's the only way. We'll be in touch, I'm sure." He stood for a moment, looking at Jennifer. When he spoke again his voice was less formal. "Look," he said. "I understand your concern about Ernie, and whether you believe it or not, I'm concerned about him, too." He looked away for a moment, then continued. "My daughter's . . . " he hesitated on the words " . . . developmentally delayed. She's only two, and we won't know for a while how much she'll be able to . . . My wife's been reading up on it a lot since we found out, but I can't seem to . . . Maybe after all this business is over she could come by and talk with you a bit? Maybe we both could?" Jennifer was taken aback. "Oh, certainly!" she said. Then, as the Mountie turned to plod back to his car she added, "Thank you," then immediately wondered what she was thanking him for.

Excited by the conversation, Ernie pedalled off behind the police car as it moved down the driveway, and followed it along the road. Jennifer turned back to the house and realized for the first time that most of the guests were on the verandah, watching the interview like an audience at a play. Anna MacEwen was presumably still lying down, and a muted hooting from the rear of the house indicated that the Lapierres were engaged in their daily practice.

As she approached the steps she knew that someone would ask what had been going on, but she did not expect it to be Simon. "Corporal Cameron wanted your help to interview Ernie?" It was more a statement than a question.

"He came back last night, didn't he?" Dr. MacEwen said. "He was outside after dinner?"

"Look," said Jennifer. "We don't know. He might have come back, and he might not have. He doesn't always tell the . . . I mean, he often says things to impress people. I'm sure Corporal Cameron will be asking other people in the village . . . I mean The Cove . . . just when they saw him, and so on."

"I thought I heard his voice last night," said Dr. MacEwen. "I didn't like to say anything at the time because I wasn't sure, but now I think the information may be useful to the Corporal. He thinks Ernie did it, doesn't he?"

"No!" said Jennifer, with much more certainty than she felt. "He is just gathering information, and he thought that Ernie might have seen or heard something useful. If he was here, that is."

"Browne did call him an idiot," Simon said helpfully. "And Ernie said he didn't like him. He . . ." The implications of what he was saying suddenly dawned on him, and his voice trailed away. Marion gave him a look that Jennifer instantly recognized as expressing emotions she often felt herself toward Simon, a combination made up of exasperation and affection in equal measure.

*   *   *

Still unsure of what he should be doing, Alan wandered into the kitchen, and to his astonishment found Steve sitting at the pine table, head down, hunched over a cup of tea. Faith was standing by the stove, facing him, and had been talking as Alan walked in. He had clearly interrupted something serious, but could do nothing about it. "Steve!" he said. "What are you . . . I mean, I didn't expect . . ."

Steve lurched to his feet. He had changed his clothes and shaved rather patchily since the previous evening; several bits of red-spotted toilet paper clung to his face. He seemed relatively sober, but as Alan came closer he caught a strong smell of alcohol. Steve's whole body trembled, and he spoke in convulsive bursts punctuated by shudders. "Jesus, Alan, what can I say? I'm sorry. Faith's been tellin' me what I done last night, and I'm real sorry, so I am." He ran his hand over his eyes and through his hair. "I've gotta get some air," he said, and reached for the back door.

Alan looked quickly at Faith, then followed him out. Outside, Steve was supporting himself against the corner of the house and retching horribly. "God, Steve," Alan said in spite of himself. "You look awful!"

"Tell me about it," Steve said, with a weak attempt at a grin. He coughed deeply and clutched his forehead with a groan. "I feel like shit, truth to tell." He slid his hand down over his nose, and winced.

Alan noticed the gesture. "I'm sorry I hit you," he said, "but I didn't know what else to do."

"Ah, that's all right, boy. Faith tells me I deserved it."

"You keep talking about Faith telling you about what happened . . . you don't remember?"

"Not a shaggin' thing," Steve said. "About four o'clock Friday morning I was with some guys on the Straight Shore, and the next thing I knows, I'm wakin' up in the cabin, freezin' to death. It's right scary. I've had the odd blackout before, but never for as long as that." He turned away to retch again, and Alan averted his eyes.

"But you must have driven!" Alan said. He had a terrifying image of Steve's old pickup hurtling down the Trans-Canada with an insensible drunk at the wheel. "All the way from the Straight Shore! You could have . . . "

Steve seemed uninterested in the possibilities. "Listen, Alan, I had to come up here and tell you how sorry I am, but I got to go and lay down. I'm really feelin' bad. Michelle's got her mother's car, and she's going to come and take me home. I'd better get out front." He began to make his way along the pathway beside the house, supporting himself against the clapboard.

Alan went back into the kitchen, where Faith was bustling about, making an unusual amount of noise. "Steve's going home," he said. "He sure doesn't look good."

Faith stopped what she was doing and stood very still. "It's a tough time for him," she said. "He's real sick, and he's still half drunk. It was hard for him to come and apologize to you. And he knows he's got to talk to Corporal Cameron pretty soon. There's people in town owes him money. If he gets his hands on a few dollars and gets to drinkin' again . . . " Her voice trailed off.

"Oh, my God! I never thought of that," Alan said. "Look, maybe you should go home, too — stay with him. Jennifer and I can . . . " Faith's look stopped him.

She did not raise her voice, but spoke with a cold intensity that Alan had never heard before. "And just what the hell am I supposed to say to him? Do you think I can tell him something he doesn't already know? We've been married for nearly twenty years. Do you think I haven't seen this kind of thing a hundred times? What am I supposed to do? Lock him up? Take his truck keys away? If he's going to go out on a tear again, there's not a friggin' thing I or anybody else can do about it. He's killing himself. I just hope he doesn't kill anybody else while he's at it. He's sure as hell not going to kill me. Or the girls."

"I'm sorry," Alan mumbled.

"Me, too," said Faith, and turned back to the sink.

As Alan left the kitchen he met Georges Lapierre hurrying along the hall. "Is good," Lapierre said. "I look for you or Jennifer. Can you come up, please, to . . . to walking place for widows? Dr. McEwen thinks he is seeing iceberg!"

Dr. McEwen was right. Far in the northeast there was a vivid speck of white against the deep, luminous blue of the ocean. Alan went downstairs to get his old binoculars, and with their help could see that the berg was moving toward them, with the wind behind and slightly to the east of it. None of the mainland visitors had seen an iceberg before, and there was much excitement. Throughout the day its progress was watched as it moved steadily toward them on the northeast wind, growing in detail and majesty as it came.

It was agreed without much discussion that they would not dress for dinner that night. Some people walked on the cliffs watching the iceberg's slow and ponderous approach, some napped, and some walked down into Cranmers' Cove. Around seven o'clock everyone gathered in the library as before for sherry, most of them in casual clothes. Dr. MacEwen was dressed exactly as he had been on the previous evening. His wife looked pale and drawn, but looked less awkward in a sweater and slacks than in her formal dress. Marion was back in jeans and a denim shirt, with jogging shoes rather than boots, and Simon was wearing his 1950s sports clothes. Alan was pouring sherry again, but no whisky. Jennifer was struck by how different this gathering was from the first: different in appearance, different in tone and, she felt with a pang of sadness, very different in relations between herself and her husband.

As soon as she entered the library, Rose Mullaly went directly to a desk where she had left a small stack of old books. "Alan," she said. "You know that figurine we've been calling a sculpture?"

"Yes?"

"I think you should put it somewhere safe. And the other one, too, when you get it back."

"I think it's still in the dining room. Shall I go and get it?

"If you like, but you should keep it safe."

"Why? What's . . . Have you found out something about it?"

"I think I have."

"I'll get it." He was back in a moment with the figurine, and placed it on the desk beside the books. He noticed for the first time that it was dotted with droplets of dried white paint, and recalled the figurine propping open the door when the dining room ceiling was painted. "Okay," he said. "What's the mystery? Is it valuable?"

"If it is what I think it is, it could be very valuable." Her excitement was obvious and infectious, and the rest of the company gathered around. "I think it's a Benin Bronze!"

She looked at the others expectantly, but no one reacted. "Dr. MacEwen?" she said, somewhat deflated. "Anna? Surely you know what I am talking about?"

Anna MacEwen merely looked stricken, but her husband said, "No. Afraid not."

"But I thought that as archaeologists . . . "

"Not our area," MacEwen said. "Sorry."

"I think you should probably explain," said Miss K, coming to the rescue.

"Yes. Well, if I'm right, it's from Benin, one of the great West African kingdoms. It was a powerful place in the early 1400s, when the first Europeans visited — that was the Portuguese — and it was still pretty important when the British destroyed it nearly five hundred years later. They made all kinds of things, but they were especially famous for their bronze work."

"You said we've 'been calling it' a sculpture," said Miss K. "Isn't that what it is?"

"Not exactly. If it is what I think it is, it's a casting, made by pouring molten bronze into a mould. But it certainly wasn't mass-produced, and it started out with a sculpture. If it's a real Benin bronze, it was made by a very complicated and careful process. First they built up a chunk of wax around a clay core, then they sculpted whatever it was they were going to make in the wax, then they dipped the wax shape into liquid clay, and kept doing that until they had built up a thick layer, only they had to add holes and channels in the clay as they went

181

along to let air out when they put the bronze in. Finally, when the clay hardened, they heated it to melt the wax out of it, then put it in a kiln and baked it solid, so it became a ceramic mould. Then they poured the molten bronze into it, and after the bronze hardened, they broke the ceramic mould off the finished product. If they made a mistake anywhere along the way, it could ruin the whole thing. The mould could only be used once, but it allowed them to put really fine detail into whatever they were making in bronze. It's called the 'lost wax' process. In French it's *cire perdu*, I think, and craftspeople still make jewelry that way, but I don't think anybody makes things as big as this."

"That's amazing!" said Marion. "How do you know all this?"

"I guess I can answer that one," Inspector Mullaly said. "It was one of those courses I . . . we took. Right, Rose?"

"That's right. Gerry took a course in the anthropology of art one summer."

"I only took it because Rose liked the sound of it. We had to stay home for the best part of the summer while she dragged books out of the library."

"I was fascinated by all the different kinds of things people made. There was a whole chapter on Benin bronze in the textbook, do you remember, Gerry?"

"Sort of."

"Well, that was what I thought of when I first saw this figurine. I looked in the *Encyclopaedia Britannica* here in the library — they've got several editions, all in perfect condition — and Jennifer ran me in to Cranmer's Cove so I could use Faith's daughters' computer to look up things on the Internet, and that sent me back to the library, and I found this!" From the books on the desk she proudly held up a slim volume with a dark brown cover. "It was privately printed in 1900, and it's called . . . " she opened the book to the title page and read somewhat self-consciously " . . . *Antique Works of Art from Benin, West Africa, Collected by Lieutenant-General Pitt-Rivers*". His name is almost as long as the title: Augustus Henry Lane-Fox Pitt-Rivers." She looked expectantly at the MacEwens, but they did not react.

"What was a general doing collecting works of art?" Marion asked.

"I don't know, exactly. I haven't read the whole book yet — I've been looking for pictures and descriptions — but he says he bought the bronze work after the British army came back from West Africa in the 1890s. They looted the city of Benin in 1897. I suppose a lot of the soldiers brought things home to England and sold them to collectors like Pitt-Rivers. And he'd have army contacts. This book was published only three years after the looting.

"Alan, I think you said that the people who built this place — the Cranmers — were an old shipping family from England?"

"Yes," Alan said. "This place was started in the 1880s, I think it was, but the family history goes back a hundred years before that. Maybe more. The fish-merchant operation here in Newfoundland was only one branch. Cranmer ships traded all over the world."

"And I wouldn't be a bit surprised if they had a hand in the slave trade in West Africa," Mrs. Mullaly said, "up until the 1830s, anyway. A lot of English shipping companies started their fortunes that way. That other figure — the one Mr. Browne was hit with — you said it looked like a European. He could have been a slave-trader."

"Was Benin involved in the slave trade?" asked Simon.

"They got drawn into it, like everybody else in West Africa. The biggest slave-dealers were probably in what used to be called Dahomey. What really makes it confusing is that when Dahomey became independent, they changed the name to Benin. It's a little country in there just below the big bulge in Africa, in between Nigeria and . . . and Ghana, I think — no, Togo is in there somewhere — but the old Benin City where the bronze work was done was east of Dahomey, in what's Nigeria now. Before the kings in Dahomey got rich on the slave trade, the kings of Benin controlled that whole area."

"But why don't we know about this?" Marion said. "I never heard anything about it in school."

"We don't hear anything about the great African kingdoms," Mrs. Mullaly said. "I think Europeans prefer to think that any civilization in the past was built by people like us. They especially don't like the idea that black people could build great civilizations without European help. They preferred to believe that black people are inferior — it helped to justify slavery, and it helps to justify discrimination now. Europeans called whole West African shoreline from the Niger River down to the Congo 'The Slave Coast'."

"They also called it 'the white man's grave'," said Dr. MacEwen, "because it was so unhealthy for Europeans."

"Pretty unhealthy for slaves, too," Mrs. Mullaly said. "But an awful lot of Europeans died there, for sure. There's an old sailor's rhyme that goes: *Beware and take care of the Bight of Benin, for there's few who comes out, though there's many goes in*. It must have been a horrible place when the slave trade was going on."

"I wonder what they meant by 'the bite of Benin'?" said Dr. MacEwen.

"I think a *bight* is a kind of . . . indentation in a coastline, only it doesn't go far enough in to be a bay. There's places in Newfoundland with it in the name, like Bumble-bee Bight and Windmill Bight. Benin City was inland, away from the coast, but it must have been pretty powerful for the name to be applied to the whole area.

The people in Benin used people from the coast as go-betweens in the trade with Europeans; they wouldn't deal with them directly."

"And they traded this bronze stuff?"

"A bit. Benin craftsmen made boxes and jewellery and all kinds of things in bronze, but in the early days Europeans didn't attach much importance to the artistry — it was too alien for them. They had the idea that 'inferior' people like the Africans couldn't do anything as well as Europeans could. But a lot of the Benin bronze work was decorated with ivory and silver and gold, and that made it valuable to the Europeans. The Portuguese were in there first, but after them there were the Dutch and the Swedes, and finally the British, so there are bits of Benin bronze all over the place in Europe going back five hundred years or more. I suppose experts could tell when the various pieces were made.

"But mostly the Benin craftsmen didn't make it for trade: most of it was for their own use, and there was a lot of it in the city itself, and some of it had been made hundreds of years before. There were all sorts of stories about how wealthy Benin was. That was probably what prompted the British to attack the place. They hauled away a tremendous amount of treasure after they slaughtered the people. When Pitt-Rivers named his book *Antique Works of Art* he really meant it: some of the pieces he bought were really old. The British Museum in London has a lot of pieces that came into Britain at that time, and so has the Glasgow Museum. And there's still a fair amount of it in private collections."

"In Canada," Marion said, "First Nations people have been getting a lot of their things back — things that were taken from them a long time ago."

"Maybe that's what happened to all the Indian clubs and medicine balls," Miss A said. "Had to give them back."

Marion took a deep breath. "I don't think so," she said. "I think it was mostly ceremonial things."

Terry had come in a few moments before to announce dinner, but he became interested in the conversation and could not resist an opportunity to tease Simon. "Yes, the missionaries confiscated a lot of things," he said, with an innocent air, "and then they ended up in museums and private collections." Almost immediately, he remembered Browne's heavy-handed taunts on the previous evening and was sorry he had spoken.

Fortunately, the reference to confiscated ceremonial material apparently did not trigger full-scale guilt in Simon; he merely looked embarrassed. "Well, it was a long time ago. The churches had some pretty . . . well, narrow ideas about spirituality. There's been a lot of changes since then."

"I know," said Miss A. "You can't go to services at our parish church these days without there being some sort native person beating a drum or something. I don't understand it at all."

Terry, still contrite, tried to shift attention away from Simon. "Do the people in Benin want their bronzes back, Mrs. Mullaly?"

"Well," she said, "the area that Benin used to control is now in more than one country, but there has been a lot of pressure to send the things looted from the city back to the area they came from. I learned from the Internet that there is something called ARM — the African Repatriation Movement — and they've been putting pressure on the British government to give back the stuff in the museums — sort of like the campaign to return the Elgin Marbles. Some people seem to think that the new Scottish parliament might be willing to give up the pieces in Glasgow."

"So I suppose that if these figurines are really what

you think they are, Alan and Jennifer can't really keep them, can they?" said Simon thoughtfully. "They'd have to give them back." No other possibility would occur to him, and Marion nodded agreement.

Alan was about to argue the point, but Mrs. Mullaly spoke first. "They wouldn't necessarily have to *give* them back. Many of the ARM people think that governments should return things from museums, but they are willing to buy things that are in private hands, because they figure the person who owns it had to pay for it. The Nigerian government has used some of its oil revenues that way."

"Ah . . . how much . . . I mean, what do you think . . . " Alan struggled to frame the question uppermost in most people's minds.

"I'd have no idea what these pieces would be worth," Mrs. Mullaly said. "I don't even know for sure that they come from Benin. But the last authenticated Benin pieces that went on auction in London — and they were nowhere near as big or as detailed as these — went for over a million pounds. The Nigerian government bought them with oil money."

There was a momentary silence while the listeners translated a million pounds into Canadian dollars, then Alan exhaled in a low whistle.

"Expensive door-stops," said Terry.

"An expensive weapon," Inspector Mullaly added.

Any further comment was pre-empted by Faith, who arrived at the library door to announce that if the supper were not served immediately it would be ruined, and that it might be ruined anyway, and it was all Terry's fault, because if he had called people to the dining-room as he was supposed to do, the food would have been on the table long ago.

The dinner was as magnificent as the previous night's, but the company was subdued. Compliments on the food were sincere but muted, and the conversation revolved around the figurines, Rose Mullaly's knowledge of African art, and colonial history. Everyone had been up late the night before, and Alan and Jennifer were both struggling with conflicting emotions, excited by the possibilities opened by Mrs. Mullaly's find, but inhibited by their own estrangement. Anna MacEwen was present, but ate little and added nothing to the conversation. Mrs. Mullaly continued to be the centre of attention. Among other things, she explained that her strong feelings about the slave trade stemmed at least partly from the fact that her ancestors had come to Newfoundland as indentured servants, a condition similar in some respects to slavery.

The dinner was coming to an end before Inspector Mullaly broke the ice by mentioning the events of the previous night. "I feel I have to say something," he said. "We've all been acting very casual about our situation. Maybe it's because we all came here expecting a fake murder for entertainment, but whatever the reason, we haven't been taking things seriously.

"Just think for a minute. Last night somebody came up behind Mr. Browne and smashed him on the head with a heavy bronze sculpture. We don't know who did it. It could have been one of us at this table, or it could have been . . . somebody else who is still out there. For the most part, we can't even come up with a rational idea for a motive. And yet nobody seems to be worried that there might be another attack — that any of us might be in danger. Why aren't we more concerned?"

Throughout the meal Georges Lapierre had provided the usual running translation in an undertone for his wife. Now she spoke to him in Bulgarian and he turned to the rest of the company. "Marya is frighten for baby. Before, she does not think murder is real. Now, she is not sure. She ask Inspector what we must do."

Inspector Mullaly had not meant to frighten any-one, but simply to draw attention to the seriousness of the situation as he saw it. Besides, he had no idea what they should do. "Tell her I don't think there is any real cause to worry about the baby. Still, I think we all should take precautions. Nobody should go outside alone, at least while it's dark. And we should all make sure that our doors are locked tonight. Perhaps tomorrow, if Corporal Cameron hasn't come back to tell us what happened, we should talk more seriously about this."

"But I have to go home," Simon said. "Tomorrow is Sunday," he added, by way of explanation.

"Alan and I will walk with you to your car," said Inspector Mullaly. "And you should go straight home and not pick up any hitchhikers." No one thought about Marion, who had intended to at least walk out with Simon when he left, and the three men went out briskly and importantly, leaving her standing alone.

Everyone went up on the widow's walk for a last look at the iceberg by moonlight, but a thin fog had devel-oped and it was only an indistinct blur in the grey-black darkness. Alan assured everyone that it was almost cer-tainly grounding itself on the reefs off the point of land that stretched eastward from the house, and would be there in the morning. After a few quiet goodnights, the company drifted off to their rooms.

When Inspector Mullaly went to his room he found the door locked. Exasperated, he gave a solid police-man's knock.

"Who's there?" said his wife.

"Who the hell do you think?"

"Oh, I don't know. Could be the murderer, I sup-pose."

"For God's sake, Rose, open the door. I can't be standing out here, not able to get into my own room!"

"Are you sorry for what you said about priests?"

Inspector Mullaly knew that argument would be useless. "Yes," he said grimly. "But not as sorry as you'll be if you don't open the damn door."

"You don't sound very sorry to me," his wife said, laughing as she let him in. "A girl can't be too careful, you know. If it isn't murderers with expensive statues, it's old reprobates in fancy dress uniforms." She cocked her head as her husband came in. "You looked pretty good, though, all the same. And you don't look too bad now, even without the monkey jacket." He grunted, and began to untie his shoes.

"You certainly put the fear of God into them down there," his wife said,

"I thought somebody had to. But you're as bad as the rest of them. You don't think it was a real murder either, do you?"

"I don't know. I'm not convinced either way."

"Well, you should be. I saw Browne lying in the driveway, remember. I'm not absolutely sure he was dead, come to think of it, but I'm damn sure he'd taken a serious blow on the back of the head. Whoever hit him certainly *intended* to kill him — or at least they hit him hard enough to. I'm sure Corporal bloody Cameron is genuine, and there is no way a real policeman would be fooling around with a fake murder. He's having a hell of a time, but the Mounties wouldn't call on the RNC for help if they were down to their last constable. I'm not surprised we haven't seen him around much. But give me some credit for knowing a real crime scene when I see it."

"I do, Gerry. You know I do. But this isn't your average crime situation, is it? You said yourself how it gets all mixed up with the mystery stuff. And if it was a real murder, then it has to be a fantastic coincidence. And there has to be a real murderer on the loose, and that's hard to believe."

"I know. But I also know what I saw." He slipped off his shoes and wiggled his toes in relief. "You certainly made them all sit up and take notice with your lecture on African art. I wonder if there's anything else in this old place that's worth a fortune. Did you really learn all that stuff about Africa from that course I signed up for?"

"No. I got some of it from the course, but I picked up a lot of it today down there in the library and from the Internet. And I'll tell you one thing I learned tonight for sure."

"What?"

"The MacEwens aren't archaeologists. They could be actors, or they could be real guests who're pretending, but they aren't archaeologists."

"How do you know?"

"A lot of things. They've been funny about archaeology ever since they introduced themselves, the way they keep saying 'not our area.' Archaeologists do specialize, but they at least recognize things from other places. I was suspicious about them all along, but this evening put the cap on it. You remember that book I found in the library?"

"The one by buddy with the long name?"

"Right. Augustus Henry Lane-hyphen-Fox Pitt-hyphen-Rivers. I looked him up on the Internet, too. I didn't find out much about him, but I did learn that he's called 'the father of scientific archaeology'. Wouldn't you kind of expect a couple of archaeologists to at least recognize his name? But I watched them when I read it out. Not a flicker."

"Wouldn't you expect actors who are going to play archaeologists to learn something about it?"

"Of course you would. But then, wouldn't you expect somebody who was going to pretend to be an archaeologist at a mystery weekend to learn about it, too?"

"So where does that leave you?"

"I've been thinking about it, and I've decided they must be guests."

"How do you figure that?"

"Well, the Missus did the same thing as I did — she handled all the correspondence, and set the whole thing up. The only thing that makes sense is if she decided on archaeology as a kind of romantic fantasy when she was writing to make reservations, and then she didn't dare tell her husband until they got here."

"The way you didn't mention dressing for dinner."

"Right. She didn't, either, come to think of it."

"But she didn't pack a dress suit for him. Anyway, why didn't she bone up on archaeology, herself?"

"Maybe she did. Maybe she read something on Egypt, and thought that was all there was to it."

"Yeah. I suppose a lot of people would accept that. It's just her bad luck that my wife is such a brilliant scholar."

"Right."

"They're from Ottawa, aren't they?"

"So they say."

"I bet he's a civil servant. Some sort of middle-range bureaucrat in charge of screwing things up for Newfoundland. He's here to see how it's working out."

"If he's a bureaucrat, he must be at the top end or else he's making some money on the side."

"What? Why?"

"How much do you think that big RV cost? You don't buy one of those on an ordinary salary."

"Oh. Yeah, I guess you're right. I suppose it's too late for you to take over my job with the Constabulary, is it?"

"Probably. I wouldn't look as good in the uniform, anyway. You certainly impressed everybody with your lecture on icebergs. Between us, we're turning into a mine of information, aren't we?"

"Yeah. Well, I learned most of that stuff last year from an article in the *Telegram* . Still, it doesn't hurt to be regarded as a local expert."

* * *

Alan also knocked on the door to the apartment he and Jennifer shared, but he did it tentatively, feeling very self-conscious, then carefully opened the door and walked into the small sitting-room, carrying the African sculpture. Jennifer looked at him from the door to the kitchen with an unreadable expression. "How does it feel to be a millionaire?" he asked with a nervous smile.

"Allie, I don't care about that. I really don't. I care about you. I care about *us.*"

"Do you still think I'm a murderer?"

Jennifer came forward toward him. "I'm sorry about last night, but I was really shocked by what you did to Steve, and then you told me that story . . . I just didn't know what to think."

"What do you think now?"

"I have to ask you this, Alan. Did you hit Mr. Browne on the head with that sculpture thing?"

Alan sighed and put down the figurine he was carrying. "I wish you didn't have to ask, but I guess I've given you good reason to. No, I didn't hit him. I might have wanted to, but I didn't."

Jennifer came forward and embraced him, and Alan hugged her tightly. She was the first to speak. "It's going to take me a while to come to terms with what you did to Steve, but I'm so glad to hear you say . . . I really didn't know what . . . "

"It's okay, Jen. I understand."

"But . . . but who? . . . "

"I haven't got a clue," Alan said. "It's got to be

somebody right here, but . . . I wonder if MacEwen is right, and poor old Miss A did it in one of her fits?"

"But that's horrible!"

"Have you got a better answer? And she did handle that sculpture as though it was nothing." They released one another. "Steve came back, by the way."

"Yes, I know. Faith told me. But he's gone again, did you know that?"

"Oh, God. I didn't know about it, but she said he might."

"He went home right after you talked to him, and he slept for a couple of hours, and then he got up and went off in his truck. They haven't seen him since. He could be anywhere."

"He doesn't remember anything, you know. I suppose it could have been him. Do you really not care about the money?"

"I don't know. It doesn't seem real, does it? None of it does."

"Well, the money might not be, I guess. Mrs. Mullaly isn't sure those things are genuine. But she thinks they are." He picked up the figurine he had brought in, took it into the kitchen, and put it in the broom-closet. "I thought I should bring this one in here, just in case.

"Imagine her knowing all that stuff! And imagine us using a couple of million dollars worth of *objets d'art* for doorstops! Anyway, I don't mind admitting that the idea they could be worth a fortune took a bit of a load off my mind. I don't think you were there on Friday night when I told them the mystery was cancelled, but I offered to cancel all charges, too. I had no idea how we were going to afford it, but I felt I had to do it. But if Rose Mullaly is right, those figurines could pay off all our debts and leave plenty of money over."

"Well, we'll just have to wait and see. Maybe Simon

and Marion are right — maybe we should give them back to . . . whoever those people in Africa are."

"Don't get carried away, now. Mrs. Mullaly did say they pay for things in private collections."

"Yes, but she also said they do it because the people who have them had to pay for them. We just got those figures with the house."

"And you don't think we paid for them? We bought the whole house, contents and all. Of course, Cranmer didn't know how much they were worth, but that's not our fault."

"Oh, I don't know," Jennifer said. "I'm just happy that we're . . . together, that's all."

"Me too. Hey, maybe we could sell the sculptures at a discount. Anyway, it's comforting to know they're there."

* * *

Miss A was restless again at bedtime, but for a different reason from the previous night. "It is very distressing, Kat," she said, pacing around the bedroom. "Everything started off so well last night, but today nothing happened. Nothing at all. No clues or anything. We don't know any more now than we did last night. I suppose if that tedious Molloy woman is right, the murder weapon could be valuable, but what has that got to do with anything? Did you notice any clues, Kat?"

"No, Lexa, I didn't, I'm afraid," Miss K said. She did not find Rose Mullaly tedious, and quite enjoyed the talk on Benin bronze, but she did not want to upset her sister any further.

"Well, we can't go on like this. I suppose that Davis fellow thinks that just because he said that the mystery weekend is cancelled and then he staged a murder, he can sit back and rest on his laurels. I kept expecting that there would be some sort of revelation today, or that something else would happen. Unless something happens right away tomorrow morning, I am going to take things into my own hands!"

Miss K thought unhappily about Dr. MacEwen's suggestions after lunch. "The policeman did come and interview Jennifer about that retarded boy," she said placatingly, "and we did learn that he came back last night."

"Oh, I know all that, Kat, but it isn't good enough. Not good enough at all. They're going to have to do much better than that! And I really have come to dislike those foreign people. He is very free with his language, I must say."

" 'Free' is not quite the word I would use, I don't think," said Miss K.

"You heard him, Kat. Everyone heard him. He said that he expected to have a Canadian piss-pot soon. I suppose it is some sort of foreign way of saying things, but it just isn't acceptable in English and in polite company. I was about to tell him so, but no one else seemed to be concerned, so I kept quiet, but I gave him a very severe look, I can tell you."

"I think he was telling us that he is hoping to have a Canadian passport," said Miss K mildly.

"Oh. I see. Well, why can't he say so properly? Remember what Father used to say about the Native troops: they could understand English perfectly well if one spoke loudly enough and clearly enough, and they only pretended not to understand in order to be annoying. I think most of these foreigners are like that."

Miss A began crossly to prepare for bed.

VII

SUNDAY MORNING

ON SUNDAY MORNING ALMOST EVERYONE WAS PRESENT for breakfast by eight-thirty, all in casual clothing except Simon, who wore his clerical suit, saying that he had to leave by shortly after ten to be in time for morning devotions at eleven. The sober effect was somewhat diluted by the fact that under his black jacket he wore a bright blue t-shirt with "Provincial Advisory Council on the Status of Women" emblazoned across the chest in red, but he explained that it was a gift from Marion: he needed only to slip on a dicky and collar to be properly dressed for church, and he had those in his car. The idea of the colourful secular clothing being present under his priestly vestments was mildly distressing to several people, most of whom had not been to church for years, but the idea did not seem to bother Simon.

Anna MacEwen was still, as her husband put it, 'resting,' and Chantal was in the kitchen again, showing every sign of being happy to be there. By general agreement, Alan, Jennifer and Terry were all present, although Terry would have preferred to be outside where he could smoke. Faith could have left the kitchen to her daughters, but insisted on supervising them.

Miss A waited until everyone had arrived, and then looked challengingly around the table. "I don't think we should wait to hear from Corporal Cameron. I think we should go ahead right now."

"Go ahead with what?" Terry asked.

"With what we came for. With the mystery. We're supposed to gather tomorrow morning and sort the whole thing out, see who has the right answer, but we have hardly talked about it. I think we should start now."

"I'm sorry, Miss Gilford," Alan said, "but I did explain. The mystery weekend is cancelled. It's over. I asked all the staff to be here this morning so that we could answer any questions, or arrange transportation to St. John's, or do anything else we can to make things comfortable for you. I was hoping Corporal Cameron would be here, but I suppose nobody can actually go anywhere until he gives permission. The one thing that is sure is that the mystery weekend you all came for is definitely cancelled."

"Indeed?" said Miss A. "And yet we seem to have an unsolved murder."

"That has nothing to do with us," Alan said, and immediately corrected himself: "Well, it has, of course, but I mean that we shouldn't interfere with Corporal Cameron's investigation. And some people do want to go and look at the iceberg," he added after a moment, realizing that all around he had not made a very compelling argument.

Miss A took the iceberg more seriously than he did, but dismissed it nonetheless. "You've just finished telling us that it grounded itself near the headland just to the east of us, as you predicted it would, and the forecast is for clear skies later this morning. We will all have plenty of time to see the iceberg in ideal conditions. I think we should get on with the mystery."

"How do you think we should go about it?" asked Simon.

Miss A took this as evidence that she had won the point. "Do you know *Clue?* The game? You play it by *suggesting* things — you know, 'I suggest that it was

Colonel Mustard in the library with the revolver' — that sort of thing."

"It isn't a revolver, you know," said Inspector Mullaly.

"Well, we know *that*," Miss A said tartly. "It was a sculpture, or something."

"No, I mean in *Clue*. They call it a revolver, because the English call any pistol a revolver, but in the little pieces they give you with the game it's an automatic."

Miss A seemed about to dismiss this bit of information out of hand, but turned suddenly and intently to Inspector Mullaly. "Why do they always say 'shots rang out'?" she asked.

It took him a moment to collect his wits. "Well, I . . . *Do* they say that? Who says that?"

"Everybody. Novelists, newspaper people, television people. they all say it. 'Shots rang out yesterday on a quiet street in West Vancouver,' things like that. But surely shots don't ring."

"Have you ever heard shots, Miss Gilford?" Inspector Mullaly asked.

Miss A was indignant. "Of course I have! Our father commanded Native troops in India. My sister and I heard shots from the time we were babies!"

"Oh. I see."

"Yes. The field guns went off with a tremendous bang — sharper and clearer when they fired live shells, but I only heard that from a distance. I heard them up close, too, but that was for ceremonial salutes, so there was nothing in the barrel. The noise was fuzzier somehow, but either way you could feel it as much as hear it. The *sepoys'* rifles made a deafening crack, and our father's shotguns more of a booming sound. His big Webley pistol was somewhere in between, and the little .22 calibre pistol he used for teaching us to shoot made a sharp, high-pitched snap, like a whip cracking.

"Bells ring. telephones ring — or at least they used to, until they started bleeping or whatever it is they do — but shots definitely do not!"

"Well," said Inspector Mullaly, "you obviously know a lot more about shots than I do. If you say they don't ring, then I'm sure you're right."

Georges Lapierre had been following the conversation with growing surprise, ignoring his wife's tugs on his sleeve and demands for translation. "Rewolwer?" he said, with some difficulty. "Shots ringing? Why we do not hear this? Now somebody is telling us Mr. Browne is being shot? Not hitting on head?"

"No," said Simon, "they don't mean that. They're talking about something else. I'll explain it later, when we have more time." Jennifer resolved to try not to be in the vicinity when the explanation was attempted. At Jennifer's request, Faith came in quietly from the kitchen and sat on a chair some distance away from the guests, speaking to no one.

"I don't think people should be allowed to say that shots ring if they don't," Miss A said firmly. "Now, do you want to hear what I think we should do?"

"Yes, of course," said Jennifer, feeling that somebody had to.

"I think we should all make suggestions about who did it, and why, and all that. It doesn't have to be our final word — we'll do that tomorrow morning, when we each have to give our reconstruction of the crime. Today, though, we can try out our ideas, and hear what others are thinking."

"Quite a few of us gave opinions on Friday night, Miss Gilford, yourself included," Terry said.

"Yes, I know, but not everyone was there. Anyway, some of us might have changed our minds. Or maybe some of us were not saying what we actually thought, but just trying something out to see what the answer was and perhaps eliminate a suspect. That's what some of us may be doing today, too."

"But this is a serious matter," Inspector Mullaly protested. "You can't treat it like a game!"

"Nonsense!" said Miss A, slipping easily into her role as schoolmistress. "Of course it's a game. It's the game we all came for. If you keep insisting that it is real, Inspector, we shall have to conclude either that you are very naive, or that you are part of the act."

"If we follow Miss Gilford's suggestion," Simon said, "I think we are each going to have to say whether we think Mr. Browne's murder is real or not. It makes quite a difference."

Miss A nodded. "Yes. Quite right. Of course, the murderer — or at least the pretend murderer — is probably right here in this room. I know that my prime suspect is — but of course . . . " she looked around the room rather coyly, " . . . I may not name that person: I may cast suspicion on somebody else to mislead the person I really think did it. Oh, it will be great fun! Anybody who is accused will have to deny it — if they can. And we are going to have to ask the people who belong to the hotel, too — Mr. Davis, Ms. Foster, Ms. Carter and Mr. Byrne. We may not believe what they say, but we have to give them a chance to say it." There were mixed feelings in the room, but Miss A was obviously enjoying herself and no one wanted to upset her.

Dr. MacEwen looked thoughtful. "So everyone will have a chance to say whether they think a real murder has taken place, and — real or not — who they think did it. And probably everybody should also have to tell where they were and what they were doing when it happened?"

"But we don't know when it happened," Terry said.

"Not exactly," Dr. MacEwen replied, "but we do know it was between the time when we all got up from dinner and when I found him in the driveway about an hour later. And we know that for at least part of that time Mr. Browne was arguing with Alan. If everyone says what they were doing in that period, we might be able to pin the time down more clearly. Of course, some people may not be telling the truth . . . " He seemed to look pointedly at Alan.

"Is that agreed, then?" said Miss A. "Let's get on with it," she added, unconsciously echoing what Mr. Browne had said on the first afternoon.

"Perhaps we should hear what Inspector Mullaly has to say," Simon suggested. "He's the professional in all this, after all."

"Well, I don't think it's right for a bunch of amateurs to be trying to assign blame for a murder," Inspector Mullaly said, "but I suppose it can't do any harm. And I suppose it could turn up some evidence that will be helpful to the proper authorities."

Miss A humphed derisively. "That Cameron fellow, I suppose. I don't expect much from *him*. Sniffling and snorting all the time."

"He can't help having the flu," said the Inspector mildly.

"Hitting, not shooting?" Lapierre said.

"Yes!" said Miss A in exasperation. "Hitting! Bashing on head!"

Other people were somewhat taken aback by her tone, but Lapierre was not offended. "Ah," he said, and nodded several times, then began to translate for his wife. Alan had been silenced, and no one else offered any objections to the plan.

"Since it was your idea, Miss A," Dr. MacEwen said, "perhaps you should begin."

"I don't mind a bit. First of all, I think it is all part of the act. And as I said before — I don't think you were here at the time, Mr. Davis — it was a very clever idea to pretend that the mystery was cancelled and then to stage a murder. A clever idea, but I'm afraid the rest of the plot is rather pedestrian.

"The idea that we should come here for a murder mystery and then a real murder should take place is simply too much of a coincidence to be believable. So I think it is an act, and that Mr. Browne was a plant." She saw Georges Lapierre raise his head and quickly added, "*Not* a vegetable from outer space, Mr. Lapierre: an actor who pretended to be a guest. I think the argument between him and Mr. Davis was staged so that my sister would overhear, and I believe that Mr. Davis took the statuette from the front porch, met Mr. Browne in the dark in the driveway and helped him to arrange the fake blood and so on, and left the figure near Mr. Browne's 'body' so that it could be found by anyone coming on the scene.

"If Dr. MacEwen had not happened on the 'body' when he did, Mr. Davis would have had to 'find' it himself, but with everybody wandering around in the fog, they could be reasonably sure that someone would stumble on it. I hope poor Mr. Browne didn't have to lie on that cold driveway for too long before Dr. MacEwen happened along. He was not very likeable before, but that was acting, too, I suppose. It certainly fooled us for a while. But he is probably quite a pleasant person, really. Most actors are, I believe." Terry looked thoughtful as Miss A went on. "Corporal Cameron and the ambulance attendants were also acting, but I have decided that they are local people who were recruited to play the parts . . . " She paused, and then in a different, younger-sounding voice, said: "Of course, the willow trees have a great deal to do with it."

"Oh, dear," said her sister. "Willow trees, Lexa?"

Miss A answered in her normal voice and with some asperity. "What on earth are you talking about trees for,

Katherine? We're trying to solve the mystery. Do try to keep up."

Everyone tried not to look at anyone else. When it was clear that Miss A had no more to say for the moment, Dr. MacEwen said, "There is one thing you have left out, Miss Gilford. Where were you when all this was going on?"

"I was . . . walking about. Katherine was not interested in leaving the verandah, so I went by myself. I did not go along the driveway to the back of the house, but I did go down the front drive and looked back at the house, and I walked in the garden. It was shortly after I came back to the house that you raised the alarm." She looked around archly, well aware that her explanation did not rule her out as the attacker.

Alan knew that some of the guests suspected him of being the guilty party in a fictional mystery, and he knew that Jennifer had, at least for a while, believed he had struck Mr. Browne in real life. All the same, hearing himself accused in this matter-of-fact way was disconcerting, to say the least. He said nothing until Terry addressed him directly. "What do you say to that, Alan?"

Alan shook his head. "I can't say any more than I already have. We had planned on two other actors being here, and they didn't arrive. You know that, Terry. Somebody really did hit Mr. Browne with that sculpture, but it certainly wasn't me. I argued with him, yes, and it turns out that we knew one another about thirty years ago in Toronto, but after we sorted that out I went out to the back of the house. I came in through the back door, and I didn't know anything about what happened until Dr. MacEwen came in."

"So who did it?"

"I haven't the slightest idea."

"We'll put you down as undecided, shall we?" Terry said.

"You also argue with Mr. Browne, Terry," Georges Lapierre said. "You are shouting, 'Go to hell with you old shit-face.' I hear this, and I tell this, but you do not say why you shout. Now you must say."

Terry glanced around. Although some people seemed mildly amused by Lapierre's account, everyone was looking at him expectantly. "Okay," he said. "Why not? Only, before I say anything, I should remind you: I know what the plan was, and I was part of it, and I know what happened to the other actors. So I'm not playing a part. Well, I *am* playing a part, I guess, but . . . I mean, right now I'm telling the truth." He paused for a moment, trying to think of a clearer way to express it, but could not. No one else commented, and he went on. "Okay. I went outside after dinner like everybody else, and I was having a quiet smoke at the end of the verandah when Browne came up and . . . and made . . . I guess you could call it an indecent proposal. I refused. He persisted, and I got angry. I don't think I said -" his lips twitched with a suppressed smile — "I don't think I said quite what Mr. Lapierre says I did, but I did raise my voice a bit."

"You say I tell wrong?" Lapierre said. "You say I make lies?"

Dr. MacEwen broke in before Terry could answer. "Do you actually mean to say that he made a . . . a homosexual advance to you?"

"He did," Terry said gravely.

Dr. MacEwen considered this for a moment, looking very concerned. "I'm sure you are aware," he said finally, "that there have been several cases lately in which men have been acquitted on charges of murder after they have killed other men who made sexual advances to them."

Terry's air of gravity deepened. "Really?" he said.

"Yes. Apparently the men were so disgusted by the implications that they . . . "

"Those were all in the States," Inspector Mullaly cut in, "and they didn't all end up as acquittals. Anyway, it's not as simple as you make it sound. What are you trying to do, give Terry a defence?"

"Thanks all the same," Terry said, "but if that's what you are doing, I really don't need it. I didn't do anything to Mr. Browne, I just told him what I thought of him and walked away."

"I do not believe," Lapierre said. Madame Lapierre spoke in her own language and he added, "Marya does not believe also. First he is telling us nothing, now he is telling us fairy story. We believe murder is part of act, and Terry is doing it. Maybe Alan also."

Terry successfully repressed a laugh, but could not entirely control a grin. "I don't think that is quite the best choice of words, considering the circumstances . . . "

"Again you say my words are not good? You are laugh at my speaking in English?"

"I'm not laughing at your English, Mr. Lapierre. It's just that . . . well, I'm sure Simon will explain when he is explaining about the revolver," He was working hard to maintain a dead-pan delivery. "But I can assure you that I am not telling . . . " he bit his lip " . . . that I am telling the truth."

"So you think it was a real murder," Miss A said. "Who do you think is the murderer?"

"I didn't say that I think the murder was real, I said that I knew what the original plan was, and that I was going to be part of it. At the same time, Miss Gilford, I find your version of events very convincing . . . " Alan drew in his breath, but Terry ignored him: " . . . although I disagree with you on one or two points. After I told Alan that the other two actors would not be arriving

I offered to try to put something together — I even roughed out a script — but he refused. I think he really did intend to cancel everything, but then he had second thoughts, and somehow he managed to make an arrangement with Mr. Browne to fake a murder after all. It seems far-fetched, but I agree with you that the idea of a real murder taking place when a pretend murder is cancelled is even harder to believe. Wasn't it Sherlock Holmes who said that if you eliminate all the other possibilities, the one that is left, no matter how unlikely, must be correct? As far as I can see, this is the only one left."

"That's great, Terry," Alan said grimly. "Thanks a lot. You're a big help."

"So you think Mr. Browne started off as a real guest," Miss A said thoughtfully, "and he was being himself all through dinner. If he *was*, he was not a nice man. Do you really think he would go along with something like this on the spur of the moment?"

"I think he *did*," Terry said. "I think he found everything too tame for him, and he liked the idea of taking a more important role in the drama. A lot of people have a secret desire to act, you know . . . although, when you come to think of it, he didn't get much of a chance to perform, did he?"

"So you think that he and Mr. Davis staged their argument so that my sister could hear?"

"Yes. And he could have gone around after dinner deliberately quarrelling with people so there would be more than one suspect when he was found murdered. Most of us didn't like him to start with. I certainly didn't, and I was really angry with him when he approached me outside, but I've given it a lot of thought — especially after talking to Alan about it yesterday — and this is the conclusion I have come to. I don't think Browne was really homosexual at all. I think it was Alan who put him up to making advances to me, because Alan knows . . . well, I just think it was Alan."

"And it would mean that Corporal Cameron and the ambulance men would have to be actors, too?"

"Well, yes, in a way," Terry said. "I'm not too happy about that part. I've been here off and on while Alan and Jennifer were working on the place, and I've seen Cameron around, and I know he's genuine. But he *was* pretty sick. I suppose he could have been home with the flu, and came up here as a favour . . . and maybe the ambulance guys . . . I don't know. It does sound pretty far-fetched. But nothing else makes any better sense. Anyway, it's pretty much the same scenario as you put forward, Miss Gilford. All I've added is the idea that it was improvised rather than planned."

"Well, it certainly adds a dimension," said Dr. MacEwen. "Did Browne quarrel with anyone else after dinner that night, I wonder?" He looked around the room and Simon and Marion looked at one another.

"Well," Simon said, rather reluctantly, "I wouldn't say we quarrelled, but we did meet him."

"Most of us thought you'd gone home," Dr. MacEwen said. "I didn't know you were still here until you came out to where the body was. So you were around all the time? And you talked to him? When was that? Where were you?"

"We met him on the stairs," Marion said. "Shortly after the dinner broke up. He was going up to his room to get something. His lighter, I think he said."

"I see," said Dr. MacEwen. "And were you going up or coming down at the time?"

"We were going up," Marion said firmly. "We were going to my room." Her tone suggested that no further questions would be welcome, but Simon apparently felt a compulsion to explain.

"We wanted some privacy . . . to . . . to *talk*," he said.

"In private. We went out on the verandah, but there were so many people . . . "

"I imagine Mr. Browne would put a different interpretation on it?"

"He did," said Simon. "He was very rude. I nearly said something."

"He was horrible," Marion said. "I told him to mind his own business, and we went along the gallery on the second floor. He went on to the third."

"So he made you very angry?"

"Yes," said Simon, "I'm afraid he did, poor man. It's sad to think that his last human interactions were hostile ones." This was delivered in a dutiful but rather stilted and self-conscious manner.

"And where were you when he was hit on the head?"

"Oh, for God's sake!" Marion said. "We were in my room, of course. We heard all the commotion when you found him, and we came out, and then Simon felt he had to go to the . . . the scene."

"It doesn't matter what religion he was," Simon said with somewhat exaggerated sanctimony. "A few prayers at a time like that can't go amiss."

"So you think he was really murdered?" Dr. MacEwen asked

The young clergyman's brow furrowed and he looked nervously at Miss A. "I don't, actually," he said finally in his usual voice. "I suppose it's all right to say it now, isn't it, Miss Gilford? I've been trying to react the way I would in real life, if it was a real murder, you see. But I suppose I don't have to any more. Or do I?" He was genuinely puzzled, but, as usual, anxious to do what was expected of him.

"This is ridiculous!" Alan said.

Simon was paying no attention. "It's really quite amazing," he said, "how pretending an emotion can call up the real thing. Is that what actors do, Terry? I was genuinely annoyed at Mr. Browne during dinner and when we met on the stairs, but of course at that time I thought he was just an unpleasant person. As soon as we heard the commotion and learned that he had been hit on the head, though, I realized that he had to be acting. But then I realized that a clergyman would have to go to anyone who had been . . . . I felt quite strong compassion for him when he was lying there in the driveway, all the same, but of course I couldn't really pray for him the way I would for a person who really . . . . Still, I had to pretend, didn't I? It would be expected."

"I can't see how you could feel anything for him at all, except disgust," Marion said. "He was a nasty old man, no matter what way you look at it."

"I really don't think you can say that," Simon objected. "He was just playing a part. He could be a very nice person, really. We'll probably meet him tomorrow, after the mystery is worked out, and as Miss Gilford says, he'll probably turn out to be a perfectly decent sort of fellow."

Jennifer and Alan exchanged a look. It had occurred to them independently that Simon and Marion might very well have really been talking while they were in her room, and probably talking very much the way they were now.

"So you think it was a pretend murder," Dr. MacEwen said. "Who do you think is the pretend murderer?"

"I still find Miss Gilford's scenario — is that the right word? — anyway, I find it very convincing. I think Alan is the pretend murderer." Simon looked at Alan cheerfully, in supreme confidence that he had arranged the whole thing. Alan shook his head in frustration.

"I don't," said Marion. "Too obvious. And I'm not entirely sure it was pretend. Either way, I think it was Terry." Terry looked at her, wounded.

Simon suddenly registered shock and dismay. "If it was a real murder," he said in a horrified tone, "I should have . . . I mean, I didn't . . . Oh, that would be terrible! It wasn't real, was it, Alan?"

"I'm not going to put up with any more of this," Alan said, getting to his feet.

"I think I should go, too," Faith said, also standing. "I knew you were going to have a mystery weekend, but I didn't think it was going to be like this. I don't like it at all."

"Just a moment," Miss A said. "No one can force you to say anything, but at least you should hear what other people have to say." They would have ignored such an appeal from almost anyone else, but out of courtesy to Miss A, they both stopped and stood near the door.

"Now, then," said Miss A, "we haven't heard from the Molloys, and . . . "

"Mullaly," the Inspector said. "And I'm certainly not going to take any part in this. I've told you what I think of it."

"And I'd rather wait," his wife said. "I do have some ideas, but I want to think about it some more first."

The elder Miss Gilford looked around imperiously. "I have nothing to say, either. But as I pointed out yesterday, Dr. MacEwen told us he would have no part in the weekend, and yet he seems to be taking a leading role. Since Mrs. MacEwen is not able to be here, I'm sure we should all like to hear what he can tell us."

Most men would have been daunted by the implications and the frigid tone in which this was delivered, but Dr. MacEwen was unfazed. "I feel it is nothing less than my duty to speak," he said, "especially since my wife, who brought us here, is indisposed. I'm sure she will agree with anything I say." Marion rolled her eyes.

"First, I should say that I have gone back and forth on the matter of whether the mystery is real or invented.

When I found Mr. Browne on Friday evening, I was convinced that it was all real. By the next morning, I had come around to thinking that it had been staged, but Inspector Mullaly made me re-think that position. Now, I am honestly uncertain. I still rather think the murder was real, but what some of you have said has given me reason to doubt." MacEwen was no longer making jokes, but spoke with a certain authority, and the people in the room listened.

"Now," he went on, "putting aside the question of whether or not there was a real murder, we must consider the question of who did it, either in fact or in fiction. And as you have said yourself, Miss Gilford, for the purposes of deciding who did it, whether it was fact or fiction *does not matter*. If a fiction is to be believable, if it is to fool us into accepting it, then it must have the *appearance* of reality. If we can work out the motivations and the actions, we can identify the guilty party, whether in real life or in pretense. What we have heard so far gives us several people who could be strongly suspected."

"Several?" said Miss A. "There are only two, surely? And one of those is not a very strong suspect, in my opinion."

"I stand by my statement, Miss Gilford," MacEwen said, "*several* people. To begin with, you have made the case against Alan very convincingly." Alan snorted. "As for Terry Byrne, I believe that Inspector Mullaly was too quick to dismiss the factor of heterosexual rage. It has been clearly demonstrated in several cases reported in our newspapers that unwanted homosexual advances can trigger a violent reaction in normal men, causing them to strike out blindly, without thought of the consequences. Although Terry has been a model of propriety so far during our stay, it is clear that he is a volatile young man. He could have been so infuriated by Mr. Browne's advances that he snatched up the first weapon that presented itself, raced after him in the dark, and struck him down, hardly aware of what he was doing."

MacEwen paused and looked around the room. In spite of his pedantic style, his words were having an effect. Most people were looking reflectively at Terry, who was staring at Dr. MacEwen in open-mouthed astonishment. "And now, of course," MacEwen went on, "aware of what he has done, he tries to make light of it, to act as though he was only mildly annoyed by Mr. Browne's behaviour." Alan began to say something, but MacEwen was not going to let anyone divert the group's attention.

"I do not say that this is what happened," he said, "but only that it *could have* happened that way. I can see that many of you agree. Now we must consider Simon and Marion." Most eyes turned to the young couple, who looked startled at the sudden attention. "Mr. Browne made clear that he was a journalist — and not just any journalist, but one who could ensure that his writing would appear in a national newspaper. I don't think that any of us was in any doubt that — provided Mr. Browne actually was who he said he was — we would see an account of our weekend in *The World*. And we had no doubt about what that account would be like: it would be cynical and sneering. It would hold us all up to ridicule. Any of us could be vulnerable, but who is more vulnerable to mockery than the clergy? And consider what Mr. Browne could do with a young clergyman and an extremely attractive young woman . . . " Marion tossed her head impatiently " . . . who is studying *sex workers*. Consider what he might make of the fact that he surprised this rather oddly assorted couple going to *her room* after dinner."

"Oh, for God's sake!" Marion exclaimed. "You're as bad as he is — was. Simon, are you going to . . . "

"Really," Simon said, "this really is . . . " he looked suddenly at his watch. "Oh, dear. I'm going to have to leave."

"You're not going anywhere until this . . . this *misogynist* is finished," Marion said grimly.

"I don't think I need to say anything more," Dr. MacEwen said. "I can see that other people present are thinking the same sort of thing as I am." He turned away from Simon and Marion. "Perhaps Mr. Browne even said something to them about his intentions to write about the weekend — but that would not be necessary. Miss Ivany is a forceful young woman, who follows her own path. Mr. Tulk is . . . " — he paused just long enough for his audience to consider what sort of person Simon was. "Perhaps the two of them stood for a moment on the landing, discussing what the consequences would be for them both if Mr. Browne wrote his article. Perhaps they watched from the shadows as Mr. Browne came out of his room with his lighter, and went down the stairs. And perhaps they decided to see that he would never get the chance to write about them. I must say I was surprised when Mr. Tulk suddenly appeared in the driveway and knelt by Mr. Browne . . . but of course he could have been there all along, behind the shrubbery in the dark . . . "

Simon stood up, looking anxiously at his watch. "I really have to go," he said piteously.

"Oh, go on," Marion said. "I hope the steeple falls on your head." Simon left the room, the very picture of dejection.

As a murmur of conversation began, Dr. MacEwen held up his hand. "Again I remind you, I am not saying that these things happened, I am merely saying that they *could* have." Without giving time for anyone to comment, he went on, "I have already mentioned the possibility that Miss A . . . " both Gilford sisters looked at him, Miss K with a thunderous scowl and Miss A with surprise " . . . that Miss A could have done it. She has demonstrated that she could handle the weapon easily . . . "

Miss A turned to her sister, delighted. "Katherine! I'm a suspect! He said he'd mentioned it before! Did you know about this? Why on earth didn't you tell me? Oh, this is very exciting!" She turned back to Dr. MacEwen. "I *am* quite strong, you know, and quick, too. I was outside in the fog . . . "

"That sounds almost like a confession," Dr. MacEwen said.

"Don't be ridiculous. It is nothing of the kind. I just want to be sure everyone has all the facts." She turned back to her sister, wriggling like a girl with excitement. "A suspect!" she exclaimed. Miss K was pleased by her sister's pleasure, but apprehensive. Jennifer knew what she was thinking, and was terrified for a moment that Dr. MacEwen would mention Miss A's affliction as he had done earlier, but he didn't. It was not necessary; everyone in the room was capable of thinking of it for themselves — except Miss A.

"Well," Jennifer said, "this has been most . . . interesting. Perhaps . . . ."

"Excuse me, Ms. Foster," Dr. MacEwen interrupted, "but I haven't quite finished. Yesterday, we were all watching when Constable Cameron came to talk to you and that retarded boy, Ernie."

"Yes," Jennifer said in protest, "but . . . "

MacEwen interrupted her again. "The boy was hanging around outside before dinner, and he could have been there after dinner broke up. Is that what happened, Ms. Foster?"

"He might have come back," Jennifer said reluctantly.

"Yes. I thought I heard his voice in the darkness, but

I couldn't be sure, so I didn't mention it at the time. He had already shown his dislike for Mr. Browne. He knows his way around the house — would know about the sculpture, perhaps has handled it before. If it was standing in the porch, as Mr. Davis believes it was, he would recognize it — and I believe he is quite capable of understanding what he could do with it. I think we cannot discount the possibility that it was Ernie who struck Mr. Browne, whether in reality or in fiction."

Jennifer was near tears. She could see that the others were taking MacEwen's suggestions seriously. "Ernie would never . . . " she began, but Dr. MacEwen interrupted her for a third time.

"But there is at least one other person," he said. "And I must say that I am surprised no one has mentioned him so far." He turned toward Faith, who had started to leave when Alan got up but had remained standing by the door. "This electrician fellow — Steve — who was here last night, he is your husband, Mrs. Carter, I believe?"

"Yes," Faith said in a small voice.

"And he has disappeared?"

"No. Well, yes."

"He returned, I believe, and then went away again?"

"Yes." Faith's voice was even smaller.

"And I understand that he says he cannot remember anything that happened on Friday night?" MacEwen turned away from Faith and addressed his next statement to the others. "As Miss Gilford pointed out, I did say that I would have no part in amateur detecting," he said, "but I cannot help but wonder why no one has suggested that Mr. Carter could have attacked Mr. Browne."

Faith drew in her breath with a gasp, and Jennifer hastened to intervene. "Oh, but that's silly. What possible reason could he have? He didn't know anything about Mr. Browne."

"Perhaps he had no reason for attacking Mr. Browne," MacEwen said. "But has it occurred to you that Browne and your husband are alike in some respects? Browne was bald, and Alan is nearly so. They are about the same height. They both have beards and curly hair on the back of their heads — Browne's was white, and Alan's is blonde going grey, but they are not so different, especially in the dark. And the two men were dressed almost identically."

Alan did not much like being compared to Mr. Browne, and he certainly did not care for being described as nearly bald; he thought of himself more in terms of a receding hairline. However, he could see where MacEwen was leading and he felt he had to say something, even if it was a mystery-story cliché. "You mean . . . " he began, but McEwen raised his voice and carried right on: "I'm suggesting that although Steve might not have a reason for attacking Mr. Browne, he had every reason to want to attack *you*. After all, you had just punched him rather violently in the nose. We must consider that he might well have attacked Browne, thinking he *was* you. No one would mistake one of you for the other in normal circumstances, but last night it was very dark, after all, and foggy. And Mr. Carter was very drunk."

"Steve would never . . . never . . . " Faith could not finish, and pushed blindly through the swinging door to the kitchen. Jennifer followed her out, and the rest sat in silence, considering this new possibility.

"Steve came back only long enough to tell his wife and Alan that he can't remember what happened," Dr. MacEwen persisted. "And then he disappeared again. His fingerprints may be on that sculpture, under mine and Lapierre's — but of course they could have got there when he was working on the renovations. Anyway, I think the police should at least find him and ask him some questions."

Dr. MacEwen apparently had no more to say, and neither had anyone else. The guests dispersed with little conversation to wait for lunch.

* * *

"Oh, Kat," Miss A said as soon as the Gilford sisters were back in their room, "he actually named me as a suspect!" A puzzled look crossed her face. "But he said he had mentioned it before. Did you know about it? Why on earth didn't you tell me?"

"I was afraid it might upset you," her sister said.

"Upset me! I would have been upset if somebody *didn't* suspect me. That's why I picked up that sculpture, you know. It was much heavier than I thought it would be, but I wanted to show that I was capable of holding it. My arm is still sore." She rubbed her bicep reflectively. "But you didn't have much to say today. Haven't had much to say since we got here, in fact. Are you feeling all right, Kat?"

"Yes, of course. I'm fine."

"I'm sorry we didn't plan things better for this meeting today. I'm sure we could have thought of some way to cast suspicion on you, so you could be a suspect, too. In fact, this whole thing has come too late. It should have happened yesterday. But it probably wouldn't have happened at all if I hadn't started things off. What on earth would they have done if I hadn't?

"It's going to have to be all sorted out tomorrow morning. I know what, though! We can make you my accomplice! Let them think that you knew I did it all along, but didn't say anything because you wanted to protect me."

This was very close to what Miss K, in her darker moments, feared to be true. "Thank you, Lexa," she said, "but I'm sure one suspect in the family is enough. Did you learn anything from your game of Clue? Do you still think Mr. Davis is the culprit?"

"I'm not so sure any more. It seemed logical, but when I heard that young waiter fellow, Terry, casting suspicion on him . . . ."

"Why should that change your mind?"

"Well, they are both part of the staff, so they must know what is supposed to happen. If Terry is putting suspicion on Mr. Davis, it must be because they want us to think he did it, so I think it must be somebody else."

"But who could it be?"

"That's the problem, isn't it? Maybe Dr. MacEwen is right and it was that electrician fellow — Faith's husband. But that would be a bit of a disappointment, don't you think? The murderer shouldn't just *appear* like that, *deus ex machina*, or whatever it is. It should be somebody in the hotel, somebody we see all the time."

She seemed not to even consider the possibility that the attack on Mr. Browne might have been real, but her sister was much less certain.

* * *

Rose Mullaly stopped off in the library to look for another book. When she arrived at their room her husband was in the act of pouring a drink from a flask of rum he had brought with him. "It's early for that," she said.

"Not all that early. We should be eating in a half hour or so, and I gather Faith is giving us a proper boiled dinner." He held up the bottle. " Want one?"

"Well, if she's really making a boiled dinner, maybe I will. But just a small one."

"My God," Inspector Mullaly said, after he had sat down with his drink, "that MacEwen is some talker, isn't he? Up to now, he's just been clowning around, but that was serious."

"Quite a list of suspects. What did you think?"

"For somebody who said he thought mysteries are silly — at least according to his wife — he certainly seems to know how they work."

"How do you mean?"

"Well, he's figured out a fancy motive for just about everybody. Miss A did it because she's got Alzheimer's or something; Terry did it because he was disgusted at being propositioned; Simon and Marion did it because they were afraid Browne would write about them . . . "

"And poor old Steve did it because he was too drunk to tell Browne from Alan. That was a good one."

"They're all the kind of thing you'd find in a murder mystery, but I've got to admit that they're all possible, too. Except the one about Terry."

"What's wrong with that one?"

"I'd say that young fellow is homosexual. If Browne really propositioned him, he did it because he knew it, too."

"What makes you think Terry is? . . . "

"I can't tell you, exactly, but I'd put money on it. That kind of thing used to be illegal when I was a young copper, remember."

"Browne didn't seem to be that way. You'd sort of expect him to hate . . . people like that."

"Yes, but he was from a different age. Like us. It was illegal when he was young, too; a lot of guys his age learned protective camouflage. Anyway, I could be wrong and MacEwen could be right. Some of his scenarios are more likely than others, but any one of them could be real."

"So you still think it was a real murder?"

"I don't *think* it, I bloody well know it. I just hope Cameron is on top of it somehow."

"He doesn't seem to have done much yet. We've hardly seen him. What kind of a way is that to run a murder investigation? In the old days, when you got involved in something, it was your family that didn't see you, not the suspects."

"The poor young fella is sick, remember. And it's a long weekend. He must be running himself half to death. Just imagine if there was a big accident on the Trans-Canada and the Mounties didn't get there!"

His wife looked at him appraisingly. "You aren't in touch with him, are you, by any chance?"

"Me? In touch with Cameron? No way. Oh, I'd help him out if he asked me, but he's not going to ask. I told you, the Mounties wouldn't ask us for help if their lives depended on it. And the last thing I want is for him to think I'm interfering. No, I'm not in touch with him."

"So who dunnit?"

"Damned if I know. I hope Cameron does."

Rose Mullaly looked at her watch. "All that talk seemed to take up a lot of the morning. There won't be much time to look at icebergs before dinner."

"The only ice I want to look at is in a glass. But there'll be plenty of time after dinner for anybody who wants to go chasing that one. It's cleared off nicely, too. We never used to get sunshine on the twenty-fourth weekend, did we? I seem to remember a lot of snow. Is this what they call global warming, do you think?"

VIII

SUNDAY AFTERNOON AND SUNDAY EVENING

RS. MULLALY'S ASSESSMENT WAS CORRECT; THERE WAS only time for some of the guests to go up on the widow's walk, where they could see the iceberg looking astonishingly large and sitting stationary less than a kilometre away, grounded near the headland that protected the hamlet of Cranmer's Cove from northerly winds. In the morning sun its stark white was streaked with soft greens and blues, deepening in the shadows near the waterline, where the beginnings of the huge underwater mass could be seen as a pale blue-green fading into the deeper blue of the surrounding water. Guests took a few photographs even though they knew it was too far away, and planned to get as close as they could to the spectacle after they had eaten.

In traditional Newfoundland speech and practice, *dinner* came in the middle of the day, and was a full cooked meal; *supper,* referred to in some areas as *tea,* came around five o'clock and often consisted of leftovers from dinner; and a *lunch* was a snack that could come at any time of day or night, but most usually at bedtime, as part of a *mug-up*. Faith was intensely conservative about some things, but because she loved cooking she had accommodated easily to the modern mainland and middle-class townie way of having an elaborate dinner at a scandalously late hour in the evening, and she managed with difficulty to accommodate to having a light meal in the middle of the day, and calling it lunch, but her accommodations would stretch only so far, and Sundays were different.

From the very beginning Faith had planned for Sundays in the hotel to be marked with a solid, traditional boiled dinner at one o'clock, consisting at a minimum of salt beef, potatoes, turnip, cabbage and pease pudding, followed by a good, stodgy dessert like Blueberry Grunt, followed by a period of convalescence, sitting drowsily around and snoozing in upholstered chairs. She was convinced that guests from other places, once having experienced this sequence, would never again arrange their Sundays any other way. It was in anticipation of this sort of dinner that Inspector and Mrs. Mullaly, familiar with the ritual, were fortifying themselves with rum in their room.

A proper boiled dinner takes some time to prepare, so Faith and her daughters had set everything in motion well before Dr. MacEwen made his accusation about Steve. This was fortunate, because Faith would have been in no state to carry out the preparations, or even to supervise. It took the combined powers of both her daughters and Jennifer to persuade her not to head immediately "into the country" to look for him, and she surrendered only to the argument that if he had really gone back to their cabin, her sudden appearance would be likely to frighten him into retreating even farther into the woods. She finally agreed to ask one of his brothers, a solid and reliable man who was never known to take a drink, to go and look for him, but no one was very hopeful. To everyone's surprise, Alan was able to get through directly from Hancocks' to Constable Cameron's cell phone, and the Mountie agreed to send out a bulletin on Steve's old truck, but more in the interest of getting it off the road than because he wanted to interview Steve. The daughters, even the vegetarian, could make a boiled dinner as well as their mother; they finished and served the noon meal speedily and competently while Faith lamented and wiped her eyes.

The meal, unusual to most of the guests, provided the basis for most of the lunch-time — or dinner-time — conversation, with Inspector and Mrs. Mullaly taking on the role of local informants on exotic Newfoundland customs. Anna MacEwen made an appearance, shaky and pale, and picked at her food while her husband explained that he felt it was time she began to come around. After the meal, he said, they were going to take a walk along the cliffs to see the iceberg. His wife looked at him with surprise and reproach, but said nothing.

Simon returned, still in his clerical clothing complete with collar and sober black dicky, and sat at the table with the others, but without Marion. She was in the kitchen, sharing a vegetarian meal with one of Faith's daughters while the other one ate salt beef and teased them amiably. Jennifer was impressed and envious at how easily and freely the girls talked and laughed with Marion — she could hear their young voices through the door to the kitchen. And it was not only youth that they had in common, but a sense of belonging that seemed to be able to transcend barriers of age, class and religion; they got along very well with Rose Mullaly, too. Jennifer felt hurt and excluded, but knew that anything she might do would only make matters worse.

Miss A made several conversational forays that signalled her feeling that they should "do something" about the mystery, but having gone through her game of *Clue* in the morning, and listened to Dr. MacEwen's lecture, no one seemed able to think of anything more they could do.

After lunch — or dinner — the MacEwens set off to look at the iceberg, but others declined their invitation to go along: no one wanted to try to make conversation with Anna. Inspector Mullaly retired to his room to read. Faith's eldest daughter had a brand-new driver's licence, and she and her sister borrowed their mother's car to take Marion and Rose Mullaly on a sightseeing tour. Miss A set off to walk to Cranmer's Cove again, planning to walk along the road to the community, then take the path over the headland to see the iceberg. Faith went down the hill to use the telephone to alert her network about Miss A's route, and Miss K, who did not feel up to walking on the cliffs, retired to the library where she fell asleep in a leather armchair. The Lapierres went to the billiard room to practise their instruments while Chantal napped, and intended to take her out to show her the iceberg when she awoke. Alan disappeared and Jennifer went to their apartment. Simon, after exchanging a few polite but distant words with Marion, drove back to the rectory.

Dinner had ended around two. It was shortly after four when the MacEwens staggered up the front stairs, Anna paler and more agitated than ever, supporting her husband, who walked as though he was not in full control of his legs, a dazed expression on his face. The short version of the story was quickly told: he had been attacked as they walked on the cliffs and struck on the back of the head, where some bruising, a bump and a small cut could be seen through his short-cropped sandy hair.

Since Ches and Walt, on Corporal Cameron's request, had relocated their ambulance to be nearer the highway, no medical assistance was available locally. Jennifer took the MacEwens off in her car to a community twenty kilometres to the southwest, where there was a nursing station and clinic, Alan went to the neighbours' to put in another call to Corporal Cameron, and as guests and staff turned up during the afternoon they were made aware of the situation.

Most received the news with shock and dismay, but some took it differently. One of these was Georges Lapierre, who met a kindred spirit as she came into the hall from her walk. "Ah! Kind lady! Mrs. A!" Lapierre exclaimed. "You are hearing news?"

"News? What news?"

"Again willain is attacking! Is hitting on head Dr. MacEwen!"

"What? Really? Where? When?" Miss A looked around for a more reliable informant, but no one was at hand. "And who is this 'Willan' person?"

"Dr. MacEwen and Mrs. is walking on cliff. Somebody is hitting on head. Is good, I think. And nobody is know who is willain."

Although she herself was delighted, a sense of propriety led Miss A to say, "Good? You can't say it is good for a man to be hit on the head." It dawned on her slowly that Lapierre was saying that the attack was the work of a 'villain', and with that realization came another question: "Is he dead?"

"No. Is not dead. Hurt on head, but not yet dead. Going to doctor with Jennifer. Is bad for somebody being hit, yes, but is good for mystery, I think. Now is *two* mysteries."

Miss A left Lapierre as soon as she decently could and went to find her sister. Miss K was extremely agitated, but Miss A hardly noticed. "This is marvelous, Kat," she said. "I was walking on the trail near the village, so I wasn't actually anywhere near where Dr. MacEwen was attacked, but they don't need to know that. I can be vague about it, and I can still be a suspect!"

Miss K was much less enthusiastic. "Lexa," she said, "It's time you stopped this silliness. This is very serious.

You must not do anything to attract suspicion to your-self."

"Oh, dear," Miss A said. "That's your 'I'm-the-older-sister-and-you-must-do-as-I-say' voice. I haven't heard that for years. I really don't know what's worrying you, Kat."

Her sister sighed. "And I don't think *you* realize how serious this is. Think of all the things Mr. Browne and Inspector Molloy said about how people are wrongfully convicted. And, just for a moment, imagine if these attacks were real!"

"Oh, well, I don't for a moment think they are real. But it doesn't matter anyway. When the *dénouement* comes I can refute any suspicion. I have plenty of witnesses that I was nowhere near the place where it happened."

Miss K was surprised. "Have you?"

"Yes. It was the strangest thing. As soon as I started up the trail beyond the village, a group of children joined me. They seemed to be following me at first, but then they caught up and the smallest one, a little girl, took my hand. So we walked along and she chattered away. I couldn't understand most of what she said — they have a very strong accent — but it didn't seem to matter. We went and looked at the iceberg, and she told me all about it — or I suppose she did: I couldn't understand what she was saying. I just kept saying 'Isn't that nice,' and things like that.

"At one point one of the older boys seemed to want to go off somewhere else, but it seems as though the rest of them had to take care of the little girl who was walking with me. One of them said one of the few things I did understand. He said that their mothers — they say 'mudders' — he said, 'Our mudders will skin us alive if we lets 'er out of our sight,' so they stayed with the little girl, and she stayed with me until we came back to where there were some houses, and they all ran off."

"And they were with you the whole time you were on the trail?"

"Yes, of course."

"That's wonderful, Lexa." Miss K gave a silent prayer of thanks for Faith and her network of 'mudders' in Cranmer's Cove.

Corporal Cameron looked and sounded only marginally better than he had the last time he visited Cranmer House. He came with a sheaf of forms around five o'clock and again labouriously took statements from everyone. It did not take quite as long as the last time, but nonetheless the questioning lasted well beyond supper-time, so that the inmates of Cranmer House ate in shifts, some people going from the interview to the evening meal or the meal to the interview.

In marked contrast to the Friday night most of the guests had lost their enthusiasm for the idea of an old-fashioned mystery, but nevertheless natural curiosity led everyone to find out what they could about the most recent attack. Those who believed the murder of Browne to have been real — by now practically everyone — were sombre and concerned; only Miss A and Georges Lapierre treated the assault on Dr. MacEwen as an opportunity for more amateur detective work. The MacEwens themselves, as befitted victims, were serious and reserved.

The nurse-practitioner had put a plaster on the back of Dr. MacEwen's head and given her opinion that he had not suffered a concussion, but to be on the safe side suggested that he not sleep for a few hours. Dr. MacEwen seemed to resent the suggestion that his injury was not very serious. What could be seen of the wounds to his head were a lump, a small cut and an area of bruising, which might have indicated two or more blows. When Dr. MacEwen insisted that he had been hit only once, the nurse suggested that he might have been struck with an irregularly-shaped object.

His own and Anna's account of the event was reticent at first: Dr. MacEwen had left the path and gone into a densely wooded area, and had been out of his wife's sight when the attack occurred. It became clear without ever being put directly into words that he had left the path to urinate. Anna MacEwen had heard rustling and thrashing about in the bushes, and then heard her husband cry out. She went in after him and found that he had fallen forward, and she had heard someone, or some*thing*, moving away through the trees as she bent to help him. They both said that she was very lucky not to have been attacked herself, and that they were both lucky to be alive. She heard voices around the time of the attack although she saw no one, and thought that perhaps the attacker had been frightened away by other hikers on some other branch of the path.

Then there was the vexing question of motive. Could both attacks be the random actions of some mad person who might strike at anyone he or she found in a vulnerable position? Dr. MacEwen himself leaned to the theory that in his review of suspects in the assault on Sidney Browne, he had identified the actual killer, who now hoped to silence him. He looked narrowly around the room, as though he believed that his assailant was present.

The others looked nervously at one another. As their stories emerged, it appeared that hardly anyone could be ruled out as a possible perpetrator. In spite of Miss K's warnings, Miss A spoke vaguely of walking on the cliff path and did not mention her entourage of children, so that it was thought quite possible that she had been nearby when the attack took place. Her sister began to wonder to herself whether the children had really been there at all, or if Miss A's deteriorating mind could be shielding her from the knowledge that she had carried out the crimes herself.

Simon, who had to excuse himself for an hour or two during the interviews to 'do' Evensong for the handful of parishioners who did not want to watch the hockey game, admitted that he had gone for a long, solitary walk in the afternoon, and could not name anyone who could testify as to his whereabouts at the crucial time. Inspector Mullaly was alone in his room. He had been sleeping, although he would not say so and insisted instead that he was reading. Miss K was asleep in the library, but also said that she was reading. Terry freely admitted that he had been asleep for most of the afternoon but, like the others, had no one who could confirm his statement.

The whereabouts of the Lapierres was obvious to everyone who was awake for the first hour or so after dinner, but then they, too, had walked along the trail, little Chantal ensuring that their progress was slow and with many stops. At first there was some question as to why they had not crossed paths with the MacEwens, but soon everyone agreed that the cliff path was in fact several trails that branched and intertwined, in some places passing through tall brush and stunted woods. Jennifer and Alan explained that it was used not only for sightseeing but also for berry-picking, which accounted for its many branches. The MacEwens and the Lapierres and any number of other people could have passed one another easily without knowing it.

Alan had the most difficulty explaining where he had been. Among other things, he had taken the remaining bronze figurine to his workshop in what had once been the stables behind the house to lock it in a cupboard where he kept his most valuable tools. What he did not wish to admit was that there was half a packet of cigarettes in a workshop drawer, left over from before he had stopped smoking, and he had stayed in the shop all afternoon, smoking and reading a book on wood finishing.

The fact that he had taken the figurine out of the house was suspicious, but the idea that he could have carried it all the way up on the cliff trail in order to hit Dr. MacEwen with it was too bizarre to be taken seriously. The Lapierres watched him sternly, still suspecting that he was attempting to introduce elements of science fiction. For them, the crimes that had occurred were satisfyingly mysterious, and if anyone attempted to say that extraterrestrial beings were involved, they would be severely disappointed. At the same time, the nagging possibility that the crimes were real made them especially cautious about the baby.

Faith's two daughters had taken Rose Mullaly and Marion Ivany for a tour of the area. When they were two kilometres or so west of Cranmer House, the girls had pointed out a trail that led to the cliff path, and from there back to the hotel, and beyond to the community. Marion, who had worn her running shoes, had decided to run back along the trail 'to give herself some time to think'. Rose Mullaly felt it was very likely that within the next few days both of the younger girls would take to running on the cliff path and thinking deep thoughts while doing so. Although they behaved with what they believed to be sophisticated offhandedness, they paid close attention to everything Marion said or did. The effect of Marion's run, of course, was to place her on the path at about the time when Dr. MacEwen was struck.

In the aftermath of the questioning by Corporal Cameron people struggled with questions of their own. Conversation, instead of being general, tended to be between individuals. Jennifer found Inspector Mullaly in a corner of the library and approached him tentatively.

"Could I ask you a question?"

"Of course. I hope I can answer."

It was obvious that she had prepared for the occasion. "In your experience, is it possible for people to do things and not know they've done them?"

Mullaly was surprised, but tried not to show it. He suppressed his immediate impulse to make a joke, and treated the question seriously. "I suppose it's *possible*," he said slowly, "but I don't think it happens very often. Can you tell me what you're thinking about?"

Jennifer tried to formulate an anonymous way of telling him what was on her mind, but failed. "It's Alan," she said after a moment. "He's told me he didn't hit Mr. Browne, and I believe him, but do you think he could have done it without knowing? Everyone seems to think he did it. Could he have hit Dr. MacEwen, too, and not know? He's told me some very disturbing things about his earlier life, and I . . . I . . . "

"Now, try not to upset yourself, Ms. Foster," Inspector Mullaly said, having no idea how to cope with the situation. Her faith that Alan would not lie to her, even if he might try to murder people, seemed curious, to say the least. "I'm sure Alan knows as much about what he is doing as the rest of us." It occurred to him that some people would not take this to be entirely reassuring, and he added: "If he says he didn't do those things, then I'm sure he didn't."

In fact, Inspector Mullaly thought it entirely possible that Alan *had* done it, and knew quite well what he was doing, but he could hardly say so to Jennifer.

"Thank you," she said, and walked away, still looking doubtful and troubled.

Inspector Mullaly prepared to leave the library, but he was not to get away that easily. "Inspector Molloy,"

Miss K said, coming through the library door as Jennifer left, and looking around to make sure that no one else was there, "I would like to ask you a question, if I may."

"Mullaly," he said. "I'll be happy to answer if I can."

"Do people ever do things . . . perhaps terrible things, without knowing they have done them?"

This seemed to be becoming a popular idea. "You're thinking of your sister, I suppose, Miss Gilford?"

The question came bluntly to a point she had planned to reach only after some preliminary discussion, and she had to steel herself to answer. "Yes," she said, finally.

"Have you any real reason to think she hit Browne, or Dr. MacEwen, or both of them? Anything beyond what MacEwen said yesterday?"

"Well . . . she did show that she could lift that sculpture thing, and she was out somewhere this afternoon, when Dr. MacEwen . . . "

"Those are reasons why it might be possible, but do you have any evidence that she did anything, or any real reason to think she did?"

Miss K gave the question serious thought, and answered slowly. "No, I suppose not."

"Miss Gilford, I think you're letting your fears about your sister's mental condition lead you think things that you really have no reason to be afraid of. Didn't Jennifer say that between her and Faith they'd see that the people in Cranmer's Cove would keep an eye on your sister when she went down there?"

"Yes, they did say that. And Alexandra did tell me a tale about being followed by a group of children, but when I saw the way people were looking at her this afternoon, I was afraid . . . And she has been acting so strangely at times . . . "

Inspector Mullaly did not think it was very likely that Miss A had struck Sidney Browne, and he was very much reassured by the mention of the children in Cranmer's Cove. He put his hand gently on the old woman's arm. "Miss Gilford," he said, "your sister's . . . trouble . . . will probably cause you a lot of anxiety in the next little while, and I'm sure we will all be thinking about you — maybe some of us will even remember you in our prayers — but I really don't think you need to worry any more about this affair. Corporal Cameron said he would come back tomorrow morning, and I'm sure he'll sort it all out."

"But who could have done these terrible things?"

"I honestly don't know, but I think you can rest assured that it wasn't your sister."

It was pleasant to hear, but Miss K was not at all sure that Inspector Mullaly knew what he was talking about. And she found the idea of being mentioned in Roman Catholic prayers rather unsettling.

*　*　*

Simon went to Marion's room and knocked diffidently on the door. She opened it warily. Dusk was gathering outside, and the room was lit only by a goose-necked lamp on a desk where she had been reading and making notes. She waited for Simon to speak first.

"Um . . . this afternoon," he said. "You said you . . . ah . . . went for a run 'to think'. What . . . um . . . did you . . ."

"You went for a walk this afternoon by yourself. Were you thinking?"

"Ah . . . well, yes, I was, in fact."

"So we were both thinking."

"Yes. I . . . um . . . wonder if we were thinking about . . . um . . . about the same thing? Maybe we should talk about it."

She opened the door a little wider, but Simon didn't move. "You don't want to come in to talk?"

"Well . . . ah . . . in the circumstances, what with one thing and another, no, probably not."

"Should we go for a walk?"

"That doesn't seem like such a good idea . . . does it?"

Marion sighed. "Let's go and see if there's anybody in the library. Or there's that sitting room on the second floor that nobody uses. Just wait 'til I put my shoes on."

*   *   *

When Miss A returned to their room, Miss K was waiting. "Well," she said, "you certainly didn't do anything to decrease suspicion, Lexa. If anything, you made yourself more suspect."

"Oh, I hope so, Kat. That's what I was trying to do." She noticed her sister's expression. "For heaven's sake, you're not still worried, are you? I told you that I have a perfect alibi if I need it."

"You're sure about the children, are you?"

"Of course I am. Don't be silly. Do you really think I could imagine something like that? You must think I'm losing my m . . . my . . . What is it they say?"

"Losing your mind?" said Miss K in deep distress.

"No, not that. Oh, I know, it's 'marbles'." She put on a hard, American-sounding voice. "You must think I'm losin' my marbles, sister!" and she laughed happily at the thought.

"Don't be ridiculous, Lexa. Anyway, it's not me we have to worry about. It's what other people might say. The police could do the sort of thing Mr. Browne was talking about, you know: put you in jail with one of those . . . those sex people Miss Ivany mentioned, and pay her to say you told her you had made it all up! They do that sort of thing, you know."

"But the children . . . "

"They wouldn't ask the children. They don't, when they are trying to convict someone."

"But we could have our lawyers do it! We could wait until they have their witness in the box, and our lawyer could say, 'Your Honour' . . . "

" 'My Lord'," said Miss K.

"Are you taking to using profanity, Kat?"

"Certainly not. But I don't think they say 'Your Honour.' I think they say, 'My Lord'. Actually, it's more like 'M'lud,' I think."

"Do they?" Miss A said doubtfully. "Well, then, our lawyer could say, 'M'Lud' — are you sure they say that, Kat? It sounds a bit silly. I think they say that in England, and they say 'Your Honour' in the United States. What do we say in Canada?

"Oh, I know, we say 'Your Worship'. That's it. So our lawyers could say, 'Your Worship, I have a dozen witnesses who can prove that the accused, Miss Gilford . . . ' — that sort of thing. It would be very exciting. You know, Kat, this is turning out to be rather fun, but I'm afraid it is too late."

"Too late? What is too late?"

"Everything. Having Mr. Browne killed on the first night was a good idea, but then things should have happened quickly. Clues and things. But now Dr. MacEwen has been attacked, and it's Sunday night, and it all has to be sorted out tomorrow morning. I had rather hoped that we would be able to do the sorting. I had imagined us in the library, telling everyone what happened and accusing the guilty party, like Miss Marple, but I can't see it happening now. We don't have enough time or enough clues. Do you think we should sneak out tonight, after everyone has gone to bed, and look for clues?"

"I certainly do not! I think we should go to bed sensibly, and hope that everything *is* all sorted out tomorrow. This has been a pleasant place to stay for a few days, but I am looking forward to going home."

"I don't think anyone has enough time," Miss A said wistfully. "Ever. I don't suppose I'll ever be charged with anything." She sighed. "I wonder what they *do*, actually?"

"Who?"

"Those sex people you were mentioning."

"Oh, Lexa, for Heaven's sake!"

* * *

When Alan and Jennifer were alone, he plugged in the electric kettle for tea and put two slices of bread in the toaster. "I don't know what to make of this at all," he said. "I'm beginning to think it has to be Steve, crazy as that sounds. Have you been in touch with Ernie? Everybody and his dog was up on the cliff path around the time MacEwen got hit. I wouldn't be surprised if Ernie was there, too."

"He was. I went down to Hiscocks' and called his aunt. It was one of the first things I did. Have you been smoking?"

"How did you know?"

"I can smell it on your clothes. I smelled it earlier, when we were talking to Corporal Cameron. Are you going to start again?"

"No, I don't think so. It made me feel sick, and I've got a headache."

"You'd better hang your clothes outside."

"Yeah," Alan said. "I can smell it, too. I guess we all used to smell like this, but we didn't know it."

Jennifer had given up smoking several years earlier than Alan, and had little patience with this suggestion. "Were you really in the workshop all afternoon?"

"Of course I was! Good God, you don't think . . . "

"No. No, but . . . Some of the others still think you did it, you know. They think you hit Mr. Browne on Friday night, and Dr. MacEwen today. Some of them think it was all part of the act, but one way or another they think you did it."

"How the hell can they still think it's an act? If you take us out, and Faith and Terry, and if Browne was an actor, and now the MacEwens, it doesn't leave more than about six people for the paying audience. That doesn't make any sense."

"I don't think Miss A and the Lapierres are thinking in terms of economics," Jennifer said, but Alan was not listening. He stopped what he was doing and furrowed his brow.

"Hey, wait a minute! You know, it could have been Terry!"

"Oh, that's silly. He really wanted this thing to work for us. He thinks the world of you, you know."

"Does he?" Alan was genuinely surprised. "But anyway, the fact that he wanted it to work is the whole point. You know, I don't think he always makes much of a distinction between reality and acting. He could have done it while he was in his character, thinking he was helping us out, and maybe his real self doesn't know anything about it. I wonder if I should ask Inspector Mullaly about it?"

"I don't think so, really. And I don't think anybody else is going to come up with that idea. It's everybody thinking it was *you* that worries me. Think of what Mr. Browne and the inspector were saying about how people get convicted. And Browne was right, no matter what Inspector Mullaly says: the police are forever putting people in jail and then paying somebody else who's in there to say they confessed."

"Cameron wouldn't do something like that. He said he'd be back here tomorrow morning. I hope to God he's got something to tell us. Do you think we should go on trying to run a hotel after all this is over, or should we sell those African statues and the hotel, and go for a cruise?"

*   *   *

Rose did not arrive in the Mullalys' room until some time after her husband had gone there. She found him lying on the bed, reading a Dorothy Sayers mystery. "Have you been holed up in here all evening?" she said.

"I'm afraid to go out. People keep asking me crazy questions. Most of them seem to think whoever is bashing people on the head is doing it without knowing it."

"That sounds promising."

"I might have known you'd say that. You don't think *I* did it, do you?"

"No, probably not. But only because I've been keeping an eye on you."

"Where've you been all this time?"

"I went down to Faith's place with her and her daughters for a while. They've got a really nice house. It's too bad Steve is the way he is. They say he's the nicest kind of a fella when he's sober, and he never hurts anybody or does any damage even when he's drinking. He usually just gets himself into trouble."

"He could have got himself into plenty this time. Have they heard from him at all?"

"No. Faith thinks he's still up in the country, but his brother couldn't find him around their cabin, so he's gone off to look in other places. And the Mounties are looking for the truck."

"But he could have been sneaking around on the cliff path when MacEwen was hit?"

"I suppose so. But so could you."

"I was reading."

"So you say, but I don't think you're telling the truth."

"What do you mean by that?"

"I think you were asleep."

"Patrick O'Brian says that nobody ever admits to being either rich or asleep. I guess you know I'm not rich, but I might have been asleep. About the only ones with an alibi are you and Faith's daughters. Come to think of it, though, you're giving each other an alibi. Maybe the three of you did it together. You figured it out, and the kids bashed him while he was peeing. It seems a bit unfair to hit a man when he's standing there with his . . . "

"You don't have to spell it out. Anyway, I think we're going to have to do better than that."

"I suppose you're right. Have you got any ideas?"

"Some. But I need to think some more about it."

Inspector Mullaly yawned. "Bed time," he said.

IX

MONDAY MORNING

*O*N MONDAY MORNING THE GUESTS TURNED OUT FOR breakfast between eight-thirty and nine, but there was little animation. Simon joined them as usual, and without spoken agreement they took their coffee into the library and sat down, waiting for something to happen. Miss A plopped down in a stuffed leather chair with an exasperated sigh.

"Well," she said, "the food has been good, and the evening of the murder was quite dramatic. And Cranmer House is a wonderful place for a mystery, but I am afraid I would have to say that over all the weekend has been a disappointment. There should have been clues and things all along, and this morning we should be able to have a proper *dénoument* here in the library, like a proper old-fashioned mystery, with at least one of us telling who did it, and how and why. As it is, we don't know any more now than we did at the first. All we have is speculations — unless somebody else has information that I don't have."

"I'm sorry, Miss A," Alan said, "that you persist in acting as though this is still a mystery weekend. It was intended to be exactly the way you describe, but I have to repeat, we had to cancel our plans. And, unlikely as it seems, somebody did hit Mr. Browne on Friday night."

"So you keep saying," Miss A snapped, "but you have

not added anything. It appears to me that the whole thing has all been a waste of time,"

"I'm sorry if you feel that way, but at least it won't have been a waste of money. I said there would be no charge for the weekend, and I meant it."

"I am not complaining about the money, and we have no intention of accepting your offer," said Miss A haughtily, "but I would be less than honest if I did not say that I am disappointed in the weekend. I suppose now we all have to wait for that wretched, sniffling Mounted Policeman."

"He did say he'd be here this morning," Alan said. "And he knows people have reservations to keep and schedules to meet."

"And I suppose he will tell us who did the murder?"

"If it *was* a murder," Rose Mullaly said.

Several of the guests raised their heads or turned toward her, but Miss A was first to reply. "Hmph. I suppose you mean he will tell us that it was all pretend — all part of the act. We already know that. At least I do."

"No. I don't mean that, exactly."

"Well, what on earth do you mean?"

"It's hard to explain . . . " Mrs. Mullaly spoke slowly and hesitantly, not sure she was ready but aware that she would not get another chance. "The trouble with old-fashioned mysteries — and most of the new ones, too — is that everything *fits*. The clues are all there, and if you put them together the right way, you get the answer.

" But most things aren't like that. With a real mystery, you've got a few facts — a few things that you know — and you have to reconstruct a whole series of events from those facts. It's like all the speculation about the Kennedy assassination. You can't . . . "

Inspector Mullaly interrupted. "She means the John F. Kennedy assassination. You should probably know that my wife is an expert on the subject. She's the only person I've ever heard of who has read the whole of the *Warren Report* from cover to cover."

"But *Warren Report* is many wolumes," Georges Lapierre protested. "Is filling many shelf in Washington. Is not possible to read all. I see this in Russian magazine."

"Well, all right, maybe not the whole report," Inspector Mullaly conceded, "but she read the published version, and a damn great thick book it was, too. The kids were young then, and Rose had a broken ankle that had to be kept in traction, so . . . "

"Yes," his wife said, "I couldn't move around for weeks. We had a baby at the time, and my mother came in to look after him and the other youngsters. I asked Gerry to bring me home something to read, and I hoped he'd come back with a nice mystery or two, but he brought me the *Warren Report*. It had just come out. I was a bit disappointed at first. I think he just picked the thickest book he could find, hoping it would keep me quiet."

"It worked, too." The inspector grinned. "She started reading it and couldn't stop. She didn't believe any of it, of course. Then she read everything else that came out about the assassination. I think she knows more about it than anybody outside the FBI."

"Ha!" she said. "Most of *them* don't know anything at all. And the ones that do know won't talk."

"See what I mean? You don't want to get her started on that, I can tell you."

Georges Lapierre had been translating as usual for his wife, and both were registering greater and greater puzzlement. "How Mr. Browne is connecting to assassination President Kennedy, please?" he asked, finally.

"I'm sorry," Mrs. Mullaly said. "We got side-tracked there. I didn't mean to make a connection. What I was trying to say is, a murder mystery is like a small version of a big conspiracy like the Kennedy thing. People have got a set of events to deal with — some are a bit vague, and there may be more than one version of some of them, but some things are pretty definite: Kennedy was shot as the limousine came down the road in Dealey Plaza — we've got pictures of that — and Lee Harvey Oswald was shot in front of dozens of witnesses in the police station — there's pictures of that, too — and so on.

"That's what we've got to work with. So we take all the events and try to fit them into a logical pattern. And that's the way most mysteries work: we figure out the motives and who did what, and when they did it, and all that kind of thing. But what I think Gerry has been trying to tell us is that real-life mysteries don't work like that. People are late turning up for appointments or they get caught in traffic, or they take the wrong turn . . . We have to improvise. People are always having to decide what to do on the spur of the moment, because things happen that they didn't expect. And some of the facts we have when we are trying to figure out a real-life mystery may not fit at all."

"I'm amazed!" Inspector Mullaly said. "All this time I thought you never paid any attention to anything I said!"

"I don't, mostly," said his wife, cheerfully. "But I think your ideas fit right into this one." She turned back to her audience. "What I'm trying to say is, we might have a few facts, but until the whole thing is explained, we can't tell what they mean. For instance, in the Kennedy case, the police say that Lee Harvey Oswald was arrested in a movie theatre. Are they telling the truth? And if he really was in a theatre, why was he there? Was he supposed to meet somebody there? Was he trying to establish an alibi? Or was it completely accidental: was he going along the street and saw somebody he knew coming and dodged into the theatre so they wouldn't see him?

"Every possibility fits some version of what happened in Dallas that day, but we can't tell which is the real one until . . . "

"So why he is in theatre?" Lapierre said, fascinated.

"I don't know," she said, "and that's the point." Lapierre translated quickly for Marya, and they both looked disappointed. "Nobody knows for sure unless they know the whole story, and the people who know that whole story are either dead or they're not talking.

"I'm not saying there's no logic to it. Each thing that happens has a cause, and everything that anybody does has a motive . . . " she looked inadvertently at Miss A, and looked away quickly " . . . but when you try to reconstruct something that happened in the past, you can waste a lot of time trying to fit something into the pattern that doesn't really belong there. The fact that you've got a few bits of information doesn't mean that they all fit together in the same pattern. I think our archaeologists would agree with that." She gestured toward the MacEwens, but Dr. MacEwen did not meet her eye, and his wife did not raise her head. "Mystery writers know it, too, of course, and they try to lead you to put the clues together one way, then they show you how they fit together better some other way. Maybe that's what happens in those cases that Mr. Browne was talking about — the police make up their minds to a certain version of events, and they manage to convince the Crown prosecutors and judges and juries, only they've got the story wrong, and there is no writer to put them right." She looked at her husband, but he made no comment.

"The only way to avoid it is to question everything. Not to take anything for granted. This weekend we all came expecting a murder mystery, so when Dr.

MacEwen found Mr. Brown lying in the driveway we all started to speak of it as a murder. But was it?"

"Oh, for heaven's sake," said Miss A. "There's no use telling us it was make-believe. We know that!"

"I'm afraid it wasn't make-believe, Miss Gilford. It was real enough."

"He isn't dead!" Anna MacEwen said suddenly, with the first real animation she had shown since the day they all arrived. "That's what you mean, isn't it? He's not dead!"

"No, in fact he's not. And if we all hadn't had our minds fixed on a murder mystery, we would have known it."

"It did occur to me," Inspector Mullaly said. "I was pretty sure he was alive when they took him away."

"Yes, but you were so desperate not to be thought of as interfering with the RCMP that you didn't make any effort to find out for sure."

"I thought Cameron would tell us," her husband said sheepishly.

"But he didn't, did he?" Simon said, clearly hoping that Rose Mullaly was right, and that he had not delivered make-believe prayers over a real corpse. "Corporal Cameron didn't say Mr. Browne was alive."

"No," Rose Mullaly said, "but he didn't say he was dead, either. I guess the fact that we all kept calling it a murder and trying to figure out who did it didn't get in the way of his investigation. It might even have helped.

"I suppose if the phones had been working, or if Cameron had been able to spend more time here, or if the ambulance men had been close by in Cranmer's Cove somebody might have thought to look into it. As it was, we all just accepted the idea that he'd been killed."

"But he's definitely not dead? You know that for sure?" Anna MacEwen asked eagerly.

"Yes, I do. I'd been thinking about all this, so

yesterday evening I got Faith to take me to her house to use her phone. A lot of the girls I went to school with became nurses. Now they're mostly retired, but a few are still holding down pretty senior positions, so it didn't take me many calls to get the story. The ambulance took Browne to the hospital at Clarenville and then the Cooper brothers went to Whitbourne to be near that stretch of highway. The doctors kept Browne in intensive care Friday night, sent him in to the Health Sciences Centre in St. John's by helicopter on Saturday, they did some emergency surgery to take the pressure off his brain, and by yesterday afternoon he was sitting up in bed and making life hell for the nurses, demanding to be allowed to smoke. His head will hurt for quite a while, but he won't die — at least not from that."

"Oh, thank God!" said Simon fervently. Anna MacEwen said the same thing at almost the same time, and began to cry.

"That's enough, Anna," said her husband.

"I wonder what sort of connection *she* had with Mr. Browne?" Miss A said to her sister in a stage whisper audible to everyone in the room. Then, in a normal pitch, she addressed Rose Mullaly: "Even if he is still alive, someone certainly intended to kill him. We still have a case of *attempted* murder to deal with."

"*Two* attempted murders," Dr. MacEwen said.

"What?" said Miss A. "Oh, yes. Two."

"If it *was* attempted murder," said Rose Mullaly.

"What else could it be?"

"Well, imagine — and I'm not saying it happened like this, but it could have — imagine that somebody noticed the two bronze figurines in the hall on Friday night. Let's say both of them were there. Maybe the person who noticed them thought they were Benin bronzes, and maybe not. Maybe he — or she, or they — just recognized that they were African and pretty old,

249

and probably valuable. Maybe our imaginary characters also noticed that the owners didn't seem to attach much importance to the figures. There were flecks of paint on them, and from where they were standing, they were obviously used as door-stops.

"Now, imagine that after dinner on Friday night, when Alan has said the mystery weekend is all off, and everyone has been drinking a bit, and there'd been all that business with Steve, and there is a lot of confusion, this person sees a chance to nab the figures. Maybe there won't be another chance, but what are you going to do with them? If you grab them, the only thing you *can* do is hide them until you can figure out a way to get them away.

"Everybody is milling around outside on the veran-dah, so it isn't safe to take them out there, and you don't dare take them to the back door because you don't know who might be in the kitchen, but maybe, at least for the moment, the main staircase is clear. So imagine that this person — or maybe there were two of them — nipped upstairs with the figurines, to their room. Or maybe they used the little elevator."

Everyone was listening closely and Rose Mullaly was gaining confidence as she went on. "Now things get interesting," she said. "Let's imagine they take the figu-rines into their room. What do they do now? They could hide them, I suppose, but they're pretty big, and with Faith's daughters going in and out doing the maid service, that wouldn't be safe. And then they'd still have to figure out some way to get them out of the house without being seen. It would be best to get them out right then, if they could: it was very dark, and foggy, and if they could get the figures outside they could hide them somewhere and maybe pick them up later, but going back down the stairs with them was certainly not a great idea.

"The grass on the lawns was overgrown — it hasn't been cut since the snow melted off — and the turf underneath is wet. Those heavy metal figures wouldn't suffer much damage landing on the lawn, even if they fell from a third-storey window, and they wouldn't make much noise, either — just a soft thump that would be masked by the fog. So let's imagine that the person — or the people — who took the figurines — let's imagine that they eased open the window, and heaved the first one out. They'd have to give it a good heave so it would land on the grass on the other side of the driveway."

Anna MacEwen had stopped weeping and had been watching Mrs. Mullaly for several seconds in horrified fascination. She turned to her husband. "Eric! She knows! She . . . "

"Anna!" Dr. MacEwen said, his voice like a whip. "Shut up! Don't say another word!" His wife put her face in her hands and began to cry again.

"Well," said Mrs. Mullaly, "there doesn't seem to be much point pretending this is all imaginary any more, but I might as well finish the story, because that, of course, was when poor old Browne came along, smoking his cigar and shining his little flashlight down on the gravel. The figurine caught him on the back of the head, and he went down like a sack of potatoes. We all tried to figure out why somebody hit him based on who he was, and what he was like, but he just happened to be in the wrong place at the wrong time. Is that the way it happened, Eric?"

"Are you actually trying to accuse me — us — with this preposterous story?" MacEwen asked. "I would advise you to be very careful what you say. There are laws about libel, you know."

"I think you probably mean slander, and I'll take my chances with that. I suppose you intended to hide the figurines in that big camper of yours, did you? I bet there are places in there to hide things that only experts could find. Alan had said the mystery was cancelled, so you could plan to pick up the figurines in the dark, tuck them away in one of your secret compartments and leave first thing in the morning. It could take some time for Alan and Jennifer to notice that they were gone, and by then the trail would be cold — and, anyway, they didn't think they were worth very much.

"Once you'd seen that the first one hit Browne, though, everything changed. You started off with the problem of how to steal the sculptures, but all of a sudden your main problem became how to avoid responsibility for what had happened to Browne. How did you deal with the other figure? My guess is that you kept it in your room that night and brought it down early Saturday morning, before anyone was up, and stuck it under the shelves in the back porch, where you could 'find' it later. And then you made sure to pick it up and handle it in front of everyone so that if anybody found your fingerprints on it there would be a good explanation. It must have been hard for you to give it up, but you couldn't risk trying to steal one of them when the other was suspected of being a murder weapon."

"I am warning you, Mrs. Mullaly, I will not stand for this sort of character assassination.

"Anyway, if anyone was going to try to steal those figures, surely it would have been you." He paused, then added sarcastically, "You *are* the self-styled expert, after all."

"Oh, yes," Rose Mullaly said. "I almost forgot that part. You and Anna are not archaeologists at all, are you? After being married to Gerry for nearly forty years I've made a few police contacts, too, even in Ottawa, so I made a few other calls . . . " She broke off and looked around at the gathering. "The phones being out of commission is a good example of what I mean. Most of us thought it was part of the plot — or at least we kept trying to fit it in somehow. But it didn't fit because it was a real accident. Right, Alan?"

"Yes," Alan said, "it was."

"But it was a great idea for a mystery. It seemed to fit right in."

"We never thought about it when we were planning for the weekend," Alan said. "It never occurred to us."

"Well, you should write it into the script for the next one."

Mrs. Mullaly addressed the MacEwens again. "So I made a few calls to police contacts in Ottawa, and guess what? I found out that you two run an antique shop there. Of course, that doesn't make you experts in Aftrican art, but you can probably recognize an item that could be valuable when you see it. You've certainly done it here in Newfoundland — Terry told Faith about all the old Newfoundland pine furniture you've got in your camper. That's what started me thinking along this line in the first place. You and Anna are not archaeologists, and you don't have a doctorate, but you do deal in old furniture and curios."

"That has nothing to do with it," MacEwen said. "We were all expected to choose our identities for the weekend. Everybody was supposed to be whoever they wanted to be, and Anna decided we would be archaeologists. And as for that furniture, we collect items wherever we go. I paid for every bit of it."

"I'm sure you did. Paid poor people who have no idea of the value of what they had. Paid people whose livelihood and way of life has been snuffed out by the cod moratorium. Do you want to tell us how much you'll make on those tables and washstands?"

"Don't be ridiculous. We will make a reasonable profit, otherwise there would be no point in doing it.

And the people we bought the things from would not know where to sell them for a higher price."

"But you couldn't offer to buy the figurines, could you? That would draw attention to them, and even though Alan and Jennifer could use the money, they are sophisticated enough to inquire into the real value. If you could get them away, though, you could probably dispose of them quietly to some collector who wouldn't ask too many questions. You didn't really know what you had, though, did you, until I mentioned the price of Benin bronzes? Imagine if you had got away with it and sold them for a thousand or so, and then found out what they were really worth! It almost makes me wish you had."

"This is ridiculous!" Dr. MacEwen said. "I'm glad to hear that Mr. Browne is alive, but somebody still has to face charges of attempted murder — Steve, or Ernie, or Miss A."

"That's another thing," said Mrs. Mullaly. "On Friday night you said very clearly that you were not going to join in any amateur detecting. But then, after what we all called the murder had happened, you were careful to point out all the possible suspects, especially the ones who couldn't answer for their actions."

"I suppose he included me with the other two just for a diversion," Miss A suggested. "I can certainly account for *my* actions!"

"Oh, Lexa!" her sister began, but Rose Mullaly cut in: "Yes," she said. "That must be it." 'Dr.' MacEwen said nothing for a moment, then said, "I was hit, too, don't forget,"

"Oh, I'm not forgetting. You were hit out on the cliff path, when nobody else was around. And then you discreetly let it be known that you were hit from behind while you were having a pee in the bushes, so everybody was polite about it, and didn't ask too many questions."

She turned to his wife, "It must have been terrible for you, Anna, was it? You had to hit him hard enough to leave a mark serious enough for him to show when you came back. You probably didn't hit him hard enough the first time, so he made you do it again: that would account for the two areas of bruising the nurse noticed on his head. You were already upset by the idea that you had been part of the cause of Mr. Browne's death, so being forced to hit your husband must have been pretty traumatic. Or maybe you enjoyed it?" Anna didn't answer, but put her face in her hands and began to weep again. Everyone else was listening open-mouthed.

"But he didn't fall down at all, did he?" Rose went on inexorably. "Maybe he was already sitting down when you hit him. The way you told it, he'd have had to fall forward into the bushes he'd just been peeing in, but I noticed he didn't bother to wash or change his clothes, either after you came in at first, or after you got back from seeing the nurse.

"We all just assumed that poor old Browne was the victim of a murderous attack, either planned or spur-of-the-moment, real or staged. We all tried to explain it that way, and Eric here helped us along by providing plenty of material to work with. But what we actually had was a theft gone wrong and some pretty cold-blooded attempts to cover it up. There was no murder, but he was prepared to make somebody else into a murderer to get clear himself."

MacEwen stood up abruptly. "Come with me, Anna," he said. "We are not going to stay here and listen to any more of this."

"But don't we have to wait for Corporal Cameron?" Simon said. He had listened Mrs. Mullaly's accounts of theft, fraud, lies and attempts to frame innocent people, but the idea that anyone could leave after being told to stay by a policeman still seemed incredible to him.

"We should keep them here," Marion said, "so Corporal Cameron can charge them. Can't we do a citizen's arrest or something?"

"Charge us with what?" The man everyone had thought of as 'Dr. MacEwen,' the rather jolly archaeologist, spoke with an unpleasant sneer. "With that unbelievable tale? I hope nobody will be foolish enough to try to stop us."

Georges Lapierre's brow was furrowed with concentration as he tried to follow the rapid flow of English. Marya spoke to him urgently in Bulgarian, and he did his best to translate. "Marya say, she understand Dr. MacEwen does not do murder. But he is thief, yes? He steal statues?"

"Steal?" Dr. MacEwen said. "If anyone tries to charge us with that, I'll have them up for false arrest so fast . . . "

"He's probably right," Inspector Mullaly said. "To be charged with theft, you pretty much have to have the goods on you."

"But if Mrs. Mullaly has the real story," Alan said, "he tried to take both the sculptures . . . " The idea that the MacEwens might have got away with the figurines before he had any idea of their value was beginning to sink in, and he did not like the thought.

"So it seems," said Inspector Mullaly, "but have you ever heard of a charge of attempted theft? Even if somebody has picked something up in a store and stuck it in his pocket, it's hard to charge them unless they walk out past the cashier without paying. If you nab them inside, they can always say that they just put it in their pocket to pick up something else, and of course they intended to pay for it. The only time you can pin shoplifters inside the store is if you find they've got stuff in secret pockets sewed into their underwear or something, and even then it can be a bit dicey if they get a high-priced lawyer."

"Good Heavens, Gerry," said his wife, "are you trying to give them an alibi?"

"Anybody who knows the difference between libel and slander ought to know what an alibi is. It's when you can show you were somewhere else when the crime took place, and I don't think any of us can do that. I *am* talking about a defence, but I don't think I'm saying anything that 'Doctor' MacEwen hasn't already thought of. You may be right, but you've got nothing concrete to tie the MacEwens to the sculptures. And, as he has pointed out himself, even if you've explained how Browne got hit on the head, almost anybody could have been responsible. Our room is on the other side of the house, but *you* could have taken one of the figurines up on the widows' walk and thrown it off there. You're the one who figured out how valuable they are, after all."

"But would I tell everybody that if I was trying to steal them?"

"You didn't tell us until after Browne got hit with the sculpture. By that time you could have been trying to cover your own tracks."

"But that's silly. How would that help cover my tracks?"

Her husband was somewhat taken aback. "Come to think of it," he said. "I don't know. But the point is, MacEwen doesn't have to prove he didn't do it, he just has to show that other people could have. And he seems to have done a pretty good job so far. I've already said that the surface of the figure that's still here isn't great for fingerprints, so that isn't likely to be much help. But even if they manage to lift some prints off the other one, what will they find? I'll bet Alan's and Jennifer's are there, and probably Steve's and Ernie's. Maybe Simon's, and maybe some other people's. And MacEwen was smart enough to handle it in front of witnesses — me included — after Browne was found, and then he handed it to Lapierre, so both of theirs will be on it, on top of the others.

"Unless Cameron comes up with some pretty strong evidence — and I don't think he's going to — there isn't a chance in the world that MacEwen will be charged with anything."

"You see, Anna?" MacEwen said. "I told you there is nothing they can do to us. We'll go and get ready, and as soon as Cameron has taken down that ridiculous yellow tape, we'll leave."

Miss A turned to Inspector Mullaly, incredulous. "You mean they're going to walk away scot free?"

"Well, *he* will, anyway, I suppose," Inspector Mullaly said with a grin. "I don't think Anna is Scottish, though." Miss A snorted impatiently and Anna gave a ghost of a smile.

"Gerry knows more about these things than I do," Rose Mullaly said, "so if he says that Eric MacEwen isn't likely to be charged with anything, I suppose he's right. But that doesn't change the fact that he did his best to commit a really terrible act. And I don't mean the theft. Even if nobody was charged, and even if Browne turned out to be alive, we'd all still wonder, wouldn't we? We could never be absolutely sure, and some of us would always be afraid that somebody we knew — maybe somebody we loved — had tried to kill people. Some of us could be tormented for the rest of our lives."

"I said that," Anna MacEwen said, in a voice scarcely louder than a whisper. She spoke to her husband, but her words were meant for Rose Mullaly. "I told you that, but you wouldn't listen."

"But I *found* him!" MacEwen said. "I was the one who got help!"

"I've been thinking about that, too," said Mrs. Mullaly. "You probably couldn't tell who it was from up-stairs, but you knew somebody'd been hit, and I think your first thought was to go down and get the sculpture. I think that when you got there and saw Browne lying there bleeding, you panicked.

"I started off feeling sorry for both of you. For you, Anna, because I think you let your husband push you around, and for you, Eric, because you aren't really a murderer, you're just swindler and a petty thief. You were genuinely upset when you came in with the news about Browne. You could have left him there, after all, for somebody else to find — or maybe nobody would. Maybe we'd all have thought he'd gone to bed, and he'd just lie there until morning. He would have died for sure, if that had happened. So in a way you might have saved his life. But then it was you who put him in danger in the first place.

"I don't feel sorry for either of you any more," she went on implacably. "You were frightened on Friday night, Eric, because it had all just happened, but you made up your mind pretty quickly how you were going to get off the hook — even if it meant putting somebody else on it. And you, Anna — I know now why you've stayed in your room crying: it wasn't squeamishness, it was guilt. I can understand how you felt, and I can even understand how you might try to avoid responsibility for what happened to Browne — it was an accident, after all. But I can't forgive you for the fact that you were willing to make innocent people into murderers and condemn other people to a lifetime of doubt and anxiety, just to get off the hook yourselves. Feeling guilty's not enough." She paused for a moment and the room was silent except for the sound of Anna MacEwen's weeping. Her husband pulled her roughly to her feet and they started for the door.

The silence seemed to stretch on unbearably until

Rose Mullaly spoke again, this time to the room at large, and in a lighter tone. "But even if they aren't charged with anything, I don't think that means they'll get away without some sort of penalty."

"What do you mean?" MacEwen said, turning back.

"In all this talk we've been forgetting about one of the central characters, just the way we did before, but I'd guess that Sidney Browne is going to be very interested in who knocked him on the head, accidentally or on purpose. He won't care a whole lot whether it was an attempted murder or a robbery gone wrong; he'll want a piece of whoever did it. I'd say that as soon as he hears what happened, he'll slap the MacEwens with a suit for damages, and I imagine the kind of lawyers he knows in Toronto would be happy to take the case for a percentage of the settlement. They're not supposed to do that sort of thing in Ontario, I'm told, but I'm sure there are ways around that.

"To make sure he covers all bases, I imagine he'll sue the hotel, too, and the only way Alan and Jennifer can get out from under is by showing that they took proper precautions, and the whole thing was the MacEwens' fault. I think the rest of us can probably help out there, and maybe Corporal Cameron, too. The rules of evidence aren't the same for a civil suit as they are for criminal proceedings, they tell me. My guess is that the whole thing will be settled out of court for a pretty fancy sum. Things like that usually are."

Finally, she addressed the MacEwens directly. "I kind of think that Browne's lawyers will figure out the value of your business in Ottawa, and your fancy camper, and the two houses in the Glebe that you rent out, and your big place on Sussex Drive, and the cabin in the Laurentians, and anything else you own, right down to within a couple of hundred dollars, and they'll triple it, and that's what they'll go for. Pretty soon your lawyers will start to pressure you to settle, because that's the only way they've got a chance of getting paid, and by the time you settle with Browne and pay the lawyers, you won't have a whole lot left. You'll probably have a big loan to pay off, in fact. So it doesn't look as though you're going to make much profit from that old Newfoundland pine furniture after all. It's all just a guess, though. What do you think, Gerry?"

"Couldn't have said it better myself."

Any further comment was pre-empted by the ringing of the doorbell and the arrival of Corporal Cameron. He knew Browne was alive, of course, and had arranged with the RCMP in St. John's to take his statement. He was pleased to hear Rose Mullaly's fuller account of a story he had begun to piece together himself, and announced that he was closing both attempted-murder investigations, would be taking down the scene-of-the-crime tape barriers he had put up, and told them they were all free to go. The figurine that had struck Mr. Browne was still in the detachment's evidence locker; he would return it to Alan and Jennifer if they asked, but suggested that it might be safer where it was until the matter of a civil action was decided.

Cameron answered a few questions, but clearly was in a hurry to leave. "This is still the holiday Monday," he said. "The traffic on the TCH will be really heavy later on, with people heading back home, and we're still short-handed. But if we don't get any serious accidents —" he knocked on one of the library tables for luck " — as of about midnight tonight, I'm going to go home and collapse into bed, and nothing is going to get me up short of a murder, so I hope you people don't have any more surprises up your sleeves."

While he was talking, the telephone crew arrived and re-attached the lines with great efficiency and only a few jokes. Shortly afterward, when no one was noticing, the MacEwens slipped away, and on the way down the driveway apparently tore the wire down again. Eric also spun the wheels of their recreational vehicle, leaving gouges in the gravel.

Faith served a light lunch, and the remaining guests insisted on settling their accounts, dismissing Alan's offer of waiving them. "Is very good mystery," Georges Lapierre said to Alan, as he signed the credit card slip. "Marya say she is glad you do not make science frictions about plant." Alan was still not sure whether the Lapierres thought the events were real or fictional.

Rose Mullaly had apparently made other telephone calls on the previous evening, because after lunch one of their grandsons arrived, evidently pleased to have been asked to drive their car out, alone on the highway for the first time, to pick them up. Rose told Jennifer privately that she could not bear the idea of riding back to St. John's on the bus, trying to answer questions from the Gilford sisters and the Lapierres. Their grandson was anxious to leave until Faith's daughters dropped in; after that he seemed in no hurry at all. In fact, when the Mullalys were ready to leave they found that the three young people had gone off in Faith's car, so that Michelle could demonstrate *her* new driver's licence.

Terry took Alan aside and apologized for doubting him. "I really thought you'd made some sort of deal with Browne, and were going to run the show yourself," he said. "It's what I would have done. But then when MacEwen got hit . . . "

"Never mind," said Alan. "I thought you did both of them as your bus-driver character."

Terry looked offended, but let it pass. "Listen," he said, "we should be able to run this one for July 1. Surely Sheila will be out by then, and it won't matter if Derm is still wearing a walking cast. It would be a shame to waste all that preparation."

"I don't know," said Alan. "We'll see."

The Gilford sisters and the Lapierres left together, driven by Terry, who promised to stop off in Clarenville, where he was to pass on a box of fancy biscuits left over from Christmas to Derm, if he was still in the hospital, and a couple of packets of cigarettes to Sheila, if she was still in the lock-up, as seemed likely. In the end, Alan and Jennifer found themselves saying good-bye to the last person to leave, Marion Ivany, who was to be driven back to the Trans-Canada and the cross-island bus by Simon.

"It's been very nice to meet you," Jennifer said, and meant it.

"It's been a very interesting weekend," said Marion, "and thank you for letting me stay. But in fact we'll probably be seeing one another again in a week or so. I'm coming back on my way to Toronto . . . "

"That's very nice," said Jennifer desperately, "but I'm afraid we're fully booked from next week on. We hope to finish the room you've been in, and . . . "

"Oh, that's all right," said Marion. "I didn't mean I'd be coming back to the hotel. I'll be staying at the rectory, won't I, Simon?"

"Yes," said Simon, "yes, indeed. At the rectory. Yes," and he smiled uncertainly.